---— ★ ———

Willow found that she could not shut out her memories or stop her imagination building pictures of the way Ringstead had died. She had once read an article about drowning that suggested it took about six minutes for a healthy adult to drown, and she detested the thought of what those minutes would have been like for him if he had known what was happening when his head was forced into the water. She tried to make herself believe that he must have been dead or at least unconscious before it happened.

———— ★ ————

"Cooper [is] the coziest of cozy Britishers now working the genre."

— *Reviews*

Also available from Worldwide Mystery by
NATASHA COOPER

ROTTEN APPLES

NATASHA
COOPER

The Drowning Pool

W💥RLDWIDE®

TORONTO • NEW YORK • LONDON
AMSTERDAM • PARIS • SYDNEY • HAMBURG
STOCKHOLM • ATHENS • TOKYO • MILAN
MADRID • WARSAW • BUDAPEST • AUCKLAND

THE DROWNING POOL

A Worldwide Mystery/April 1998

First published by St. Martin's Press, Incorporated.

ISBN 0-373-26271-X

Printed in U.S.A.

For the Monday bridge players

ONE

Night One

THE PAIN RELAXED its clawing hold. Willow brushed her damp forehead with the back of her hand, exhaled and tried to smile reassuringly at her husband.

'What's all that noise?' she said as the memory of the repeating physical clamour inside her gave way to real sound. 'Someone's yelling outside.'

No one answered and she left Tom's side to waddle over to the window. She leaned gratefully on the deep white-painted ledge as she felt the next contraction beginning. When it was over she looked out of the window and saw a small crowd of women in the hospital forecourt shouting and waving banners in the face of two security guards dressed in grey-and-yellow uniforms. Another man, whose face she could hardly see but who appeared to be dressed in a plain grey suit, was standing watching the fracas from the shadows cast by the canopy over the main door into the hospital. He emerged into the light as a woman screamed.

'It's just the demonstrators, dear,' said a student nurse with kindly patronage. She was easily young enough to be Willow's daughter. 'Don't you worry about anything except your baby.'

'But who are they?' said Willow crossly just as another contraction grabbed her.

She groaned, longing to fall back on the floor and beg to be knocked out with drugs—or even a bang on the head—so that someone else could take control and stop her feeling anything at all. But she had read the latest books and was determined to follow their austere instructions to do without drugs and stay upright for as long as possible. She felt Tom's hands on her back and heard his voice, trembling slightly, saying: 'Pant, Will. Come on: breathe. Just pant.' He panted with her in the approved style of their joint antenatal classes and she felt a flicker of amusement even through the extraordinary pain that was beyond anything any of the books had led her to imagine.

When she could, she said: 'I'm far too heavy for you to hold.'

'Come back to the bed, Will,' he said, looking over his shoulder towards the midwife, who nodded. 'Come on. Before the next one. You don't have to lie down, but…'

'It's safer to be there,' she said with a faint smile. 'I know, Tom.'

'Ah, here's Mr Ringstead,' said Tom, greatly relieved to see the most senior of the hospital's obstetricians.

At six-foot-four, with a craggily handsome face, powerful shoulders and an unruly shock of greying blond hair, Alexander Ringstead cut a magnificent figure. On the few occasions when she had seen him, Willow had always thought he looked an unlikely inhabitant of a world full of women, but he seemed quite at home with them. He had been amazingly kind to her at one of the antenatal clinics, not only reassuringly knowledgeable about what she was going through but also quite unshocked by everything she said to him. She had attended all the subsequent clinics in the hope of seeing him again, but she had usually had to make do with a junior doctor or one of the midwives.

Even so, she shared none of Tom's relief at the sight of Mr Ringstead. He was far too senior to attend any normal birth and his sudden appearance made her think that there must be something very wrong with her—or the baby.

'You're doing fine,' he said with a gloriously confidence-building smile before she could ask any questions. 'Now lie down for a minute so that I can check that all is going as it should.'

Willow lay down and waited for bad news. After a brief examination Ringstead let her get up, just in time for the next contraction.

'Here we go again,' she said, feeling a worse pain than any so far.

Leaning back against Tom, she could not help remembering stories she had heard of three-day labours. She did not think that she could last much longer without drugs, let alone through the rest of the night. Then the contraction eased and she tried to persuade herself that Ringstead might be worried about nothing more than her age.

'What is it?' asked Tom.

'I was thinking that if twenty-six-year-olds are "elderly primagravidae", I must be a positively senile primagravida,' she said, managing to laugh.

'You and me both,' he answered, sounding less strained. He wiped her forehead with a refreshingly cool cloth and brushed her hair back from her face with a hand that no longer trembled. 'Don't worry. You took the folic acid, had every possible test, ate all the approved foods and none of the wrong ones, gave up drink, did everything. Isn't that right, Mr Ringstead?'

'Absolutely. You'll be fine,' he said, smiling impartially at them both. 'And forty-four is no age these days. Everything's going as it should.'

There was another burst of shouting outside.

'Who is it making all that noise?' Willow asked breathlessly.

'WOMB,' said the obstetrician in his driest voice. 'Women Overtake Male Birthing, or so I understand. Now I'm going to have to go on to my next mum, but you're not to think that I'm deserting you. Sister Chesil will look after you.'

'Yes, I know,' said Willow, half-reassured that he saw no need to stay and yet wishing that he was not going to leave her to the dragonlike Sister Chesil.

Of all the midwives Willow had met during her antenatal visits to the hospital, Sister Chesil was the only one she had

never liked. She was efficient and knowledgeable but she had
an air of grievance about her that set up all sorts of alarm bells
in Willow's mind, and her mouth was set in lines of bitter
anger. In all their meetings, Willow had never once seen her
smile at anyone.

The consultant had hardly gone before the next contraction
stopped Willow thinking about anything else.

'It won't be long now,' said Tom doggedly, feeling the effect of what was happening to her through his hands. 'Ringstead said so. Stick with it, Will. Come on. That's right.
You're doing so well. Come on, old girl.'

Only about ten minutes later, after she had sworn at him
for trying to reassure her when he had no idea what she was
feeling, a completely different sensation took hold of Willow.
She opened her mouth to say something but could not. Sister
Chesil, apparently understanding exactly what was happening,
got Willow on to the bed at last.

Tom wiped her forehead once more and removed some
strands of the sweatily lank red hair, which had fallen into her
eyes. He looked terrible and she wanted to say something to
help, but she needed everything for herself and the violent
things that were happening to her body.

'I can see the head,' said Sister Chesil some time later.
'There. It's crowned. It really won't be long now. You're doing well. That's right. Well done.'

Teeth digging into the tip of her tongue, tears of effort and
pain gathering in her eyes, Willow felt her child leave her at
last and looked down. She saw movement and heard a gasp.

'Don't hit it,' she said through the heavy breaths that were
taking her to some kind of recovery.

'Don't worry, Will. They know what they're doing,' said
Tom, who had read all the books after she had finished with
them and knew what she was talking about.

With him at her side, Willow watched as their tiny, bloody,
waxy daughter was laid very gently on her stomach. She put
one hand tentatively on the child's sticky black hair and then

slid it down over the back and legs and slowly pulled her up towards her breast.

'She's got the right number of arms and legs anyway,' she said to Tom, trying to sound funny, but her voice broke.

He put one hand on Willow's head and the other on her crooked arm as the midwife laid a warm blanket over Willow and the baby. Willow looked at the midwife for a second and to her astonishment saw the woman smile at last. It was not long before her lips snapped back into their familiar discontented lines, but for a moment she had definitely smiled.

'She's wonderful,' Tom said, swallowing painfully as he looked down at his daughter. 'And so are you, Will. I...I don't...' He managed a gasping kind of laugh. 'I can't quite work out what on earth to say.'

Willow turned to smile at him. He still looked terrible, but some of the fear had gone from his brown eyes.

'No,' she said. 'We're neither of us quite...normal just now.'

'Exactly.'

Later, when the baby had been labelled, washed, weighed and checked, the midwife brought her back to be fed.

'Now it's perfectly easy,' she said as she helped Willow to arrange the baby against her breast. All the bracing briskness was back in the midwife's voice, and there was no longer any evidence that she had ever smiled at all. 'Come along. Don't tense up like that.'

Easier said than done, thought Willow as she did her best to obey the impatient instructions. But she had never been able to relax to order and she soon found it difficult not to join in the baby's breathless lamentations. Tom stood beside them, looking on in helpless misery.

'It's normal,' said Sister Chesil firmly. 'She'll learn. You both will. Try again. There.'

Willow blinked as two hard little gums grabbed her nipple and pulled. It dawned on her with a kind of shock that her mother, too, had been through all this. All sorts of unexpected feelings were washing about in her brain and she did not have the strength left to deal with any of them.

She gazed down at the baby and paid no attention to anyone or anything else. She did not even notice Sister Chesil nodding in silent approval as the baby began to suck. After a moment she nodded once again and left the room.

Tom watched his wife and daughter, aware of some very mixed feelings of his own. Relief that it was all over was much the strongest and, recognising it, he let himself sit down at last. Almost at once Willow gasped. The baby, dislodged, let out a sharp wail.

'What is it?' Tom said, leaping to his feet again as he saw his wife's terrified expression.

'I'm bleeding.'

For an instant, which felt like minutes, no one moved or spoke. Then Ben, the medical student who had been watching everything Ringstead and Sister Chesil had done and feeling even more spare than Tom, pulled forward a bucket just as Tom shouted: 'Fetch Ringstead.'

The student nurse ran out of the room.

Sister Chesil returned a few minutes later, breathing fast. She paused for a second in the doorway.

'My god! It looks like a butcher's shop in here,' she exclaimed as she moved forward, but she sounded reassuringly unhysterical. Tom and Willow began to breathe again. Calmly pressing her hands on Willow's abdomen, the midwife added: 'Ben, take the baby.'

Nurse Brown peered round the door of the delivery suite a few minutes later. She still looked frightened enough to set Willow's heart hammering again in spite of Sister Chesil's reassuring matter-of-factness, and her voice was shrill as she said: 'I can't find Mr Ringstead. No one knows where he is. What...?'

'Stop talking at once,' said Sister Chesil harshly, 'and go and fetch Doctor Kimmeridge.' She looked up at Tom and Willow, who were both staring at her as though she were their only saviour, and said more conversationally: 'He's the registrar. Have you met him yet?'

'No,' said Willow, her voice shaking. 'What's happening? I mean, why am I bleeding like this? Is it…?'

'It happens sometimes. Don't fuss.'

Fuss, thought Willow in a mixture of outrage and supreme anxiety. I'm pouring blood and you tell me I'm making a fuss?

Then she remembered Mr Ringstead's surprising appearance in the delivery room and anxiety overcame all her outrage as she realised that the bleeding could have been what he had feared. It must be serious. She wanted to shout out her need for reassurance. But she said nothing and became aware that the midwife was talking to her.

'You'll like Doctor Kimmeridge,' Sister Chesil was saying cooly as she continued to press down on Willow's uterus. 'He'll be here in a moment. You did well, you know, to have such a quick labour.'

'Was it quick?' said Tom, as eager as the midwife to distract Willow from what was happening. He hoped he did not sound as scared as he felt, but he thought it unlikely. He was appalled by all the blood and by what it might mean. He made an effort to control himself and added: 'It felt enormously long.'

'For a first baby at forty-four it was remarkably quick. Ah, Doctor Kimmeridge, good,' said Sister Chesil, as the heavy doors to the delivery suite were pushed open. Willow looked up and saw a thin, slight, dark-haired man with a sardonic expression on his sallow face. He seemed to be doing his best to look gentle as he said: 'We'll soon have you settled.'

Eventually they managed to do enough to persuade Willow that she might not after all be bleeding to death.

MUCH LATER, bathed, dried, anointed, padded up and dressed in a celebration nightgown from some enormously luxurious shop Tom had found, she was taken into a bay of six beds in one of the main maternity wards on the floor above the delivery suites. A perspex, wheeled cot was put ready beside the bed. Nurse Brown laid the child carefully in Willow's arms and left them alone with Tom at last, shutting the checked curtains as she went.

Willow was surprised to find how much she still hurt, but there was an odd displacement in her brain, as though the torn and wrenched bits of her body were detached from her. She felt as though she and the child were floating together in a private warmth, and she kept looking at Tom to make sure that he was still there and part of it all. It seemed impossible that he should not feel what she felt and yet she knew he could not.

He looked achingly tired and was obviously still anxious, but even as she watched him his eyelids began to close. He was very pale, too, and Willow was irresistibly reminded of the way he had looked when he had spent a week in a coma after being shot by a gang of frighteningly young drug-dealers.

As a police officer he had always been at risk, but she had believed that he was much too senior to become involved in the sort of street crime that led to most serious assaults. It was ironic that on that occasion he had been no more than a passer-by, not even investigating the drug-dealers he had been unlucky enough to meet.

It had taken him a long time to recover completely from what they had done to him and even after he had been pronounced fit for work again he had not been returned to operational duties. Instead he had been given promotion and a desk job at Scotland Yard. He hated it, but Willow felt that there were several compensations.

His eyes opened as he felt the strength of her attention on him. He saw that she was smiling.

'What's funny?' he said, rubbing his forehead as though his head ached.

'Only that you and I seem to spend an inordinate amount of time sitting by each other's hospital bedsides.'

His tired eyes brightened for a moment and he laughed quietly.

'True.' He put one finger very lightly on his daughter's head. 'But this stint has been a bit more productive than usual, hasn't it?'

'Yes.'

'Was it…? No, that's a stupid question. Sorry. I didn't mean to…'

'I know. Don't worry. It was ferocious and I'm glad it's over.' She bent her head so that her lips could brush the baby's hair, no longer sticky. 'But I wouldn't have missed it for anything.'

Tom sank back in his chair and the plastic cover squeaked. Willow sneaked another look at him a few minutes later and saw that he was drifting off to sleep again. A sudden raucous shout from the demonstrators outside the hospital woke both him and the baby. Willow wished she had a bucket of cold water to fling over the banner-wavers as though they were a pack of howling stray cats. It seemed outrageous that they should be disturbing her family at such a moment.

Sister Chesil came back just then. Seeing that most of the other women in the ward were asleep, she very quietly asked Willow how she was feeling.

'Weak,' Willow whispered. 'And it still hurts.'

'That's normal. But I've brought you some tablets.' She held out a small white plastic cup with two bright capsules in the bottom. 'You take those, while I put your baby back in her cot.'

Willow was reluctant to let her daughter go, but it seemed the right thing to do, and so she relaxed her arms and let Sister Chesil take the shawl-wrapped bundle and lay it down in the cot. Willow took the pills and allowed the midwife to push back the sloping bedhead so that there was room for the pillows to lie flat.

'You ought to sleep now. The demonstrators have been moved off and you must take advantage of the quiet while you can.'

'Has Mr Ringstead reappeared?'

'Doctor Kimmeridge has done all that's necessary for you,' said Sister Chesil repressively, as though the consultant's movements were none of Willow's business. 'There's no more serious bleeding down there and nothing for you to worry about.'

The midwife glanced at Tom. Seeing that his eyelids were slowly shutting once more, she added: 'You should follow your husband's sensible example and get some sleep.'

A small snore, more like a snuffle, emerged from Tom at that moment and the midwife nodded in satisfaction.

'I'll do my best,' said Willow, as usual envying Tom's ability to drop off even in the most inauspicious circumstances.

'Sleep well now,' said Sister Chesil as she disappeared through the curtains

An hour or so later Willow woke from a dream-filled doze as there was yet another commotion, this time only just outside her ward. She thought the demonstrators must have found their way in and moved her head so that she could see through a gap in the checked curtains. She could just see the swing doors of the ward being pushed open by one of the nurses, who seemed to be talking to someone out in the passage. Her striped uniform dress was stretched tight over her buttocks as she pushed backwards, and her waist looked very small in its deep red-elastic belt. After a moment Willow heard a breathless and troubled youngish voice saying: 'They've found him, you know.'

'Where?' came an urgent, older, female voice. 'Where?'

There was an indistinct mumble of words and then an exclamation:

'God, how terrible!'

Willow struggled to hear what else was being said, but there were too many different voices, most of them only whispering. Then a man's voice said much more loudly: 'I told you, he was face down in the birthing pool. Of course he was dead. How couldn't he have been?'

Another mumble of more distant voices made it impossible

for Willow to hear anything more until the male voice said: 'I know. It's appalling that no one even thought to look in there. What were you all doing? Somebody ought to have thought to look.'

Wondering whether they were talking about a baby and how anyone could have left him alone in the birthing pool, Willow pushed herself up against her pillows to make sure that her own daughter was still in her cradle. It looked as though she was peacefully asleep.

'He must have been like that for ages,' said one of the shriller female voices from outside the ward, breaking into the peace of the dimly lit room with its sleeping women and babies. 'How could it have happened?'

'The police are on their way,' said Sister Chesil's unmistakably authoritative voice. 'We'll know more when they've seen him. It's silly to speculate without information. Get back to work all of you.'

'What?' Tom had woken up and was rubbing his eyes with the knuckles of both hands. 'What's up, Will?'

'I'm not sure,' she said, staring at him. 'But someone's dead. The police are coming.'

'What? Nonsense. Don't be so silly.'

'I'm not,' she said, angry that he should have contradicted her so automatically and in such a dismissive tone of voice. 'They're talking about it outside. A nurse has just said that someone's dead, drowned in the birthing pool. The police are on their way. I don't know if it's a baby or whether it's... Tom, d'you think it could be Ringstead?'

'Surely not. I'm sorry if I sounded sharp, but you must have misheard, Will. Perhaps you were dreaming. Look, I'll nip out and check.'

He turned back with one hand on the blue-and-green curtain. 'You don't mind if I go, do you?'

'No. I want to know what's happened, too—and who it is.'

TWO

Night One and Day Two

THE SQUEAK of the ward doors swinging open woke Willow again half an hour later, and she was blinking as Tom pushed his way back through the blue-and-green curtains. He stood for a moment watching her and she noticed that his eyes were alert and his mouth looked hard.

'So what's happened?' she asked before he could speak. 'You've got your professional look on.'

'Have I? Sorry. That's the last thing you need.' Seeing that she was about to argue, he smiled deliberately and tried to think of something that might distract her from the news he did not want to tell her. 'You know we're going to have to decide what to call our daughter now that she's a real "human bean".'

'I know,' Willow said, stifling her impatience with difficulty. 'But we can't decide something that important in the middle of all this or we'll make a mistake we'll regret for ever. Look, Tom, I need to know what's happened. Who's dead?'

'I don't think it's good for you to think about it now. Too worrying, Will, and you shouldn't be worried at all tonight.'

'Nothing could be more worrying than not knowing. Tom, stop protecting me, please. It'll drive me mad. Just tell me what's happened.'

He looked at her for a moment and then shrugged.

'I'm afraid it's Ringstead, Will. They don't yet know exactly what happened, but he was found face down with his head in the birthing pool.'

'Drowned?'

'Probably, but they won't know that for sure until they've done the autopsy.'

For a moment she could not speak. When she could she asked what else Tom had discovered.

'No details yet,' he said. 'A team's arrived from the local AMIP, and the inspector wants to talk to me. I'll know more when I've seen her, and I'll come back and tell you anything I can then. If you need me before that, send one of the nurses. They'll know where we are. I'm so sorry, Will. On this of all nights.'

'It's hardly your fault,' she said and then, seeing his expression, quickly added: 'I know that's not what you meant. I'm sorry, too. But must you get involved with the AMIP team? It's not your case and you look worn out. Couldn't you go home and get some sleep?'

Tom's face creased into the old smile and Willow felt herself smiling in response.

'Thanks, ducky, but I can cope. All the AMIP bunch will want is an account of everything I heard and saw this evening. It won't take long. I'll have a word with them and then get my head down. You ought to sleep, too. Try not to worry too much about poor Ringstead. I don't want you lying awake in misery when you should be triumphant.'

'I'll try not to.' Forgetting all her earlier irritation, she searched her mind for a way of reassuring him and eventually found something that might do. 'There wouldn't be much point in any case. It's over for him. Whatever it was that led to his death, it can't hurt him any more.'

'Yes. There is that.' Tom's mockery and his toughness alike disappeared in a wave of tenderness. 'Will, I...'

She held out one of her hands as he hesitated.

'I know. Me, too. Take care, Tom. Don't let them exploit you. You're a desk man now, not operational.'

He bent down to kiss her and then left. She did her best to sleep but was not successful for a long time. Alexander Ringstead must have died just as her daughter was being born, and no amount of rationalism could make that any different.

Falling asleep eventually, she missed Tom's promised return by only a few minutes. He stood at her bedside, determined not to wake her and yet longing to be able to talk to her again. After a while he left the ward as quietly as he could to go home and snatch a little sleep himself.

Willow woke later to a cacophony of chatter, crying babies and clattering cutlery and opened her eyes to see a woman in a pale-green dressing-gown standing at the foot of her bed with a tray in her hands.

'Hello,' she said.

'Hello,' answered Willow, pushing the hair out of her eyes and trying to think who the woman could be.

'I brought you some breakfast.'

'Thank you; but why you? Don't the nurses do it?'

'Not often. They're so busy these days that we tend to help out once we can move reasonably comfortably again. I'm in the next bed there. I had my baby two days ago and I'm used to being up and about. How are you feeling? I gather you had quite a rough time.'

'Not really compared with some stories I've heard, but I didn't sleep very well: thinking too much about poor Mr Ringstead, I suppose.'

'I'm not surprised,' said the woman, putting the tray down on Willow's table and swinging it across her bed. 'Everyone's talking about it. Isn't it awful?'

'Do you know what actually happened?'

'They say he was drowned in the birthing pool. That's all I know.'

'Oh, God!' said Willow, putting a hand over her eyes for a moment. 'But how could he have drowned? It's so shallow. He was a big man. He must...' She broke off, reluctant to admit the thought that had been with her ever since Tom had told her that it was Ringstead who had died. She looked up at the other woman, who nodded.

'I know,' she said, looking sick. 'He must have been murdered.'

'Unless he had a heart attack and fell in,' said Willow, feeling as though she were fighting for some hopeless cause. 'Or perhaps he did it himself. Even that would be less awful. At least, I think it would.'

'Oh, I think that's very unlikely. What a way to choose! After all, he could have got any number of sleeping pills and things that would have been much easier. Besides, he wasn't the suicidal type at all; so cheerful and sure of himself.'

Willow looked towards her sleeping baby. She had always known that she would be bringing a child into a world full of violence, but she had never dreamed that it would come so close so quickly.

'God knows how they're going to cope without him here. It wouldn't surprise me if the whole place fell apart,' said the other woman, unaware of the effect she was having on Willow. 'I'm glad I'm going tomorrow. What about you?'

'I don't know,' said Willow, and then added as she tried to comfort herself: 'But Doctor Kimmeridge is very good. I'm sure he'll hold things together.'

'He's only a registrar. One of the other consultants will have to take over and none of them are a patch on Mr Ringstead.'

'How do you know anything about them?' asked Willow. 'I thought everyone on this ward came under Ringstead. I haven't even heard any other consultant's name being mentioned.'

'Nor have I this time, but I had different ones for each of my other two babies. And people talk, you know. Take it from me, Ringstead was one of a kind. They'll never find anyone else as good.'

The woman seemed belatedly to realise how worried Willow was becoming and added in a more soothing voice: 'But you needn't worry. All the tricky bits are over for you now.'

'Are they?'

It was a long time since Willow had felt quite so ignorant.

Her steady progress to a relatively senior position in the civil service had left her not only well informed and articulate, but also convinced of the value of her own judgment. Her subsequent—unexpected—success as a romantic novelist had brought her confidence of a different kind, and a series of haphazard but ultimately successful investigations of serious crime had only strengthened her opinion that she knew what she was doing, who she was, and where she was going.

The birth of her baby had changed all that, and she felt as though she had emerged into an entirely new world with rules and dangers of which she knew very little.

'I'd better get on with the other trays,' said the other woman before Willow could ask anything.

She smiled bravely and poured herself a cup of strong Indian tea as she contemplated her breakfast tray. Looking at the flaccid toast and swamped cereal, she could not help yearning for the sort of perfect, imaginatively cooked food her housekeeper, Mrs Rusham, made for her and Tom every morning. Pushing the thought away, she ate what was in front of her.

Then came the tricky business of getting out of bed and discovering which bits of herself hurt most. It was a relief to lean over the cradle and watch her daughter's huge eyes widening. The baby could not possibly have recognised her so soon, Willow told herself firmly, but even so it was an unexpected relief not to be greeted with screams of panic or dismay. Willow picked her up out of the cradle, carefully supporting her worryingly floppy head and laid her on the bed to change her.

Having dealt with the dirty nappy reasonably well, Willow got back into bed with the baby in her arms and tried to feed her. That was less successful. The two of them struggled for some time. The baby howled in frustration and Willow winced each time her sore nipples were squeezed between the extraordinarily hard gums her daughter had been given and tried not to panic.

Eventually they both gave up. While the baby lay crying against her, Willow mopped her own eyes on the sheet and told herself that they would get it right next time.

'How are you this morning, Mrs Worth?'

Willow took the sheet away from her eyes and saw Doctor Kimmeridge standing by her bed with an unknown nurse and a young male medical student in attendance. Unfairly angry with Kimmeridge because he had seen her in tears, Willow said stiffly that she was perfectly all right.

He told her to give her baby to the nurse and lie back. Willow closed her eyes as he examined her. When he had finished, he asked whether she had any questions.

Willow sat up and straightened her nightgown with jerky movements.

'Yes. I want to know exactly what happened to Mr Ringstead and whether he drowned or died in some other way before he fell in the pool.'

'That's not what I meant,' Kimmeridge said quite sharply. 'I know nothing about that. I'm concerned only with your health and that of your baby. Now, have you any sensible questions?'

Willow shook her head, blinking at the irritability in his voice, which seemed excessive even in the circumstances. As he stalked away to his next patient, the young Irish nurse waited behind to say in a soft brogue: 'Don't mind him too much. It's been a terrible strain for him having to field all Mr Ringstead's patients like this.'

She must have been in her early twenties and would have been very pretty if her eyes had not been swollen with tears. Her hair was mouse brown but it gleamed with health under her stiff white cap, and there was a sprinkling of freckles over her small, straight nose. The plastic label on her blue-and-white-striped dress announced that her name was Brigid O'Mara. She looked intelligent and kind, and it was obvious that she was devastated by Mr Ringstead's death.

'He hasn't had any sleep yet, and he's as worried as the rest

of us. Are you sure there's nothing you want to ask? Most
new mothers are full of questions and you didn't look happy
when we arrived.'

Willow gave in and let herself describe the abortive feed
and ask for some advice.

'Don't worry about it too much,' said Nurse O'Mara, showing no sign of the impatience that Sister Chesil had not
bothered to hide the previous night. 'Most new mothers have
trouble feeding their babies at first, but you'll soon get the
hang of it. Everyone does.'

Willow sighed, hating the mixture of pathetic gratitude and
even more pathetic anxiety that she felt.

'I'll have another go in a minute,' she said.

'Good. And try not to get upset if it doesn't work at first.
That'll only make your baby nervous and both of you even
more tense. Remember that it always takes time and don't
think you're getting it wrong. I'll be back in a while to see
how you're getting on, but I must go now or Doctor Kimmeridge will be getting impatient.'

'Will he have to carry Mr Ringstead's responsibilities for
ever?' Willow asked, almost clutching Nurse O'Mara's
starched apron in her anxiety not to be left alone with the
hungry baby.

'Oh no. He's just holding the fort until they bring in another
consultant to take over. Now I must be off. I'll come back as
soon as I can.'

The baby soon began to whimper and then burst into full-
blown crying. Willow scrambled out of bed to pick her up and
then took her back into the warmth of the covers.

'Push your breast a bit further in,' said a kind voice a moment later. Willow looked up and, through watering eyes, saw
the woman from the next bed watching her with sympathy. 'If
her gums are further in, they won't hurt so much.'

'Ah,' said Willow a moment later. She slowly relaxed.
'That's better. It works.'

'Of course it does. Are you all right now?'

'Yes, thank you.'

'Pleasure.' The other woman walked back to her own baby and efficiently hoisted him into position and started to feed him.

Willow soon forgot about everything else in the fascination of her first successful unsupervised feed. When Nurse O'Mara came back, Willow greeted her with a broad smile.

'So,' she said with obvious pleasure. 'The feed went better, did it?'

'Yes, much better.'

'Well, good for you then.'

'Thank you,' said Willow, just as a clamour of hoarse, angry shouting burst out below her window, vividly reminding her of the previous night. 'Is that those wretched rioters again?'

'I'm afraid so. The Funny Feminists.'

'What?'

Nurse O'Mara looked at Willow with all the brightness fading out of her face again. Her lower lip began to tremble. She coughed, swallowed and then said in a reasonably controlled voice: 'That's what Mr Ringstead always called them. Sorry.' She reached for a Kleenex from the box on Willow's locker, wiped her eyes and then blew her nose. 'Whenever I think of the things he used to say, it makes me cry.'

'I can imagine,' said Willow gently. 'He had quite a sense of humour, didn't he?'

'Yes.' Nurse O'Mara gulped and tears welled over her swollen eyelids.

'What are the Funny Feminists here for?' Willow asked, partly out of genuine curiosity but more as a way of helping Nurse O'Mara overcome her distress.

'They want to change the way the hospital manages births,' she said, sniffing as she pulled out another paper handkerchief and shredded the edge. She breathed carefully and then managed to smile.

'Why? Everything seems to me to be very well managed.'

'I'm glad you think so. But they think that doctors sometimes interfere too much and make it harder for women to give birth naturally. They claim that sometimes means they need more pain relief, which in turn can lead to a need for forceps at the end, and that does carry more risk than a natural birth.'

'Nobody interfered with me,' said Willow just as a snuffling sound from the baby made her forget about the demonstrators and Nurse O'Mara and even Mr Ringstead. As her daughter looked up at her, Willow stroked her face and decided that Tom was right: they would have to find a name for her quickly. She was a person, not a thing, and she needed a name. Willow did not notice Nurse O'Mara backing quietly away.

When Tom looked in briefly on his way to a lunchtime meeting, Willow told him some of the names she had been considering. He laughed and told her with all the old, easy, friendly teasing in his voice that no daughter of his was going to prance about London with a name like Tullia or Laetitia.

'On the other hand,' he added, gazing down at the dark-haired baby nestling against Willow's shoulder, 'I can see her as Lucinda.'

'Can you?' Willow moved so that she could see the baby's face. Her eyelids fluttered upwards and once again the huge, black-looking eyes gazed up into Willow's green ones.

'Lucinda,' said Tom again. 'Yes, I can. I've never known anyone called that. It's pretty and it suits her, Lucinda Wilhelmina.'

'Absolutely not,' said Willow with more energy than usual. 'My name is much more idiotic even than Tullia. I've been trying to imagine what my parents could have been thinking of to saddle me with it.'

'But Will is all right, and it suits you.' Tom bent down to kiss her. 'I'm...'

'Going to have to go. Yes, I know you are. Don't worry about it. We'll both still be here when you're free again.'

Tom looked at her. 'You know, I wish you had let me book you into a private wing somewhere. I could have afforded it—

and even the interest on your latest royalty cheque would have paid for it twice over.'

'We're fine here. Don't worry. Obstetrics is one of the things the NHS does particularly well, not least because it can't be rationed. I know you wanted me to be in carpeted, hushed and private splendour with nurses who look as though they've just had a makeover and colour counselling, but this is fine. And if we don't all fight for the National Health…'

'We'll lose it. Okay, my love, you win. No soapboxes. They'll bore Lucinda.'

'And you, too, probably. I'll save it for when you think I'm strong enough to hear that sort of insult directly.' Willow laughed at his surprise. 'I'm still me, Tom, even though I've just given birth. Go on, off with you. And don't let them get you down too badly at the meeting. I hope it doesn't go on for half the night again.'

He shuddered and turned away, looking back to say over his shoulder: 'I quite forgot: Mrs Rusham is anxious to come and see you this afternoon, but she's worried that it might be too much for you. I said I thought it would be fine but that you'd ring if you were too tired to see people.'

'No. I'd like to see her.'

'Good. She's longing to bring you a hamper of delicacies. She doesn't seem to trust anyone else to feed you adequately, although I must say you look perfectly healthy to me.'

They were both laughing as Tom eventually forced himself to go. His place was soon taken by an unknown nurse with Willow's lunch. She looked down at the sandwich and small bowl of tinned fruit salad, and teased herself with thoughts of what might be in her housekeeper's hamper.

THREE

Day Two

WILLOW AND LUCINDA both had a nap after lunch but Willow's was much shorter than the baby's. By three o'clock she was awake and bored. All the other women in the bay had visitors sitting by their beds, and Willow lay against her pillows unashamedly listening to their conversations. Everyone seemed to be talking about Mr Ringstead and what might have happened to him.

Willow soon learned that he had been a man of considerable power. Until then she had not known that his full title had been Clinical Director of the Obstetrics, Gynaecology and Paediatrics Directorate or that he had been in charge of ten other consultants, twenty junior doctors and about a hundred nurses.

Nearly everyone seemed to have liked him and no one had a bad word to say for him, even though one or two of the older nurses who came into the bay were reluctant to answer questions. Willow could not work out whether that was because they disapproved of gossip or had some reservations about Mr Ringstead. The students and junior nurses, on the other hand, had obviously all adored him and were more than happy to talk.

The liveliest of them was a brown-eyed young woman with very smooth dark hair called Susan Worbarrow. Like Nurse O'Mara she had been crying, but she was dry-eyed by then and she answered a whole series of questions from the husband of the woman in the bed directly opposite Willow's. Willow listened in growing frustration until the man eventu-

ally asked the question in which she herself was most interested.

'Did he have any enemies?'

'Only the managers,' said Susan Worbarrow lightly. 'They
don't like anyone on the clinical side, of course, but they specially loathed Mr Ringstead because he stood up to them every
time they tried to make him cut his budgets, and he tended to
make frivolous jokes whenever they were being particularly
serious.'

She turned as she spoke and saw that Willow was alone and
eavesdropping.

'Hello,' she said brightly as she crossed the floor. 'No visitors yet? You look rather glum. I'm sure your husband will
be in later.'

'I'm not at all glum,' Willow assured her. 'But I couldn't
help hearing what you were saying just now. Is it really true
that the managers are trying to cut the obstetrics budget?'

'Yes, but you needn't worry about it. You and your baby
will be long gone by the time any cuts are actually introduced—even if they ever are.'

'I'm glad to hear it,' said Willow with some fervour. 'But
why are cuts being made at all?'

'Because of the fruiting bodies in the basement.'

'Fruiting bodies?' Willow's overactive imagination was
providing her with some quite horrible pictures of what must
have been happening in the basement.

'Yes. It's a fungus. Dry rot. Not the white thready kind that
creeps under floors, but great orange blobs that emerge on the
surface. They're all over the basement.'

Willow knew that at any other time she would have been
amused by her own misunderstanding, but no jokes about bodies—fruiting or otherwise—could have made her laugh just
then.

'Are you saying that because they're going to have to spend
money on the building they're going to ration obstetric care?'
she said in outrage.

Susan Worbarrow relaxed against the edge of the bed as though she were settling down for a long chat.

'They'll have to. The hospital is run by an NHS trust now and the trust is running out of money. All the directorates have got to do their bit and Obs and Gynae is no exception.'

'But how? If women have babies, they have babies. It's the one speciality for which you can't operate a waiting list.'

Susan Worbarrow's face broke into the widest smile Willow had yet seen from her. It looked out of place with her swollen eyelids.

'That's just what he said. Mr Ringstead, I mean. When they told him how much money he was going to have to save, he asked them point blank if they were expecting him to start rationing care here.'

Willow noticed that three of the other women and their husbands were all listening. One of the men, who was holding his baby and looking most uncomfortable with it, said: 'And what did they say to that?'

'Well,' said Nurse Worbarrow, turning to flash a dazzling smile at him, 'a friend of mine overheard a couple of consultants saying that the business manager of the directorate looked all sort of superior and pleased and he said he was glad that Mr Ringstead had got the point at last. He also said that he'd drafted a long list of the various savings that could be made, and he passed a copy of it over the table.'

'And then?' said Willow.

'Well,' Susan said, turning back to Willow again, 'Mr Ringstead laughed and said he didn't think he'd bother to read the list since all he would need to know was how many babies the hospital could afford in each twenty-four hours. Everyone looked surprised then, especially Mark Durdle, the business manager, but Mr Ringstead kindly explained that once the quota was full, he'd just tell any other mothers who went into labour to cross their legs and hold on until the following day.'

One of the women was looking outraged, but all the others were giggling.

'Oh, dear,' said Willow when she could speak. 'And I suppose the meeting collapsed as they all burst out laughing.'

'Not exactly,' said Susan Worbarrow, twisting her face into a clownlike mask. 'Lots of them did think it was quite funny, even though they tried to pretend they didn't, but Mark Durdle went white and started shaking with fury.'

'But why? Anyone could have seen that Mr Ringstead was just teasing him.'

'I know. But that's why he was in such a bate. Life is deadly earnest for him and he thought he was being mocked and humiliated.'

'Well, he had a point there, didn't he?' said Willow.

'Maybe. Anyway, it didn't end there. Mr Ringstead was enjoying it all too much to stop and so he said: "I'll just make a note of how many babies it should be in every twenty-four hours. Would six do you, Durdle, or should it be only four? Tell us and we'll fix it. Whatever you want. It won't be any trouble to us and I'm sure the women will cooperate".'

'Oh dear,' said Willow again, laughing still. 'And I suppose it was all round the hospital in no time at all.'

'Well, you know what hospitals are like, and the managers aren't very popular at the moment. As soon as we heard about it we started crossing our legs whenever we saw Durdle. He hates us.'

'I'm not surprised,' said Willow at her driest.

Everyone in the ward was laughing by then, but they all sobered up as the senior midwife on duty that morning appeared in the doorway. Comfortable-looking though she was with her plump figure, round face and greying hair, Sister Lulworth managed to express icy disdain as she glanced from one bed to the next.

'Nurse Worbarrow,' she said a moment later in a voice that made several inhabitants of the ward flinch and look as guilty as rule-breaking fourth-formers. 'I should like to see you in the nurse manager's office at once.'

She swept out. Susan Worbarrow did not look much chastened, but she did as she was told.

'Poor girl,' said the curious husband when the swing doors had closed behind her. 'She's in for it now.'

'Oh, I should think she'll survive. She seems pretty tough,' said Willow, feeling a little guilty for having encouraged the story but glad to have heard it.

Her housekeeper appeared in the doorway just then, with a heavy-looking insulated picnic box in her right hand. Willow waved. Mrs Rusham smiled and came over to the bed, where she looked carefully at her employer's face.

'You look better than I expected,' she said before adding with more warmth than she usually showed: 'Was it very bad?'

Willow hardly knew how to answer the most personal question Mrs Rusham had asked during the ten years they had known each other.

'No,' she said, not wanting to embarrass either of them with too much detail. 'Aspects of the process were a trifle grim but it's done now.'

'I'm glad.' Mrs Rusham let her eyes slide sideways so that she could look at Lucinda. 'And how is she?'

'She seems pretty well. Would you like to hold her?'

Without waiting for anything more, Mrs Rusham put down the picnic box and efficiently picked Lucinda up. Having tidied the Shetland-lace shawl that she herself had knitted, she settled in a chair beside the bed and gazed down at the baby's face. Willow watched in surprise as tears gathered in Mrs Rusham's fierce dark eyes. They did not fall.

'Have you decided what to call her?' she said after a long silence.

'Lucinda.'

'That's pretty.' Mrs Rusham looked up with an infinitesimal smile on her thin lips. 'You're right. She does look well. And no jaundice.'

'No. Amazing really, considering how old I am.'

'I've brought you a picnic,' said Mrs Rusham sedately. 'I thought you might like some food that was a little more interesting than the hospital's likely to provide.'

'You are wonderful. The meals here are adequate, but that's all. They've been making me long for your cooking. It is really kind of you to have taken the trouble.'

Mrs Rusham's face flushed slightly and she shook her head.

'It was no trouble,' she said gruffly, adding almost at random: 'It will be pleasant to have a baby in the house.'

Willow's face softened in amusement and affection at the typically Rushamian understatement.

'It'll certainly be a change. Noise, nappies and broken nights.'

'I can always help babysit for you or take over night duty if you get too tired.' Mrs Rusham looked surprised as she spoke, as though taken aback by her own forwardness, and Willow hurried to reassure her.

'What a wonderful offer,' she said lightly. 'I shall certainly take you up on it.'

Mrs Rusham pushed her left wrist out from under Lucinda's back so that she could see her watch over the baby's head. 'I'd better be getting back now. There's a lot to do to get the house ready for your return. Shall I put her back in the cot?'

'I'll take her,' said Willow holding out her arms.

'I am glad that everything's turned out satisfactorily,' Mrs Rusham said when she had handed Lucinda over. 'I had thought it was a rather risky thing for you to be doing.'

'At my age,' said Willow, nodding. 'I know you did. I did too. It probably was mad, but we wanted to, and all is well.'

'Yes,' said Mrs Rusham, still looking at her and apparently not knowing what else to say.

'Thank you for coming,' said Willow.

Mrs Rusham nodded abruptly and then turned and hurried out of the ward. As she pushed open the swing doors at the far end of the long room, a tall, broad-shouldered, grey-haired man in a long white coat was revealed, talking to one of the nurses.

For a moment Willow thought that he was Alexander Ringstead. Then he turned and she saw that his face was completely different. Surprised by her own irrationality, she got painfully out of bed and, holding Lucinda in her left arm, pulled her curtains shut with her other hand. But she found that she could not shut out her memories or stop her imagination building pictures of the way Ringstead had died. She had once read an article about drowning that suggested it took about six minutes for a healthy adult to drown, and she detested the thought of what those minutes would have been like for him if he had known what was happening when his head was forced into the water. She tried to make herself believe that he must have been dead or at least unconscious before it happened.

He had been a big man, several inches over six foot and with broad shoulders and a solid-looking chest. He must have weighed a good fourteen or fifteen stone; perhaps even more. If he had been conscious, he would not have submitted to six minutes of such torture without a struggle that would have made a great deal of noise.

Willow thought back to Lucinda's birth. Her own sensations, the emotional as well as the physical, had been so colossal that it was possible that she might not have heard anything, but there had been plenty of other people around who were not in the process of giving birth and would surely have investigated any unusual sounds.

Lucinda moved then, snuffling and sticking her flat, wet, very pink tongue in and out between her anxious, questing lips. Willow smiled, tried to force out of her mind all thoughts of death and made herself concentrate on feeding her daughter.

They both did fairly well and Lucinda eventually lay back, sucking her lower lip in obvious satisfaction. Willow wanted to get out of bed and run down the ward, crying out: 'We can do it; we can do it. It works.'

'Hello?' said a tentative, young male voice from outside her curtains. 'Er, Willow, is that you?'

'Come in,' she called and smiled at the sight of her latest visitor, a thin, lanky seventeen-year-old boy, who was blushing at the sight of her unbuttoned nightgown.

'Rob!' she said, doing it up as quickly as possible with only one hand. 'How wonderful of you to come! Mrs Rusham has only just gone, but she brought a picnic box full of goodies. Why don't you open it and see what you can find while I tidy myself up? I expect you're hungry, aren't you?'

'I'm always hungry,' he said more cheerfully, dropped his heavy nylon bag of school books loudly on the floor and bent to unlatch the insulated box.

Willow smiled at the top of his untidy head. They had met two years earlier, soon after his mother had killed herself. He was much more at ease with himself than he had been then, but there was a wariness at the back of his casual attitude to life that was far too old for his age. Like Tom, Willow had grown extremely fond of him, and he had come to depend on them both for a lot of things his guardian seemed unable to provide. Willow told herself that they must not let the birth of their own child change anything for Rob.

'It's a pretty good haul that Evelyn's provided,' he said, looking up from the big green-and-white picnic box. His face was flushed but that could have been because he had been hanging down head first into its coldness.

'What would you like, Willow? There's smoked salmon and something that looks like salmon pâté, or perhaps it's crab.' He sniffed it. 'Crab. Sandwiches filled with all the usual amazing things, some pies that look savoury and a lot of cakes, puddings.'

'I can't imagine she didn't put in anything a bit healthier. Isn't there any fruit?' said Willow amused all over again by the bond Rob had struck up with her housekeeper. She had never been able to bring herself to address Mrs Rusham as Evelyn without an invitation and had not received one.

'Yeah, but you don't want any of that now, do you? What about a florentine?'

'Good idea!' said Willow laughing at his determination to fatten her up. 'What about you?'

'Sandwiches first and then one of these strawberry thingies, if that's okay?' he said, looking sheepishly at her. 'Though I shouldn't really because Evelyn must have made them for you. Oh, how's your baby? Sorry, I should have asked before.'

'She's fine.' Willow looked down at Lucinda. 'About to go to sleep again. Let's have tea and then you can make her acquaintance later. Now, how's school?'

'Not so bad,' he said.

Willow pressed him and listened to a highly coloured account of his last week's work, sport, trouble with the masters, and interest in one of the brighter girls in the year below his. Never having had siblings of her own or known any boys of Rob's age, Willow had taken some time to learn how he thought and could be approached, but by watching him and Tom talk, she had gradually done it.

As he talked, Willow commented, asked what she hoped were all the right questions and watched him eat Mrs Rusham's delicacies as though he had not seen any other food for forty-eight hours. Eventually he stopped, grinned at her from under his lanky fringe and added: 'They all say I talk too much. Sorry.'

'I like it, Rob,' said Willow truthfully. It was all too easy to remember the sullen, closed-in appearance he had presented after his mother's death. 'And there's generosity in letting me know such a lot about yourself and your life. Don't worry.'

'How *is* the baby?' he asked with an air of conscientious politeness.

Willow pulled the shawl down a little so that Rob could see Lucinda's face.

'She's fine, doing well, feeding properly—though perhaps not well enough to rival you yet.'

He smirked but then his face changed as he added: 'And

what about you? Tom said everything had gone well when he rang me this morning, but it must have been awful with your doctor dying like that.'

'That was awful,' agreed Willow, but she was surprised. 'Did Tom tell you about him?'

'No, he didn't say a word. But I heard some nurses talking about it while I was trying to find out where you were. He was your doctor, wasn't he? This Ringstead bloke?' Rob frowned.

'Not exactly mine. He was the consultant who was technically in charge of me, but I hardly ever saw him for more than a minute or two. One doesn't, you see, unless there's a particular problem that the midwives and junior doctors can't cope with.'

'How did he die?'

'I don't know,' said Willow. 'No one seems to know for sure yet and I still can't quite believe it's happened at all.'

Remembering her vision of Ringstead walking along the passage only a little while earlier, she shivered and held Lucinda more tightly.

'I know that he's dead, but it doesn't always seem quite real. A minute ago I even thought I saw him. I feel as though part of my brains have gone AWOL, although they must be as firmly fixed in my skull as usual.'

'Actually they're not all that firmly fixed,' said Rob with a faint smile. 'They sort of float, bathed in liquid. All brains do. Didn't you know that?'

'Yes, I suppose I did. But I'm surprised you do.'

'Well, I'm thinking of going in for them. I thought you knew that I'm aiming at medical school if my A-level grades are good enough next year.'

'Yes, I did,' said Willow, 'but I hadn't realised before that it was brains that interested you.'

Rob flushed again and looked much more like the difficult unhappy boy of two years earlier.

'I'd like to understand about them,' he said gruffly. 'Really understand, you know. About how personality works and free will and all that. I don't mean genetically, but in terms of the chemical and neurons and things. I want to know what effect changes in the neurotransmitters have and just exactly what the hypothalamus does. That sort of stuff.'

All the mischief had gone from his eyes as he stared down at his scruffy trainers. He picked at one of the spots that disfigured his strong chin.

'I can't think of anything more absorbing,' Willow said quietly, remembering the years of psychiatric illness that had preceded his mother's death. 'Or more useful. Look, could you bear to have a go at holding Lucinda for me? My pillows are digging into my back. I need to sort them out.'

'Won't I break her?'

'No, of course you won't. And if you're going to be a doctor, you'll have to get used to holding babies, even if you're going in for brains in the end.'

She watched while Rob sat stiffly with the baby in his arms. When Lucinda waved one of her arms out of the shawl, he stroked it warily and then felt her grasp his finger and drag it towards her mouth. He pulled away, but then touched her cheek.

'Have you really no idea what happened to your obstetrician?' he asked, not looking at Willow. 'That's unlike you.'

'I haven't been able to find out anything yet,' she said. 'Nobody seems to know. Or at least if they do know they haven't passed it on to any of us.'

'One of the nurses I overheard was saying that he must have been murdered but one of the others thought he might have done it himself.' Rob frowned. 'I sort of hoped you might know.'

Wishing that the nurses could have kept their thoughts to themselves, Willow repeated most of what her neighbour had pointed out that morning.

'I don't think that a doctor with access to every possible drug would ever have thought of killing himself like that,' she said, watching Rob relax. 'You really needn't worry about suicide. He could have had a heart attack or a fit of some kind and fallen into the pool unconscious. Or he could have been knocked down and held under the water. But I can't think of any other possible explanation.'

'Have you got any idea who could have done it—if it was murder, I mean?'

'Not yet,' said Willow. Then she smiled. 'And I can hardly go round the hospital asking questions in this state.'

'I could do it for you,' said Rob, sounding as though he were serious.

'No, you couldn't. You've got far too much to do. Your A-level work is very important. You can't possibly take time off to fossick about in a mystery that's none of our business and probably isn't even a mystery any longer. The police may well have solved it already.'

'Oh yes I can,' he said, ignoring her last comment. 'The exams aren't for more than a year. Look, as a future medical student, I can ask all sorts of questions around the hospital that you couldn't possibly ask, even if you hadn't just had a baby. There was an open day here a couple of weeks ago for people who are thinking of applying here. I didn't go because I don't particularly want to come here, but it means that I can wander about and talk to people. If anyone challenges me I'll just say I missed the open day and am trying to catch up so that I can decide whether to apply here or not. If they're suspicious, they can check with school and find out I'm telling the truth. How's that?' He smiled, inviting approval.

'Not bad,' she said, giving him as much as she could. 'But I honestly don't think you should bunk off school even if you *have* got a year to go before A-levels. They're far too important. The whole of the rest of your life depends on how well you do.'

'I've got lots of time. And *you* want to know what really happened to him as well, don't you?'

'Very much,' she said truthfully, 'but, Rob, you must be

careful. Talk to Tom and ask him anything you want, but don't talk to anybody else. Anything they told you might not be accurate, and wrong information is worse than none at all. Much more worrying.'

Rob looked mutinous. Willow thought that any more good advice would only increase his stubbornness and so she simply suggested that he should return Lucinda to her cot and have something else to eat from Mrs Rusham's box. He wolfed down four more sandwiches.

Tom shouldered his way through the curtains just as Rob was shaking the crumbs from the last sandwich off his loose black trousers. Tom, who was carrying a big bunch of roses, laid a carelessly affectionate hand on the boy's shoulder before coming to kiss Willow.

'Good to see you, Rob,' he said when he had straightened up. 'I'm glad you've made Lucinda's acquaintance.'

'She's lovely,' said Rob, looking wistful. 'I do think you're both lucky.'

Willow glanced at Tom, hoping that he would understand what she wanted to ask. After a moment he pushed his lips forward in a familiar expression that meant he was taking some proposition seriously, and nodded. Willow smiled brilliantly and turned to ask Rob if he would like to be one of Lucinda's godfathers.

He blinked, smiled, tried to speak and failed. Having shaken his head, and looked down at her face as though for inspiration, he eventually managed to make his voice work.

'I should be honoured,' he said with a formality the others had never heard from him. Then he added in a much more characteristic rush: 'And I'd like it, too. I really would. It'd be great.'

'Good,' said Willow. 'Then you'll be officially part of the family as well, which will be very nice indeed.'

'Thank you very much.' He scrambled to his feet, and clumsily offered his hand to Tom, who shook it in a comfortingly manly fashion. 'I'd better go though now, and let you have a bit of peace, hadn't I?'

'No need,' Tom was saying, but Rob swung the big bag of prep up from the floor, waved at them all and was gone.

'He's such a good boy,' said Willow, watching the curtains fluttering in his wake.

'I know. That was a nice gesture of yours, Will.'

FOUR

Day Three—Afternoon

ROB WAS BACK just as Willow was waking from her post-lunch sleep the following day. He was carrying a mobile he had made to hang over Lucinda's cot. It was a simple contraption of plastic-coated wire, fishing line, card, and foil of various colours, but it had a carefree kind of glamour that made Willow smile. Rob held it up just above the cot and Willow watched the coloured shapes fluttering in the warm air currents. A movement from Lucinda suggested that she had noticed them too.

'It's brilliant,' Willow said, genuinely impressed. 'How did you know what to make?'

'The art master's just had his second baby and knows what they like when they're hardly seeing anything yet. I nipped back to school last night and caught him just as he was leaving. He gave me a lot of help. I finished it before early school this morning. I'd have been here sooner, but I had classes this morning that I couldn't cut.'

He laid the mobile carefully on Willow's small bedside locker, but it slithered off on to the floor. He picked it up, straightened its strings anxiously and then, after a moment, hung it over the knob of the cupboard.

'I'm glad you didn't cut any lessons,' said Willow, frowning. 'Your…'

'A-levels are far too important,' he said mockingly, wagging his head from side to side and putting on an idiotic smile. He looked much more cheerful than he had the previous day.

'Okay, okay. I know,' said Willow, smiling at him. 'It's

none of my business and I'm not your Aunt Agatha or even one of your teachers.'

'Too right. But look, Willow, I've started talking to people and I think you're right. This Ringstead bloke can't possibly have killed himself.'

Willow looked carefully at Rob, but the only emotion she could see in his dark eyes was satisfaction. That seemed worth encouraging.

'Why not?'

'Well, apart from what you said about him having access to drugs, drowning himself in something as shallow as that pool would be far too difficult, too painful, and too likely to be interrupted. It's not like filling your pockets with stones and jumping into a deep lake.'

'No. I can see that.'

'And in any case, he'd suddenly got very happy recently, which doesn't sound as though he could have wanted to bump himself off.'

'How do you know that? I haven't heard anything like it at all.'

'I've been listening to hospital gossip,' said Rob looking even more pleased with himself. 'And everyone says that although he'd been in a pretty bad mood, snappy and irritable, he'd got much happier and been singing in the corridors recently and making jokes instead of tearing strips off people.'

'And does hospital gossip suggest any reason for the change?' asked Willow with a slight smile.

Rob's eyes glinted. 'Yeah. He'd lost weight and been wearing new cufflinks—great heavy gold ones—and much jazzier ties than usual. They think he'd got a new girlfriend, much richer than the old one, who was a nurse here.'

'Aha!'

'Yeah. So you see why it's unlikely he wanted to do away with himself.' Rob lowered his voice to a whisper. 'Although it sounds as though there are quite a lot of other people who won't be too unhappy now he is dead.'

'Like who?' asked Willow, wincing internally at her lapse from good grammar. She spoke in her usual voice, knowing from long experience that a whispered conversation arouses infinitely more interest in potential eavesdroppers than one conducted at a normal pitch.

'Well, for a start, there's his registrar—a man called Kimmeridge.'

'Oh, come on.' Willow might have taken exception to Doctor Kimmeridge's brusqueness, but she could not believe that he would have drowned his boss. 'Who on earth suggested him?'

'A couple of nurses I had lunch with.'

For a moment Willow was too surprised to speak. Looking thoroughly pleased with the effect he had created, Rob dragged forward a chair and sat down very close to the side of her bed.

'I went to the staff canteen here,' he said casually, as though it had been the most ordinary thing for a schoolboy to do, 'and got a tray and just sat down next to them. Nobody seemed surprised or bothered. They were talking about Ringstead when I sat down and I just let them get on with it. Apparently Kimmeridge thought Ringstead was blocking his chances of promotion with bad references and things. Kimmeridge is quite experienced enough to be a consultant and he's said to be very good at his job, but he's never even got on to the shortlist anywhere he applied. He's stuck as a registrar and jolly angry about it.'

'Did the nurses think it was Ringstead's fault that Kimmeridge is stuck?'

'I don't think so,' said Rob. 'The general view seemed to be that the people who appoint consultants here and in the other big hospitals he'd applied to are all snobs and he isn't public school enough for them. They don't like his Leicestershire accent and he doesn't suck up to them and hasn't enough important friends, unlike your man who seems to have cultivated them. But Kimmeridge blamed him and that must be what counts.'

'I'm amazed,' said Willow. 'And frightfully impressed with you, Rob. You've been absolutely brilliant.'

'Yeah,' he said, glowing with pleasure. 'And there's plenty more.'

Willow laughed. 'I'm not sure I'm capable of absorbing much more.'

'No, no, you must listen to this.'

'Of course I will. I was only joking.'

'Good. Your man thought some of the ambulance crews had a scam going and he'd been trying to get three of them suspended just before he died. They must have wanted him stopped.'

'What sort of scam?' Willow's mind went from stolen petrol to fiddled expenses and false overtime claims.

'According to the nurses, he'd decided that whenever they picked up someone from a house that was obviously empty and had expensive things in it, they'd tip off some mates of theirs to go round and burgle it,' said Rob joyously.

Willow realised that the whole business was turning into a game for him and she was prepared to encourage that, even though the reality of what had happened to Ringstead made it impossible for her to find any entertainment in the circumstances surrounding his death.

'Apparently there'd been a spate of break-ins round here,' Rob said, quite unaware of what she was thinking, 'and your bloke thought it too much of a coincidence that so many patients brought here by ambulance found they'd been robbed when they got home. He'd started to ask around and check with people who'd been discharged to find out whether their houses had been burgled and if so which crew had brought them in. He hadn't bothered to do any of it discreetly, and he'd caused a lot of bad feeling.'

'I'll bet.' Willow thought for a while. 'Hmm. You've done awfully well, Rob.'

He sat up very straight. His thin chest seemed to have filled out too, and all his joints had become much less floppy than usual.

'I've been thinking,' he said. 'It would have been really easy for an ambulance-driver to dress up as a porter and push a trolley along the corridors until they found your man. Then all they'd have had to do was say that there was an emergency in the birthing pool and run on ahead so that they were there ready to tip him in and hold his head under.'

'I suppose so,' said Willow, blinking at the evidence of Rob's unexpectedly vivid imagination. 'The police must know all this already if the nurses are gossiping about it in the canteen. I wonder…'

'I'm sure I can find out more,' Rob said at once, looking slightly less pleased with himself. 'I've got to get back to school in a minute but as soon as I can I'll do some more digging. I know we can find out before the police do. I know we can.'

He glanced at the enormous sports watch that looked so incongruous on his spindle-thin wrist and added: 'Hell! I have got to go. There's a match this afternoon and I'm playing. But I will find out some more. Don't worry.'

'I'm not worrying, Rob. At least not about getting more information. You've been brilliant, but I don't think you should even think about asking more questions.'

He seemed to deflate in front of her and she silently cursed herself for spoiling his pleasure. She quickly thought of something she could safely ask him to do that would not take up too much time.

'Look, on your way out do you pass those demonstrators outside?'

'Yeah,' he said sulkily. 'Why?'

'I'd like to talk to one of them, find out a bit more about what they've been up to. They were making a tremendous noise on the night it happened. I'm wondering if it could have been some kind of decoy operation.'

Rob grinned again and Willow relaxed.

'I get you,' he said. 'I know, I'll tell them you're thinking of joining them as soon as you're up and about. Don't worry, Willow, we'll crack this between us. I know we will.'

He heaved up his bag of books and blew her a kiss as he strode out between the curtains. She could not help laughing.

'Dear Rob,' she said aloud, hoping that he would get to his match in time.

She was just settling back against her pillows when his dark, untidy head appeared between the curtains again.

'I quite forgot to say, Aunt Serena knows a bit about your obstetrician, but she wouldn't tell me any of it and so I said you wanted to see her asap. You'll get much more out of her than me. 'Bye.'

He was gone again before Willow could say anything at all. She wondered how his guardian, a busy and distinguished barrister, would feel about being ordered to the hospital by her seventeen-year-old nephew. She and Willow knew each other and were friendly enough when they met, but they were not much more than acquaintances.

Nurse O'Mara was passing the foot of Willow's bed and stopped to say: 'You're looking a bit down in the mouth. Are you worrying about anything now?'

Willow shook her head, dredging up a polite smile.

'No. Not really. I was just thinking about poor Mr Ringstead and trying to imagine what could have happened to him.'

'Well you shouldn't be. I know it's tempting, but it doesn't help him at all and it'll only upset you, which isn't good for Lucinda,' she said, sounding as though she were twice Willow's age instead of half of it. 'As Sister said to us yesterday, the police are doing everything they can and we must just wait until they have something to tell us. Now, when did you last feed Lucinda?'

'An hour ago,' said Willow, no longer bothering about whether or not she was being polite. She had never enjoyed being told what she should or should not think about. 'And I changed her and washed her, and there's nothing else she needs for the moment.'

'Now, now,' said Nurse O'Mara with a patronising note that set Willow's teeth on edge. 'There's no need to get angry with me. I'm only doing my job. But it's all right. Don't worry. We all understand how difficult it must be for you and how strange you must be feeling.'

'Difficult?' repeated Willow, feeling even more irritated. 'Why? Because I'm so much older than everyone else here?'

As Nurse O'Mara's pretty, freckled face began to flush, Willow decided to pursue her small advantage.

'I'm only in a bad mood because someone told me that Mr Ringstead had been unhappy a while ago,' she said less sharply. 'Even though I didn't know him at all well, I liked him such a lot that it makes me feel as though I must have been very selfish not even to have guessed there was anything wrong with him.'

'I see. I'm so sorry,' said Nurse O' Mara, sounding normal again. 'I thought you were just being nosy.'

'I know that Sister doesn't want you all gossiping about him, but I wish you'd tell me what he was really like and what had happened to him recently. It would make me feel so much better.'

'Well now. I suppose it's true that he had been a little bit depressed a while ago. I hadn't really thought about it. He'd been so much more cheerful recently.'

'Do you know what it could have been that had depressed him? Or why he'd started to cheer up?'

Before either of them could say anything else, they heard the unmistakable sound of Sister Lulworth's slightly squeaky rubber-soled shoes. Nurse O'Mara looked worried and seized the chart that was hanging at the end of the bed. Seeing her obvious nervousness, Willow decided to forgive her.

Sister Lulworth glared at her as though she were quite un-convinced by her performance with Willow's charts, and sent her away. When she had gone, the midwife closed the curtains and asked Willow a series of detailed questions about herself and Lucinda.

Willow realised that she must be beginning to get over the birth when she felt a strong resistance to discussing the workings of her bowels with one of the women who had seemed the nearest thing to her saviour only a couple of days earlier. She told herself to behave and answered as civilly as she could before submitting to yet another physical examination.

She detested every minute of it and said nothing until it was over. Then she was allowed to retrieve some of her dignity while the midwife went to wash her hands. When she came back and began to write up the results of the examination, Willow decided to try a new tack and said, as though the thought had just occurred to her. 'Do *you* know why Mr Ringstead had got so cheerful recently?'

Sister Lulworth looked up, her round grey eyes bright with intelligence and humour.

'Whatever makes you ask that?'

'I just can't help thinking about him,' said Willow, for once trying to sound pathetic. 'Someone said he'd been very happy recently and in a way that makes the fact that he's dead even worse, if you see what I mean.'

'Although if one has to die,' said the midwife, 'wouldn't it be better to die happy?'

'I'm not sure. I'd have to think about that. But what *had* made him so happy?'

'You're an obstinate one, aren't you? Were you a breach baby yourself?'

'I don't think so,' said Willow, surprised by the question. 'And what's that got to do with anything anyway?'

'Oh, I've noticed breach babies often grow up to be very stubborn,' said Sister Lulworth. There was plenty of amusement in her smile but no mockery.

Willow found herself responding with more friendliness than she usually felt towards anyone who laughed at anything about her.

'It's true that I take a certain pride in not letting anyone stop me finding out something I want to know,' she admitted, watching Sister Lulworth's eyes narrow as she laughed, 'but I've no idea whether my birth had anything to do with it. I don't know anything about that. It was not something my mother ever talked about.'

'What, never? You do surprise me. Most mothers do, especially with their daughters.'

'Mine had never wanted children,' said Willow automatically. It was a truth she had lived with for as long as she could remember and she had never even questioned it. 'Perhaps that's why.'

'I'm sorry,' said the midwife gently. 'Have you ever thought that could be why you left it so late to have your own child?'

'Certainly not,' said Willow in a voice that her erstwhile civil service superiors would have recognised. She liked Sister Lulworth, and trusted her, but she did not welcome that kind of comment from anyone.

'I just thought you might like to talk about it,' said Sister Lulworth casually. 'Talking about things that worry us can sometimes help.'

'I don't need any help,' said Willow, feeling her eyes prickling and hating herself for it. 'Except in finding out what happened to Mr Ringstead. I must have been almost the last person to see him, but no one will tell me anything about what was done to him.'

'D'you feel he deserted you perhaps just when you needed him most? Is that what troubles you so much?'

'I thought you were a midwife,' said Willow, sounding more contemptuous than she intended, 'not a psychiatrist.'

'I'm only trying to help.'

'I know. I'm sorry,' said Willow. 'But I get so frustrated at being blocked all the time. Everyone here wants to know why he died. It's not only me. And it's perfectly natural. I can't think why no one will talk to me about him.'

Willow was surprised and rather ashamed to hear her voice

rising with every word, but it had one good effect. Sister Lulworth pulled forward a chair, sat down and laid her cool, plump hand on Willow's arm.

'There's no need to get upset,' she said. 'I'll tell you anything I can, although I don't know very much. We've none of us got anything to tell. That's why no one will answer your questions. What is it that you specially want to know?'

'How exactly he died and when and why.'

'That's my point. I don't know any of those things. All I've been told is that he was found face down in the birthing pool at three o'clock that morning. I was at home in bed when they found him and so you probably know quite as much as I do.'

'Except about what he was really like. No one will tell me that either. I heard that he'd recently become very much happier than before. Do you know why?'

'I'm not sure. He never confided in me, but it seemed to me as though he'd got something that he had wanted for a long time.'

'What sort of thing?' asked Willow quickly. 'Professional or personal?'

Sister Lulworth said nothing and so Willow tried again: 'Was he married?'

'He had been.'

'You mean he was divorced? When did that happen?' asked Willow, lying back against the pillows as she began to get some real information at last. 'And why?'

'Almost five years ago now. I don't know why, but I suspect his wife found it hard to take the fact that he had to work such long hours that he never had much energy to spare for her.' Sister Lulworth smiled as she got up and pushed the chair neatly against the wall. 'I must go now.'

'Before you do,' said Willow quickly. 'Did he have any history of epilepsy or anything like that? Fainting? Blackouts?'

Sister Lulworth stood up and ran both hands down over her pristine apron, outlining her short, strong thighs. She turned up the small silver watch she wore on the breast of her blue-spotted uniform. Willow thought she looked tired and felt a little conscience-stricken at adding to the burdens of her job. She opened the curtains, saying as she did so: 'Not that I ever heard of. I really am going to have to go now. Will you be all right? Is your husband coming in to see you?'

'Yes, he should be.' Willow realised she was not going to get any more information and accepted the fact philosophically enough. 'I know he had to be out of London for work today, but he should be coming this evening.'

'Well, try and rest until then. I expect you're very tired. The night staff said you didn't get much sleep last night.'

'Lucinda did wake up several times.'

'She will do that for a while, but she'll settle down eventually and so will you. She won't frighten you so much for long. Probably in a few days you'll wonder what all the fuss was about, and then you'll forget all about Mr Ringstead.'

'She doesn't frighten me now,' said Willow, wondering why she had ever thought she liked Sister Lulworth, but she was talking to an empty space.

When Lucinda woke and started crying Willow picked her up, changed her nappy and took her back to bed for a feed that was only quite successful. Every time Lucinda turned her head away, Willow thought about Sister Lulworth's assumption that she was a reluctant parent because she herself had been unwanted as a child.

'I am not reluctant,' she said aloud, almost overcome with the need to make sure that Lucinda never, ever, doubted that she was wanted and loved. Willow kissed her head and soothed her as well as she could before laying her gently back in her cot.

'Will?'

She whirled round at the sound of Tom's voice and held out her arms. Tom hugged her, looking over her shoulder at the interested women in the beds nearby. He was surprised by his wife's unusual demonstrativeness and then, feeling her trembling, troubled. Without letting go of her completely, he managed to pull the curtains nearest them with one hand; then he led her back to the bed and made her lie down while he pulled the rest.

'What is it, Will?' he asked, crouching beside the bed, so that he could hug her again.

'No more than a spot of post-partum anxiety,' she said as casually as possible. 'And all my old hatred of criticism.'

'Who's been criticising you? Tell me their names and I'll go and biff them at once.'

Recognising an effort to cheer her up, Willow wrinkled her nose and smiled.

'Sorry. I've just come over extraordinarily weedy. I'm sure it's only that my hormones are doing peculiar things to me, but I don't seem to have any control over myself any more. And people seem to be suggesting that I'm not having the right reactions to Lucinda and I... Oh, Tom, I can't bear it.'

She buried her face in his shoulder and knew that she was behaving like one of the sillier heroines of her earliest novels. That thought helped her get back some of her much-prized self-control and she soon stood up straight again and wiped her eyes.

'Now,' she said with an assumption of her old manner, 'tell me how the AMIP bunch are doing with the official investigation into Ringstead's death.'

'I don't know, I'm afraid.'

As Willow's eyes flashed, Tom quickly added: 'I'm not stalling. I just haven't heard anything. I told them what little I could and answered all their questions, and then I went off to concentrate on my own work. Haven't they interviewed you yet?'

'No. As the woman who was in that bed yesterday said, I'm one of the last people to have anything useful to say, having been just a bit preoccupied at the crucial time.'

'You're telling me,' said Tom, painfully getting up off his knees and finding one of the visitors' chairs. 'Ugh! I'm getting old and stiff. You know, it was pretty hard seeing what you were going through and not being able to make it any different. Does it still hurt much?'

'Not too much, but I am pretty bruised and the tears still sting horribly when I pee. But they're healing. And once I get used to this business of feeding my breasts won't hurt so much.'

Tom winced.

'It's natural, as everybody keeps telling me,' said Willow drily.

He stayed with her for two hours and helped her raid Mrs Rusham's picnic box, finding some quarter bottles of champagne neatly laid at the bottom under a layer of ramekins of pâté.

'Oh, good!' said Willow as he lifted them out.

'Won't it affect your milk?' he asked, laughing.

'No. I'm sure it won't,' said Willow, thinking how brilliant Mrs Rusham had been to have included champagne in the picnic box. It was just what she wanted to take away the taste left by Sister Lulworth's kindly attempts at therapy. 'Didn't they give nursing mothers stout in the old days? I can't see what harm it would do.'

'But we neither of us know. Perhaps I ought to ask.'

'Surely Mrs Rusham knows and wouldn't send anything I oughtn't to have,' said Willow, touching the gold-coloured foil. Then anxiety overtook her, too, and she took her hand away from the bottle as though it were full of anthrax germs. It was still hard to accept the fact that she and Tom, both experienced in most aspects of life, were completely at sea when it came to Lucinda and her needs.

He nodded and disappeared for five minutes. When he came back he was smiling broadly.

'They say it's fine and will do all three of us good,' he said, easing the cork out of the first of the small, dark-green bottles.

The wine fizzed exuberantly and he tipped it into Willow's empty water glass.

'There.'

She took a healthy swig and then accepted a smoked-salmon sandwich from him and sighed in pleasure.

'Isn't Mrs Rusham wonderful?' she said when she had finished the lot. 'D'you know? I'd forgotten that all these goodies were here. Are there any more of those florentines?'

'Sure.''

'Golly, it is good when the angst dissipates,' she said, letting her head flop back on to the pillows and smiling up at Tom.

FIVE

Day Four—Morning

'IS IT MRS WORTH?'

Willow looked up from Lucinda's face, relaxed in milky satisfaction against her breast, and saw a completely unknown woman standing just inside the curtains. Looking as though she were about thirty, she had an astonishingly beautiful, broad-cheeked face, long thick dark hair and warm brown eyes, but her hair was wild and her clothes looked extraordinarily unlikely for a hospital ward. Not only was she wearing torn strawberry-pink leggings on her long, slim legs, but she also had on a sagging black cotton sweater and heavy black hiking boots. She carried a dirty-green parka under one arm as though she were going camping and there was a twisted gold ring on the third finger of her right hand. Her nails, which were cut short, were very clean.

'Yes?'

'Hi. I'm Ros from WOMB. I've just been told you wanted to see me, but it doesn't seem like a good moment. Shall I go?'

'No, no, please don't,' said Willow quickly. 'She's just finished. It is kind of you to come. Very kind. I was only letting her take her time.'

Having mopped her overflowing breast and hooked up the huge nursing bra she wore under her nightgown, Willow settled Lucinda back into her accustomed post-feed position.

'I was only surprised because Rob said he would talk to you yesterday afternoon.' She hoped that there was nothing wrong. 'He must have forgotten.'

'I wasn't here yesterday,' said Ros, who did not look at all put out by the sight of Willow's manoeuvres, 'so I don't know what happened then, but he came running over a few minutes ago and told me you wanted to see me. He was breathless and I thought it must be very urgent. So here I am. What is it I can do for you?'

'Oh, dear, I am sorry,' said Willow, relieved to see that her new visitor was amused by the summons rather than irritated. 'I'm afraid there's nothing dramatic at all. I just thought I'd like to find out more of what you're about. You see I was actually in labour three nights ago when there was all that trouble, and...'

'There was rather a lot of noise, wasn't there? I'm sorry about that.' Ros pushed her hair away with one hand, twisting it all over her left shoulder in a loose, shining rope. 'We all are, because one of the many things we've been battling to get across to the male medical establishment is how frightening noise and bustle are for the newly born, and how unpleasant for their mothers.'

'I can imagine,' said Willow with a dryness that made the other woman flush and fiddle with her ring.

'But we couldn't help it that night,' Ros said earnestly. 'You see, the hospital security men suddenly got amazingly aggressive. They were yelling at us and trying to drag some of us away physically and banging and crashing about all over the place. It's difficult not to yell back under that kind of provocation.'

'Yes, I'm sure,' said Willow, glad to feel that her brain was working again. 'Why had they suddenly got belligerent? After all, you've been demonstrating before and since and no one's tried to stop you, have they? What was different that night?'

'Can I sit down?'

'Of course; I should have said. Do please.'

'Thanks,' said Ros, slumping into the chair and leaning her chin on her hands. In spite of her careless pose, she still looked wonderful.

'One of our people had had a meeting with the hospital administrators that afternoon, and apparently it all got rather adversarial. They'd let us do our thing without interference until then, but somebody at the meeting must have lost his temper and told the security guards to get rid of us. It looks as though wiser counsels have prevailed again since.'

'What was the meeting about?'

'Why d'you want to know?' said Ros, sitting up and staring suspiciously at her.

Unwilling to explain that she thought WOMB could have been providing a decoy operation for whoever had murdered Mr Ringstead, Willow shrugged.

'Curiosity, really,' she said, hoping that she sounded convincing. 'I'm interested in your organisation and what you're trying to achieve, and what you're up against as you do it. I rather like the idea of it, you see. I've never been a great one for female company before, but now that I've had a baby I find I want women around me, knowledgeable women, I mean. D'you see?'

Ros's face relaxed. She bent down to dig into the small orange rucksack she had with her and brought out a professionally printed, full-colour leaflet with a striking, bright blue outline of a pregnant woman on the dazzling yellow cover. The sketch appeared to have been achieved with a single flowing line. It was at once stylish and touching. Willow was surprised by the quality of the leaflet's paper and the clarity of its colour printing.

'Here,' said Ros. 'This will explain what we're about and you'll see that it's absolutely normal to want women around you. One of the things we're campaigning for is to have well-informed, friendly women available to support mothers during and after labour, instead of hierarchical male doctors who are too busy and self-important to give enough time to listen.'

'That sounds wonderful—just what I need. So why should the administrator have got so angry with you?' Willow took the leaflet from Ros and put it carefully on top of her book so that she could read it later.

'It was to do with a couple we're sponsoring.' Ros looked reluctant to say any more. Willow did not help her by changing the subject or even looking away. She simply raised her red eyebrows and waited.

'They had a baby here about two months ago and he's severely brain-damaged,' Ros went on after an uncomfortable pause. 'The hospital is denying liability, even though it's fairly clear that there were some serious mistakes made during delivery.'

'That's standard practice, isn't it?' said Willow. 'As in car accidents. I think insurance companies insist that you never admit liability even when it's clear that you drove into someone else.'

'Yes, but it's so silly and causes such trouble in medical cases. If all the money that's paid to lawyers could be handed directly to victims of negligence, everyone would be better off.'

'Except the lawyers.'

'Exactly.' Ros looked at Willow with clear approval and spoke more energetically. 'WOMB supports the idea of a national no-fault compensation scheme so that victims of medical accidents can be given the money they need without going to the courts, but until it's in place victims of negligence or accidents have to sue, and a lot of them need help to do that. We're helping this particular couple.'

'I see,' said Willow, remembering the fruiting bodies and the trust's financial crisis.

'We have a lawyer on the committee, who's advised us that the parents have a good case, but, like the rest of us, she's concerned that they may not have either the sophistication or the emotional stamina to deal with all the hassle they're likely to get before any compensation's paid. They have no financial resources of their own at all. He's unemployed, and she's had to give up her cleaning job to look after the baby. Our lawyer felt a compromise might be possible; you know, that if we leaned on the hospital they might settle, which would mean that the poor parents would get their money much quicker and without all the legal nonsense.'

'That sounds sensible, too,' said Willow. 'And even though I don't suppose the trust has any money to spare, I can't see why the manager should have lost his temper. Which one of them was it?'

'The director of finance. I think the problem was that our lawyer had taken the parents with her to the meeting and it was the first time they'd heard anyone spell out quite how hopeless their baby's chances are. They seem to have believed that he might improve as he gets older. And, you see, I think they'd believed what Ringstead told them.'

'Which was?'

'That it was just a terrible accident of nature, not anyone's fault.'

'Couldn't it have been? Accidents of nature do happen, don't they?'

'Yes, they do. And it still isn't absolutely clear what happened in this case, but our information suggests that it could have been a muddle of contraindicated drugs. All I know for certain is that at some time, for some reason, the child was starved of oxygen and his brain was terribly damaged as a result.'

Willow looked down at Lucinda again, suddenly unable to think of anything except her safety. As she stroked Lucinda's cheek, the big eyes opened again. For an instant Willow thought that Lucinda was aware of who was holding her and then she turned her head inwards a little towards Willow's body.

'I say, there isn't anything wrong with her, is there?' said Ros clumsily. Her face was bright red.

Willow saw the pulse beating in the gap between the plates of Lucinda's skull and could hardly bear to admit how fragile she was. Letting her lips brush the soft furriness of the small head, Willow felt the steadiness of the pulse underneath her lips. Her arms tightened involuntarily around Lucinda and she felt tears rising in her eyes.

'She's fine.' Willow coughed and shook her head. 'Sorry. I just get a bit overwhelmed by it all sometimes. She's had all the neurological tests and shown all the right reactions. But I keep worrying.'

'Of course you do. Anyone would.'

'Yes,' said Willow and then forced her mind back to the easier topic. 'So what did the parents do in the meeting when they heard how bad it all was?'

'The mother was nearly ill with hysteria and the father got into what sounds like a ferocious rage. You see, being not all that articulate, he didn't know how to handle himself. He was yelling and screaming and hitting out in all directions. He even broke a bit off the desk. The finance director, presumably scared witless, called security and had him bundled out of the room. Then he tried to have us moved on as well, as though it was all our fault.'

Thinking that he had had a certain amount of justification for that view, Willow frowned.

'What is it?' asked Ros, flinging her heavy hair over the other shoulder and crossing her legs. Her boots looked even more incongruous than they had when she was standing up. As she moved, her cotton sweater was pressed against her front and Willow noticed that she was not wearing a bra. Something about her looks, and the perkiness of her breasts, suggested that she was not following any tenet of 1970s feminism but something much more traditional.

'Was Mr Ringstead involved in the birth himself?'

'As the responsible consultant, he was technically in charge,' said Ros, running her fingers through her hair again, 'although it was a house officer who was doing the actual delivery. When he belatedly started to understand how serious the problem was, he sent for Ringstead, who set about getting the baby resuscitated.'

Lucinda moved then and opened her eyes again. Willow looked down and smiled at her. After a moment Ros got to her feet.

'I shouldn't really be here at all so soon after you've been delivered, worrying you with WOMB policy and stories of damaged babies. I'll get out of your way now. But when you've read our leaflet, if you want to know anything else, or if you do want to join us, just get your son to come and tell me—I'm there every third day—and I'll come up and see you.'

'My son?' For a moment Willow could not think what Ros was talking about and then she remembered Rob. It was odd to realise that she was old enough to be his mother.

'What's the matter? You look very worried.'

'What?' Willow saw Ros looking anxiously at her and quickly smiled, banishing all her mental pictures of the ostensibly cool and efficient—but in most important ways incomplete and hopeless—person she had been twenty-six years earlier when Rob was conceived. 'No, he's no relation of mine; just a friend. But thank you very much for coming. I'll read the leaflet and be in touch. How much is the subscription?'

'Whatever you can afford.' Ros looked at Willow's flowers and her delicately embroidered pure-white lawn nightgown. 'Maybe twenty-five pounds? There's a form thing on the back of the leaflet. I'll see you again.'

'Goodbye,' said Willow, watching her walk out of the ward with surprising grace in her clumping boots.

When Lucinda was satisfactorily back asleep in her cot and Willow had taken the opportunity to have a bath, she put on another of the stack of clean nightgowns Tom had brought with him that morning and got back into bed to read the WOMB pamphlet.

There turned out to be very little in it that she had not already read in all the books she and Tom had studied so closely during her pregnancy. As Brigid O'Mara had told her, the founders of WOMB were anxious to promote passive rather than active management of labour, to warn of the dangers to babies of many of the drugs that had been routinely used in hospitals for years, and to recommend a much less medical atmosphere for maternity wards.

'After all,' the editorial ended, 'pregnancy is not an illness. Most women will suffer less and produce healthier, calmer babies if they are allowed to give birth under the care of a midwife in surroundings as much like their own homes as possible. An atmosphere of noise, hard surfaces and medical drama is not helpful.'

That seemed unexceptional, and would presumably have pleased the hospital managers. A midwife and some soft surfaces must come considerably cheaper than teams of doctors, quantities of drugs and banks of sophisticated machinery. On the other hand, Willow could well understand why the managers had taken exception to members of WOMB seeking out patients of damaged babies and encouraging them to sue the hospital.

She could also understand, with deep pity, how parents might hate the doctors responsible for their child's brain damage.

'How are you this morning, Mrs Worth?'

Willow looked up and saw the thin, dark-haired registrar watching her as she read the pamphlet. Realising that he was just the man she needed to tell her more about the child in question, she smiled at him.

'I'm fine, Doctor Kimmeridge. And so's Lucinda. She's asleep at the moment. D'you need to wake her?'

'Not just now. Tell me, though: how are the two of you getting on?'

Willow's smile faded at his question. She thought that Sister Lulworth must have told him that she was worried that Willow was not bonding correctly with Lucinda.

'Perfectly well, thank you.' She saw her frosty tone registering with Kimmeridge and wondered what he would say next. Deciding that she did not want to hear it, she hurriedly added: 'I gather that poor Mr Ringstead was battling with the hospital administrators over cuts in the obstetrics budgets.'

'Yes, that's right,' said Kimmeridge, coming nearer. Willow gave him high marks for not leaning over Lucinda's cot to check that all was well. 'Money is tight at the moment, but you needn't worry about it. Everything that you and Lucinda need will be provided.'

'Oh, I know,' said Willow quickly. 'And that wasn't why I was asking. We've both been treated in the most exemplary fashion. It's just that I'm interested in how a department like this could possibly cut costs. After all, as I gather Ringstead said himself, none of you could exactly tell women in labour to cross their legs and hang on until the budget allowed another birth.'

'You were on very good terms with him if he passed that gem of his well-known sense of humour on to you.' Kimmeridge looked puzzled and a little suspicious. Willow did not disabuse him. After a moment he seemed to make some kind of decision and said in a businesslike voice: 'The only area of major cost-cutting, apart from downgrading some of the specialist nursing posts, is in the resuscitation and care of highly premature babies.'

'You mean the managers want them to be left to...' Unable to finish the sentence, Willow herself got up to check that Lucinda was all right.

'It's not as callous as it sounds, Mrs Worth. Many obstetricians as well as administrators believe that very premature—or very damaged—babies should not be treated. If they're born before about twenty-four weeks they don't have much of a chance. Even if they are successfully resuscitated and nursed through the first few months, they tend to suffer serious health problems for the rest of their lives—and a large proportion of them are permanently brain-damaged. Life caring for such a child can be virtually unbearable for the parents, and I for one believe that it must be pretty good hell for the child as well.

There are a great many considerations other than the balance sheet here.'

'Really?'

'Of course there are.' Kimmeridge might lapse easily into irritability, but he could sound quite kind, too. 'Mr Ringstead believed that if a life could be saved it should be, however limited or full of suffering it might turn out to be; but other people have different views. Is it fair, for one thing, to put a baby through procedure after procedure, knowing that it's never going to be able to lead a normal life and may well die after months or years of pain? And is it fair to put the parents through it?'

'I expect,' said Willow, dragging the words up from her deepest, least examined feelings, 'that all they mind about just at the beginning is keeping the child alive. And who can judge the quality of any baby's life in any case?'

'There aren't any easy answers. I suspect there aren't any right ones either.' Kimmeridge seemed both friendly and surprisingly ready to talk. 'A few years ago most of the dilemmas simply didn't arise,' he went on, 'because we didn't have the technology to keep such premature babies alive.'

'In the abstract,' said Willow at her driest, 'it's an interesting question, isn't it? But I suspect faced with actual people, suffering people, it must be agony for you to have to make that sort of decision. I can't think how any of you manage to keep going at all.'

Kimmeridge's face looked harder as he leaned sideways to pick her chart from the rail at the end of her bed.

'All doctors have to put boundaries between themselves and their patients. Otherwise their judgment becomes unreliably swayed by emotion and that leads to all sorts of trouble.'

'I suppose so. And presumably for a lot of the time you're too busy to think about it all.'

'There is that too,' said Kimmeridge more lightly, checking some figures on the chart. 'Which reminds me that we'd better get back to work. Tell me how you really are.'

'Fine.' Willow was much more interested in finding out what Kimmeridge thought about the baby whose case WOMB had taken up than in her own health, but before she had formulated her next question, Kimmeridge said: 'I'm not asking out of curiosity or politeness, Mrs Worth. My job here and now is to help you. And, believe me, I can. But you must talk to me.'

Willow laughed, but to her horror the sound she produced was more like a sob. She was not prepared to risk crying in front of him again and pulled herself together with all the savagery of which she was still capable.

'There's nothing physically wrong with me at all,' she said carefully. 'My emotions are extremely volatile, but so far I'm managing to contain them.'

'Good for you, but don't bottle up too much. A lot of it's better out than in.'

She managed to smile then, wondering what he would have said if she had told him that most of what was wrong with her was anxiety about the future and what she might come to feel about her daughter. So far there was not much of a problem, but she could not help thinking that there might come a time when Lucinda's existence curtailed her freedom so severely that it would be impossible not to resent her. Willow took her upper lip between her teeth and bit it hard.

The appearance five minutes later of the talkative Nurse Worbarrow provided a welcome distraction. She was carrying an enormous informal bunch of flowers tied with raffia and she handed Willow a small white envelope.

'This came with them.'

'Thank you,' said Willow, opening the envelope to read:

Congratulations. And Welcome to Lucinda. Don't worry at all about not finishing the synopsis. There's plenty of time.

Much love, Eve.

Smiling at her literary agent's reassurance, even as she wondered whether she would ever be able to write anything else again, Willow put the note on her bedside table and took the flowers from Nurse Worbarrow.

'Goodness, aren't they lovely?' Willow said, looking more closely and admiring the artless pink-and-white-and-grey arrangement of wild roses, lamb's-tongues, single peonies and sweet peas.

'Yes. Much the prettiest of any that have come in all week,' said the young student nurse. 'So much more stylish than all those loathsome yellow and purple chrysanths. I'll get a vase for them, shall I?'

Willow thanked her and reread Eve's note, trying to believe that there was absolutely no reason why Lucinda's presence should make any difference whatsoever to her writing talent.

'Or to my detective skills,' she muttered.

'Sorry, what was that?' asked Nurse Worbarrow, coming back with a large glass vase of water. 'I missed it.'

'Nothing. Talking to myself again,' said Willow. 'Losing my marbles, probably.'

'I shouldn't worry about that,' said Susan Worbarrow with another of her dazzling smiles. 'Sister Lulworth was saying only today that you're much too clever for your own good.'

SIX

Day Five

THE FOLLOWING DAY, after much more sleep than she had had
during any night since Lucinda's birth, Willow felt better and
more in control. They managed the first feed of the day without any serious difficulty, and Willow chatted to Lucinda,
changed and washed her, and put her back in the cot almost
without having to think about any of it.

The hospital's breakfast tray was its usual depressing self
and so, having drunk a cup of strong hospital tea, Willow had
a look at what was left in Mrs Rusham's picnic box. There
was plenty and she breakfasted on a florentine, a peach and
then a mango, which left her with yellow streaks of juice down
her expensive nightdress.

Amused by the mess and feeling unreservedly fortunate
again, she tidied up the picnic remains, shoved the box back
under the bed, and, bursting with energy and confidence, collected a clean nightdress and went to have her bath hours
earlier than usual.

Back in bed, clean and cheerful but with nothing to do, she
decided to sort out the few facts she had accumulated about
Alexander Ringstead and his death. Rob had donated a couple
of felt-tipped pens and one of the pads he lugged about with
his books in the tattered nylon bag, and so she was well
equipped.

By the end of a pleasantly industrious hour, she had a neatly
written account of the information and gossip she had already
been given by Rob and the nurses, together with a list of
questions that still had no answers. Several of them could be

given only by the business manager who had been so effectively mocked by Mr Ringstead, but Willow could not think of a suitably discreet way of approaching him.

She had to break off her self-imposed work first for Sister Lulworth and then for Doctor Kimmeridge, who appeared with four medical students in tow, looking much more confident than he had the previous day and also very much brisker.

As Willow listened to his description of her condition and answered his young students' stammered questions about it as pleasantly as possible, she thought of one way in which she might be able to approach the manager and waited impatiently for Kimmeridge and his entourage to finish with her.

They had not been gone long when she saw Nurse Worbarrow at the entrance to the ward and waved enthusiastically. After a moment the student nurse saw Willow's gesture and came over to her bedside.

'So,' she said, her face alight with pleasure, 'I hear that you're doing really well now and will be off home with Lucinda very soon now. That's great news. Are you pleased?'

'Very,' said Willow, unable not to respond to such sunniness, but there was work to be done and she did not want to waste any more time. 'I'm feeling pretty well now, and a lot of it's thanks to all of you. You know, I've been thinking that I'd like to do something to help. I hear on all sides how much money the hospital needs now that dry rot's been found in the basement, and I want to help. Is there any kind of fundraising campaign?'

'Oh, yes. There's a committee of ladies.' Susan Worbarrow's eyes gleamed with mockery: 'You know the sort: rich and with too much time on their hands. But I shouldn't be rude about them; they're raising lots of money and it's in a very good cause.'

'How are they doing it?'

'They have sales and balls, concerts, lunches and stuff like that. Other people who don't have enough to do pay to go to them all.'

Willow raised an eyebrow.

'They call themselves the Friends of Dowting's Hospital. There are usually leaflets around with lists of what they're doing. I'll find you one. You could always go along to some of their parties when you're up and about again.'

'I might be able to do that.' Willow managed not to say that she would have more than enough to do when she left hospital, not least in concocting a synopsis for her next novel that would satisfy her agent and both her British and American publishers and then write the whole book, while caring for Lucinda at the same time.

'But I'd rather give some more direct help specifically for this department. I suppose I ought to have a word with one of the managers about the best way of making a donation for the obstetrics unit. Do you think any of them would be prepared to talk to me?'

'I can't exactly see them turning you down if you're wanting to give them a cheque,' said Susan Worbarrow, laughing at her. 'Would you like me to ask Mark Durdle to come and see you?'

'I'd much rather go to him.' Willow looked down at her lace-covered bosom. 'Although I suppose I can't really wander round the hospital dressed like this. D'you know where my clothes are?'

Nurse Worbarrow waved casually towards a row of locked cupboards at the end of the bay.

'Well that's okay then. Is his office a long way from here?'

'No. Just beyond the nurse manager's on the far side of the lifts.' Nurse Worbarrow began to look faintly alarmed. 'But I'm not sure that Sister Lulworth would approve of you going walkabout.'

'I don't see how she can stop me, short of a rugby tackle, and that doesn't seem very likely,' said Willow drily, raising an appreciative smile from Nurse Worbarrow. 'Look, if I do go and see him today, would you keep an eye on Lucinda for me? I'd hate to think of her crying and not getting any answer.'

'Of course I will. I'd be glad to.'

Thinking she could see a hint of surprise behind the smile of approval, Willow realised that the nurses—even those as junior and rebellious as Susan Worbarrow—must be watching her for evidence of the way she was or was not bonding with Lucinda. The prospect of interrogating one of the administrators began to seem thoroughly attractive. It might, Willow thought, reinforce her shaky sense of herself, particularly if she could do it dressed and made up to look like a normal inhabitant of the world outside the hospital.

'By the way,' she said more briskly, 'someone said to me the other day that Doctor Kimmeridge would never get promotion in this hospital. He seems thoroughly in charge at the moment. D'you know why people think he's never going to be a consultant?'

'People shouldn't gossip so much,' said Nurse Worbarrow piously. Willow just laughed.

'Well, they shouldn't.'

'No, but, as you and I know very well, it's one of the greatest pleasures. Come on, tell me. You know you want to.'

As Susan frowned, Willow wondered whether her teasing had gone too far, but in the end Susan's natural inclination to tell anything and everything she knew pushed past some of her inhibitions.

'There's a lot of competition for consultants' jobs,' she began, 'and people who get them have to fit in with the hierarchy. I'm not sure that Doctor Kimmeridge has shown that he'd be able to do that.'

'Why?'

'Well, he's always stood up for his ideas very firmly even when they were quite different from Mr Ringstead's.'

'Would that have mattered? I should have thought it would make Ringstead respect him.'

'Maybe. But their arguments did sometimes get quite

heated, and it's not altogether wise to shout at your consultant when you want him to support your next application for promotion,' said Susan before hurriedly adding: 'Although I have a feeling that Doctor Kimmeridge's religion might have had as much to do with it as anything else.'

'His religion? Why on earth?'

Susan shrugged. 'Doctor Kimmeridge is a Catholic and most of the consultants here are said to be Freemasons. That may just be gossip, too, but if it's true it would explain everything.'

'But I thought there were Catholic masons nowadays.'

'Are there? I didn't know that.'

'Yes. It must be something else. Poor Doctor Kimmeridge. Does he have any family? A wife and so on?' asked Willow, making the most of her opportunity for eliciting gossip before Sister Lulworth appeared and sent Nurse Worbarrow away.

'I don't know. He never talks about his private life. But that wouldn't have any bearing on his chances either way, would it?'

'Probably not. But I'm interested in everything about them all,' said Willow. 'Sister Lulworth was telling me that Mr Ringstead's marriage broke up because of the hours he had to work here and I just wondered whether any obstetrician could manage family life as well as working here.'

'Oh, yes. Lots of them do. But not Doctor Kimmeridge. Between you and me, I think he takes life too tragically to be married to anyone except a saint, and there aren't many of them around, certainly not in this place.'

Before Willow could ask what she meant, Susan Worbarrow had to answer an urgent-sounding call from the far end of the ward. Willow added a few more questions to her lengthening list and began the still painful business of getting out of bed, put her feet into her slippers and shuffled out towards the nursing station to find out how to get in touch with Mr Durdle.

There she found Sister Lulworth talking to two women, one dressed in a simple navy-blue suit, the other in police uniform.

Willow noticed even without thinking about it that the uniformed woman was a constable.

'Mrs Worth,' said Sister Lulworth with a smile. 'What are you doing up and about out here? Is there a problem?'

With a sideways glance at the two police officers, Willow condensed her explanation of the urge to make a substantial donation to the dry-rot fund.

'And Nurse Worbarrow suggested that I speak to a Mr Durdle about the best way to go about it. I wondered if I might telephone him from here to make an appointment?'

An expression of faint distaste crossed Sister Lulworth's usually pleasant face as she contemplated the thought of Mr Durdle.

'Yes, if you wish. There's the phone, and there's an alphabetical list of internal extensions on the wall.' Sister Lulworth looked at the two police officers. 'Shall we go into my office?'

They followed her, the CID officer looking back in some curiosity. Willow was not sure whether that was because she herself had already been identified as a Scotland Yard wife, because of her urge to spend money on the hospital, or because of the way she looked, still huge and saggy under her fine nightgown. She met the stare with a challenging expression of her own and was glad to see the other woman's gaze slide away first.

Willow dialled the number given for Mr Durdle on the list beside the telephone and when he answered she went through her introduction once again. It was beginning to sound quite convincing.

Even so, Durdle seemed surprised by her suggestion, but he agreed to see her at four that afternoon.

'If that would suit you,' he added politely. 'But there's really no need for you to come to my office. I could so easily pop along to your ward.'

'Four is fine,' said Willow, calculating that both she and Lucinda would have had their post-lunch snooze and had time to get in one feed before she would have to dress for the meeting. 'And I'd rather like to get away from the ward for a few minutes and remember what it's like not to be surrounded by babies.'

Mr Durdle laughed politely and said that he looked forward to meeting her.

Willow put down the telephone receiver, remembering that four o'clock was prime visiting time for friends who did not work in offices, and for Mrs Rusham. She decided that if any of them were to come they would just have to entertain each other until she got back.

As it turned out, by four o'clock no one had turned up to see her. Even Tom had missed his usual flying visit around lunchtime and there had been no sign of Rob. Willow asked the woman in the next bed to keep an eye out for him in case he did appear, and then went to fetch her clothes from the cupboard.

Wearing the dark-blue maternity dress in which she had arrived at the hospital, with her hair brushed and a little makeup on her face, she had a look of herself in the mirror over one of the basins. With her pale-red lashes coloured with mascara and some bright lipstick giving her mouth almost equal prominence with her big nose, she thought grimly that she would just about do.

Even so, she felt most peculiar as she went down the long passage to the swing doors that led out of the obstetrics unit, and her shoes seemed horribly hard after the flapping bedroom slippers. She forgot it all, though, when she met Mark Durdle.

He proved to be a surprisingly young man, perhaps thirty, and there was something about him that seemed familiar. Willow was sure that she had seen him somewhere before, but try as she would she could not remember where.

He had a suavity that she had not expected after the story Nurse Worbarrow had told about his humiliation at Mr Ringstead's hands. His suit was well cut and made of good grey flannel, and his black-leather shoes were well polished and not at all down at heel. His grey-and-white shirt was unaggressively striped and his dull-purple tie looked carefully chosen to express authority without clashing with his pinkish complexion.

It gave Willow a moment of amusement to realise that even though the nurses did not look as though they had been to colour counsellors, their business manager certainly did.

Having smiled at her like a film star with his brilliantly white teeth wide apart, he invited Willow into his office, offered her a cup of Earl Grey tea, and asked how he could help her.

Willow sat down with care, accepted the tea, repeated her wish to do something for the hospital and asked what he would suggest.

Durdle stood up and, with his back to her, reached up to a shelf above his desk on which were ranged several boxes with the name of a printer emblazoned on their sides. His jacket rode up a little as he stretched upwards, but not enough to reach the waistband of his trousers or reveal any bunched shirt. He took the lid off one of the boxes, from which Willow got a flash of yellow just before he replaced it, and moved on to the next box.

'That's it,' he said, removing a grey folder elegantly printed in black and gold, which he offered her. Willow swallowed a mouthful of the fragrant, wonderfully unstewed tea, and took the folder.

'That's got all the details of the appeal. You'll see there the names of the committee members who are running it, and some of the sorts of activity that are available. Now this,' he reached into one of the other boxes and took out a less glamorous piece of paper that looked like a muddy photocopy made on a cheap machine without enough toner, 'is a list of the next three months' fundraising occasions. Do keep it. If you do decide to make a donation—and may I say how grateful we are for any help at all—you could simply send a cheque to me. If you were considering a longer-term commitment, you could complete the form of covenant at the end.'

He proceeded to explain to Willow exactly how much the hospital would benefit from a four-year undertaking to pay a set amount each year, paused and then asked her kindly if she had any questions.

'Yes, actually, I have got one or two,' she said with what she hoped was appealing hesitancy. 'During one of my visits to the clinic, Mr Ringstead said something to me about the fundraising. In fact, it was really his interest in it that set me off thinking about it, and after he died…oh, wasn't it awful?'

'Yes,' said Mr Durdle unemotionally. 'Dreadful.' He smiled again, but that time he kept his teeth clamped together.

Willow watched him, trying to see past his well-managed presentation of himself to the man he might actually be.

'Well, you see,' she said as she let her mind play about with suspicions and possibilities, 'when I heard what had happened to him, I really felt that I absolutely had to do something, as a kind of memorial perhaps. I don't quite know why, but in a funny sort of way I felt almost guilty that he'd died.'

As she watched Durdle's well-combed eyebrows lift, Willow wondered if she was overdoing the silliness of her chatter. She gave a nervous-sounding giggle. 'Stupid, isn't it?'

'No, Mrs Worth, it sounds to me like a most normal reaction, especially from someone who was his patient and clearly, if I may say so, cared for him. It seems admirable to me.'

'I think all his patients must have cared for him. He was the kindest man.'

'Yes.' The cool monosyllable told Willow nothing at all about Durdle's real views of Ringstead. She tried to think how she might arouse some more useful reaction.

'Was he especially involved in the fundraising or is it hospital policy for consultants to ask their patients for donations?'

'Certainly not.' Durdle sounded outraged, which made Willow's mistrust of his tidiness ease a little. 'The National Health Service is and always will be free at the point of delivery. Anyone who might happen to choose to make a contribution to the hospital's appeal would of course be received with gratitude, but no patient should ever be made to feel that it was expected. I'm immensely surprised that Mr Ringstead should have done such a thing. I've never heard of him doing anything like it before.'

For the first time he seemed agitated. Willow was pleased that he minded about the principles of the National Health Service as much as she did. But she was also smitten with conscience since Ringstead had never even mentioned the fundraising to her.

'I may have misunderstood him,' she said quickly. 'I was concentrating so hard on what would happen during my labour and everything that I probably didn't even hear what he actually said.'

'I expect that was it.' Durdle sounded no more relaxed. 'Of course Mr Ringstead was devoted to his patients and to the hospital, which might have made him say more than he should. He always found it hard to accept that funds must be carefully managed and he could never bring himself to admit that even though medical needs are important they're not the only ones that matter.'

By the time he reached the end of his little speech there were distinct sounds of indignation in his well-managed voice. Willow was interested to see that he could not completely hide his dislike of Ringstead even though he was talking to a patient and virtually everyone else in the hospital was still showing signs of grief—or at least regret.

'What other needs could there possibly be in a hospital?' she asked, watching him closely.

'Several,' said Durdle, once more sounding in control of his feelings.

'I don't understand,' said Willow. 'If I'm going to make a donation, I need to know what it'll be spent on. I mean, I want patients to benefit. That's why I want my money to go specifically to the obstetrics unit.'

'Believe me, Mrs Worth, patients will definitely benefit, however the money is spent.' Durdle sighed and then remembered to smile again. 'But since Mr Ringstead could not always understand that, I'm not surprised that an outsider like yourself should find it difficult, too. You see, as an NHS trust we have to compete for patient referrals. That means that we have to show general practitioners that their patients will have a better time coming to this hospital rather than to, say, St Thomas's or St George's or any of the other big teaching hospitals. That's our chief aim whenever we make changes, and they are always designed to benefit patients.'

'But surely the quickness and efficacy of treatment is likely to be the most attractive aspect of anything you could offer,' said Willow, forgetting to sound silly in her real interest.

'Yes indeed, but there are other considerations as well.'

'For example?'

Mr Durdle looked at the clock above his desk and turned to smile widely at Willow once more.

'Well, to take a trivial example, car-parking. It is infinitely easier for patients and their visitors if the hospital can provide them with space for their cars. In the old days only consultants had that, and several of them like Mr Ringstead found it hard to accept that nowadays patients' car-parking is more important than their own.'

There was enough irritation in his voice to suggest that he and Mr Ringstead had fallen out over the car-parking. Durdle coughed and smiled a cool little smile.

'But that question had been settled long ago. As you probably know the patients' carpark is fully operational.'

'And must be making you money,' said Willow with a false smile of her own. 'Since we all have to buy tickets to leave our cars there.'

'And thanks to the Friends of Dowting's,' he went on without commenting, 'we are facing a less difficult future than we seemed to be when the dry rot was first discovered.'

'So Doctor Kimmeridge told me,' said Willow, thinking that if she were not going to find out anything useful, she might at least do something to boost Kimmeridge's standing in the hospital. As no more than a business manager, Durdle probably had nothing to do with promotion or recruitment, but Willow had long ago learned that an atmosphere can be created around a person—for good or ill—by the attitude of a very few people.

Suddenly noticing the surprise on Durdle's smoothly shaven face, Willow realised that she must be staring at him blankly and hastily rearranged her expression.

'Have you any more questions?' he asked, taking another, more obvious, look at his clock. 'If not, I really ought to be getting on with my work, and I suspect that the nurses will be worrying about what's happened to you.'

'Of course, Mr Durdle. How inconsiderate of me! You've been so wonderfully helpful. May I take these leaflets with me so that I can take the time to decide, and perhaps talk it over with my husband, too?'

Willow thought of adding, 'men understand these questions of money so much better than we girls,' but she did not think she would be able to say the words with any degree of credibility.

'And any of the other leaflets that you think would be useful to him,' she said, going as far as she could.

'There aren't any others,' said Durdle coming round his desk to open the door, probably to make sure she really did leave his office. 'But, do please, take those.'

Willow glanced towards the shelf with the boxes from which he had taken the grey folder and the photocopy and shrugged, assuming that the others must be filled only with stationery. She thanked him once again and walked back to the ward with the brochure under her arm, adding up the little she had learned and hoping that she had not completely lost whatever knack she had once had of making people talk usefully to her.

At the entrance to the maternity ward she heard a wailing cry that she knew was Lucinda's and started to run. When she reached her bay, she saw the curtains drawn back around her bed. Tom was standing by it with Lucinda in his arms, and an expression of helpless desperation on his face. Boiling with guilt, Willow flung the bits of paper on to her bed and cooed reassuring endearments to both her husband and her daughter. Tom sighed in relief and passed Lucinda over.

Willow sat down on the edge of the bed, fumbling with the buttons at the front of her dress while holding the baby and jiggling her in a soothing fashion that did not soothe her at all. After a moment or two and a lot of frustrated crying from Lucinda, Willow handed the baby back to Tom while she freed herself.

Eventually, as Willow gritted her teeth to bear the agonising, hiccupping sobs, Lucinda seemed to recognise that she was not being assaulted by the offered nipple and began to suck. Willow and Tom both exhaled in enormous sighs and let their muscles sag in relief.

'Thank heavens,' said Tom. To Willow's gratitude, he did not ask her where she had been or why she had not been attending properly to her child. All he said was: 'Nice Nurse Susan said you'd be back in five minutes and she was right, but it felt like years. You look fantastic, by the way, glowing. Much, much better than I've seen you since we came here.'

'Do I?' said Willow, looking up from Lucinda's ecstatic face. 'Good. All's well, Tom.'

'Yes, it does seem to be. I… Well, you know.'

He quickly took a bunch of sandwiches out of Mrs Rusham's picnic box and ate his way through them, while Lucinda absorbed her own nourishment with apparent pleasure. When she had had as much as she wanted and was back asleep in her cot, Willow and Tom sat peacefully talking to each other. She did not admit quite how much time she had spent trying to find out what happened to Mr Ringstead, but she did ask what the police had discovered.

'Not a great deal as far as I can understand,' said Tom. 'Although it looks as though it must have been murder.'

'Why?'

'First, because the autopsy showed no sign of any heart damage or any kind of seizure that might have made him fall unconscious into the pool and second, because there were marks on the back of his neck—bruises—that suggest he was held down,' said Tom, quietly, as though his tone might lessen the horror of what he was telling her.

'What sort of marks? Enough to show who could have done it?'

'Not quite enough. Someone with strong hands, not particularly large, with spatulate fingers and very short nails. There are no cuts in the skin, only bruises. Therefore it was someone with nails cut right down as short as possible.'

'Or bitten.'

'As you say. But that hasn't got them very far yet. Apparently no one who shouldn't have been up here in this part of the hospital was seen at or near what must have been the crucial time, and none of the staff who belong here was unaccounted for.'

'Although,' said Willow, leaning back and letting her shoes drop to the floor as she swung her legs up on to the bed, 'it can't have taken all that long and doctors and nurses are in and out of the wards and delivery suites all the time, fetching things, and seeing other patients. I don't actually see how anyone could be sure of who was where precisely when. Do you?'

'Not precisely, no. But whoever did it would have been pretty wet, and...'

'Oh,' said Willow at once, 'was there much mess around the pool then?'

'So I understand.' Tom was beginning to look resigned. Willow pretended not to notice.

'That's interesting...'

'Will, don't...'

'Are you about to tell me what I may and may not do, Tom?' she asked quietly.

Recognising the danger in her voice, he shook his head.

'Certainly not. What I was going to say was don't you think

it would be better if you left this one to the police? I know you can't bear to see people thrashing about—oh, dear—fumbling and taking longer than you would to do any kind of job, but this *is* their job, and just at the moment, yours is…well, Lucinda, don't you think?'

Willow was silent, trying to subdue a fountain of angry, hurt, anxious thoughts that rushed up into her brain. After a long moment, she said with a kind of desperation: 'You're right, of course, but I panic whenever I think that I've got to be different now because of her.'

Tom came to sit beside them on the bed and put both arms around Willow.

'You're not and you don't have to be, but your body has just been through a lot. It must have taken most of your strength; you're probably still in a great emotional turmoil about it all. I certainly am. I just think… Be careful, that's all. Please.'

'It's just that I keep wanting to prove that I've still got a brain,' she said, hating the fact that she sounded so pathetic. 'And that I'm not about to lose myself in nappies, feeds and mush.'

'You're not. You just need to give yourself one or two more days to recover. They were telling me before Lucinda started yelling for you that you ought to be able to come home in another couple of days, provided everything's still okay then.'

'Were they?' Willow leaned against him. She suddenly felt extraordinarily tired when she thought of the prospect of looking after Lucinda without the nurses there to check that she was doing it properly. Glad of Tom's physical support, she made herself say: 'Good.'

SEVEN

Days Six and Seven

THE FOLLOWING MORNING Willow was at last questioned by two members of the police investigation team. Glad of the opportunity to find out how much they knew, she invited each woman to take a chair and smiled helpfully. 'Thank you, Mrs Worth,' said the CID officer. 'I'm Inspector Boscombe and this is Constable Rodwell. As you probably know, we are investigating the death of Alexander Ringstead on the night of the twelfth of May.'

'Yes,' said Willow, continuing to smile. 'But I'm afraid I won't be able to tell you anything much because I was in labour at the time. In fact I think his death was only discovered because he'd disappeared when I started to haemorrhage and they needed him to deal with it.'

Willow's smile disappeared as she heard a faint sound of resentment in her own voice. She remembered Sister Lulworth's exasperating diagnosis of her reaction to the news of Mr Ringstead's death and felt vaguely ashamed of herself. Holding on to Lucinda more tightly, she wondered, not for the first time, whether her vigorously defended independence and self-sufficiency had been nothing more than a terror that she would not be able to bear being deserted.

'So I understand,' said the inspector, clearly unaware of Willow's mental turmoil. 'What I wanted to ask you was whether you heard, saw, overheard or noticed anything unusual about him or about anyone else here earlier that evening.'

Her lips moved in what might have passed for a smile, but

her eyes did not change. Willow decided she did not like her.
Constable Rodwell balanced her notebook on her knee and
prepared to write down anything useful Willow might produce
in the way of evidence.

'I was preoccupied for most of the time I was here,' she
said, sounding at her most distant and controlled. All her
doubts and fears had been pushed aside. 'I'm not sure that I
would have noticed anything unless it was seriously out of the
ordinary. As far as I could tell Mr Ringstead was normal:
confident, not hurried or distrait in any way, and as kind and
funny as always. Tell me, did the autopsy give you any evidence as to exactly how or when he died?'

Suddenly distracted by a small, infinitely endearing gurgling
sound, Willow withdrew her attention completely and gazed
down at her daughter. When she looked up again she saw that
the inspector was distinctly irritated.

'Sorry,' said Willow. 'You were saying?'

'I wasn't. But the time and causes of Mr Ringstead's death
need not concern you, Mrs Worth. You and your baby are in
absolutely no danger.'

'It never crossed my mind that we were,' said Willow, raising her red eyebrows. 'But I cared about him and I can hardly
bear not knowing what happened to him, you know: whether
he was murdered or not.'

'I can see that it would be less upsetting for you if he'd had
an accident,' said the inspector. 'But I'm afraid I can't give
you any comfort on that score.'

Having recognised the sense of what Tom had said the previous evening, Willow had been all ready to share the little
she had learned or guessed about Ringstead's life, preoccu-
pations and enemies, but Inspector Boscombe's air of superiority made her decide not to volunteer anything.

It was only later, when Willow had recovered from her fit
of petulance, that she remembered she did not actually have
any real information to pass on. All she had were snippets of

gossip, a few vague suspicions and somewhere a list of questions she had not yet asked.

As the interview proceeded on its stilted way, Willow gave the inspector a full account of everything she could remember from the night of Ringstead's death. Unable to pinpoint the times when different members of the medical staff had come into the delivery room, Willow did her best to put names to them and at least list the order in which they had appeared.

Inspector Boscombe asked her to clarify one or two things she had said and then asked a series of questions that seemed to have no bearing on anything Willow thought relevant to the enquiry. She knew that she was being childish in restricting her answers to a simple 'yes' or 'no', but at that moment she did not care. She shook her head as the inspector asked whether there was anything else she wanted to say and then watched the two women leave with a kind of stubbornly angry pleasure that at least they had not got anything out of her.

Having changed Lucinda's nappy again, Willow got back into bed and was just starting to write up notes of her meeting with Durdle when she heard the slurred, squeaking noise of someone in trainers crossing the ward. She looked up to see Rob, who raised a floppy hand as soon as he saw her watching him. Then he looked away flushing, as though he did not know what to do with the eye-contact they had established. But he smiled again when he reached her bedside. Willow patted the inky, grimy hand that he had allowed to drop, apparently almost by mistake, on to the pillow near her shoulder and suggested that he say hello to his goddaughter.

While he was doing that, Willow leaned over the edge of the bed to pull out the new picnic box Tom had brought. Rob finished making his obeisance to Lucinda and inspected Mrs Rusham's bounty.

'I'm getting hold of some more data on the ambulance crews for you,' he said thickly through a mouthful of egg sandwich.

He glanced over his shoulder to make sure that no one else

was listening. Both occupants of the beds nearest Willow's had left with their babies earlier that morning and she had not yet done more than greet the newcomers. One seemed to be asleep and the other was reading. No one showed any interest in Rob or Willow. She looked at him expectantly.

He swallowed, took another huge bite of sandwich and started chewing. Willow reminded herself that he was a growing boy who needed nourishment, and waited with as much patience as possible. When he had satisfied the most desperate gnawing hunger, he put his becrumbed hands on his knees and started to tell her what he had discovered.

Worryingly, he told her that he had borrowed 'from a mate at school' a scanning device that would allow him to listen in to the frequencies used by mobile telephones. He was planning to try to pick up the suspected ambulance-driver's calls and find out for certain whether there had been any foundation to Mr Ringstead's suspicions.

Forgetting all her instinctive questions about how Rob's friend happened to have a sophisticated listening device and also how it worked and exactly what it could do, Willow decided that she would have to remind Rob that listening in to other people's telephone calls was illegal. But he was so eager to find out whatever he could about Ringstead's death and so easily discouraged that she could not bear to sound as though she were belittling his achievement.

She wanted to let him have his triumph for as long as possible and listened admiringly as he told her that he had got hold of a copy of the drivers' rota and so knew when his targets would be visiting houses that might prove tempting for their burgling accomplices. Unfortunately part of the drivers' shift would coincide with various classes that Rob could not miss. However, he assured Willow, outside those hours he would be listening as hard as possible. He said he was sure he could get her something useful.

'Oh, Rob, I'm not sure this is such a good idea,' she said, biting her lip.

At once his face took on a familiar mulish expression. She reached out to touch his hand, but he snatched it away and turned sideways in his chair, crossing his arms across his chest.

'I'm more impressed than I can say by what you've found out,' she went on as warmly as possible. 'Of course I am. But I'm also appalled at the risk you're taking.'

Rob half turned back towards her.

'I'm worried because I care what happens to you. I'm sorry if that makes me seem clucky, Rob, but I can't help it; I also care a lot about whether you stick to the right side of the law.'

He took a quick look at her from under his fringe, trying to smile.

'I know scanners aren't legal,' he muttered, 'but I thought it'd be sort of worth it to know whether your man was right to be suspicious.'

'It would be worth a lot,' she assured him. 'But your safety is worth much, much more. Rob, don't think I'm trying to interfere, but could you bear to take care? Quite apart from what might happen to you if you were to cross anybody ruthless enough to kill a man like Mr Ringstead, Tom would be so hurt if you got into trouble with the police.'

Rob frowned but he did not say anything.

'You've made such a difference to our lives, you know…' Willow said quietly and then lay back, watching Rob and not bothering to finish her sentence.

'I just wanted to find out,' he muttered. 'That's all. I thought you'd be pleased.'

He looked as though he might crack under any more pressure, and Willow did not know what to say next or how to deal with what had happened. The responsibility for his feelings weighed heavily on her and then made her angry with him. She knew that she was not being fair—after all, Rob had never asked her to worry about his feelings—but she could not help it.

Ideas about Lucinda and her right to be loved began to

hover at the edges of Willow's mind and she could feel her skin tightening around her face like a cold, wet, clay mask.

'Has Will been involving you in one of her nefarious plots?' said Tom quietly, making both of them jump. There was a lightness in his voice, but when Willow looked at him she saw that there was absolutely no amusement in his eyes. She wondered how long he had been standing there and how much he had heard or seen.

'No, of course not,' said Rob at once, but his deep blush gave him away.

'Don't worry, Rob. It's my fault for encouraging you.'

'No, Willow. You…'

'Yes. Now, hadn't you better get on back to school? Isn't it chemistry this afternoon?'

'Yeah. Right. Sorry. Thanks.' He seized his book bag, looked at Willow in dumb gratitude and gave Tom a half-hearted wave.

When he was well clear of the ward, and the doors to the passage had stopped swinging behind him, Tom looked at his wife:

'Well?'

'You're right, and I'd just been trying to explain to him that I should've stopped him sooner. I don't terribly want to tell you what…'

'Will, you'd better tell me the lot.' Tom did not sound angry or even critical, and she had long ago given up trying to imagine what he was feeling when he made his face and voice blank like that. It only led to trouble.

'Okay. Rob has been asking around the hospital canteen in case he could pick up anything about Ringstead. He, Rob I mean, was bothered that Ringstead might have killed himself and I think he wanted to get proof that he'd been murdered.'

She bit her lip and then added: 'He also knew that I very much want to find out exactly what happened and am frustrated because I can't get about the hospital to ask questions.'

Tom sighed, but he did not say anything. Willow was

shocked to discover just how much she wanted him to absolve her from what she was coming to think of as a serious crime. She noticed that she was not angry with Tom for his as yet unspoken criticism and filed away a faint sense of progress in herself.

'What I didn't realise was that Rob has a friend who has some kind of scanner. Rob's borrowed it and is intending to listen in to mobile-telephone conversations between some possibly dodgy ambulance drivers and their probably burglarious accomplices. Apparently Ringstead thought they'd been doing over empty houses of patients the drivers had brought in here. But I had no idea Rob would…'

'You needn't tell me that. I know you'd never have encouraged the boy to break the law. Or anyone else for that matter. But, Will, I wish you'd nipped his interest in the bud. He shouldn't be playing around with something like this. It's far too dangerous.'

Hating the knowledge that she wanted to excuse herself and apologise to Tom, Willow explained with as much dignity as she could collect that she had not wanted to upset Rob by criticising what he wanted to do. Tom came to sit at the edge of the bed. He stopped her in the end by telling her that he knew exactly what she was talking about, adding: 'It's hellishly difficult to find the right line between protecting him against his wilder instincts and humiliating him by treating him as a child, which he isn't. Heavens above, legally he'll be an adult next year, and he could be married already. We do tend to forget that.'

Willow nodded.

'Precisely. But don't worry about this—I've told him about scanners and…'

'I know. I heard. And I'll have a word with him later. Although, in fact, you know, he couldn't have heard anything very significant. The sort of scanner a schoolfriend might have can only pick up random frequencies. Rob wouldn't be able to listen to calls from a specific number, and even if he did hear something interesting, he'd lose the call as soon as the phone changed cell, which they do frequently.'

'I hadn't realised you knew such a lot about it,' she said, not pleased to have been made to feel such an ignoramus.

'It's my job, ducky.'

'I suppose so. But you're not really telling me that mobile calls can't be listened in to, are you? What about those various royal scandals? Someone was listening to their telephone calls.'

'Of course it's possible,' said Tom, sitting more comfortably at her side. 'But you'd need an expensive piece of kit called a cellular telephone intercept.'

'How expensive?' There were several boys at Rob's school who had access to what Willow thought were startling amounts of money.

'Twenty grand or so.'

'Ah. Unlikely then that Rob's mate has one of those.'

'I should damn well hope he hasn't,' said Tom, looking grim. 'I must have a word with the boy.'

'But you won't say anything to Serena, will you? After all, it was my fault that Rob ever got interested in scanners, and it'll only worry her if she starts thinking he's got criminal tendencies again as she did when he kept truanting and no one could work out what he was up to.'

'Sure. Now, more importantly, Will, how are you and Lucinda?'

'We're fine. She's starting to feed really well and she doesn't sleep at all badly.'

'And what about you?'

'I sleep; not perfectly, but well enough, and I can always snooze in the day.'

Tom frowned. 'That sounds as though you're worrying about something.'

'Only about four hundred and ninety-nine different things,' she said, pretending to find it funny.

'Anything I can help with?'

She shook her head, feeling ashamed of most of her anxieties.

'Don't keep me out, Will,' said Tom after a long silence. 'I know I'm not particularly relevant to you and Lucinda just now, but I hate it when you make me feel quite as spare as this.'

'It's not that,' she said at once, appalled at his misunderstanding. 'I *am* bothered about Lucinda and whether she'll be healthy and happy and all that sort of thing, of course. But I'm also worried that I seem to be so stupid.'

'You must know that's nonsense. You? Stupid? What on earth do you mean?'

Seeing that all the professional coldness had gone out of him, Willow gave in and told him about her incompetent investigation into the possible motives of people who might have wanted Alexander Ringstead out of the way. Tom's face began to relax as he listened to what she had actually been doing. At the end of her story he even laughed.

'Well, if it's been keeping you happy, I suppose it's no bad thing.'

'It hasn't really,' said Willow, wrinkling her nose. 'It's vilely frustrating not to be able to find out the sorts of things I could ask if I were in my usual state. All I've learned is that his death wasn't an accident, which you told me. Those wretched colleagues of yours wouldn't even tell me that much. However, given the fact of the bruises on the back of his neck, it seems clear that he must have been tipped into the pool by someone who hated or feared him.'

'I'd have said that's a pretty fair assessment,' said Tom. He was looking quite happy again. Willow made a face at him.

'And therefore he must have been threatening someone, either here in the hospital or in his private life; or perhaps someone he had injured was taking revenge. Although I suppose it is just possible that he could have been the victim of a randomly wandering homicidal maniac, or a murderous Martian.'

'Again, fair enough.' Tom's smile showed that he understood that her silly joke was supposed to show that she was trying not to mind having failed to reach a conclusion.

'Well, that's it. And in this state I don't see how I can get much further.'

'Thank God for that. Don't look so cross: I'm not mocking you, Will.'

'Or not much,' she said and watched amusement switch on lights in Tom's eyes.

'Fair enough. But this is serious. Listen, Will, irrespective of anything I might feel at the way you take such risks muscling in on cases like this, Lucinda needs you safe and healthy.'

Willow was silent for so long, staring down at the furry head of her daughter that Tom said gently: 'Isn't that fair, too?'

'Yes, I suppose it is.'

'But?'

'No buts at all.' She looked up and smiled.

Tom looked unconvinced by her smile, but he dropped the subject then and they spent the rest of his free time side by side on the bed with the curtains drawn around them. When he got up to go Willow kissed him and almost promised to ask no more questions about Ringstead's death. But there seemed to be no point in raising the subject just to put it to bed again; and besides she was not sure that she would be able to keep such a promise, however much she might want to comfort him for his feeling of exclusion from her new life with Lucinda.

Even so, she might have managed to leave it there for good had Rob's aunt not dropped in to see her and inspect Lucinda the following evening. Serena Fydgett was a barrister and was still dressed in the black suit and plain white shirt she had worn to court. Her hair was dark and her skin very pale. The only real colour about her came from the huge bunch of pale pink roses she was carrying.

'I know it's absurd to stick to the old superstitions about

colours for babies,' she said, laying the bouquet down on the overfull table beside Willow's bed, 'but these just were the best and freshest the florist had.'

'They're lovely,' said Willow with a private smile as she remembered reading about the origin of 'blue for a boy; pink for a girl'. According to the book male babies, being so valuable, had had to be protected from the evil eye with 'something blue'. The evil eye was apparently quite welcome to do whatever it wanted to girls and so all they got was meaningless pink.

In spite of her determined clinging to rationality, Willow decided to buy Lucinda something bright blue as soon as she was on her feet again.

'It's sweet of you to have come, Serena,' she said. 'How are you? Good day in court?'

'Not at all bad,' said Serena before settling down to give Willow an entertaining account of her client's effective manipulation of his less-than-experienced prosecuting counsel.

'But all that is by the way,' she said eventually. 'How does it feel having had a baby at last?'

'I'm still not quite sure,' said Willow lightly. 'My emotions are doing the most peculiar things. One minute I'm elated beyond belief and the next pathetic and teary. And terrified. Whenever I remember that I'm easily old enough to be her grandmother, I wonder what on earth I'm doing. In fact, I can't help feeling that I'm taunting nature or fate or something.'

Willow laughed to show that she did not really mean anything so absurd, but something in Serena's eyes suggested that she was not convinced.

'Goodness knows what'll be done to me in retaliation,' Willow went on, still trying to sound frivolous. 'Or to other people.

'I suppose it's not surprising that you've been getting fanciful. Giving birth must be the most enormous shock to the system. Did it hurt much?'

'Yes, frightfully,' said Willow more cheerfully. 'Still does in fact.'

Serena laughed nervously and Willow noticed that she was looking at Lucinda with an ambiguous expression, partly wistful and partly wary.

'Do you want to hold her?'

'Would you mind?'

'What, in case she gets infected by lawyerliness? Not at all. I can't think of anything better for her. So profitable!'

Willow put her daughter into Serena's arms and saw tears gathering in her eyes, just as they had in Mrs Rusham's. They did not leak over her eyelids and Willow was not sure that Serena herself was even aware of them. Eventually even the fascination of Lucinda's changing facial expressions seemed to pall, and Serena looked away, saying: 'Rob told me you wanted to talk about poor Alex Ringstead. Wasn't it dreadful?'

'Yes.'

'I knew him a bit, you know.'

'Did you?' Curiosity got the better of Willow's uncharacteristic yielding to Tom's wish to protect her from herself. 'Yes, of course, you did. Rob said. I'd forgotten. My brains really have gone squashy. What was he like in real life? He was wonderful as a doctor, but what was he like as a friend?'

'Pretty good company, I suspect. I didn't know him well enough to claim him as a friend, but I met him at quite a few fundraising dos for the hospital and he was always good fun.'

'How on earth did you get involved with them?' said Willow, trying to pretend that she was not full of glee at the possibility of learning something useful at last. Her doom-laden fears of nature's revenge on her and her child had disappeared for the moment. 'You've never acted for the hospital, have you?'

'No, never. But the campaign is being run by Mary-Jane Roguely.'

Willow looked puzzled.

'You know,' said Serena impatiently, 'the wife of Sir George Roguely, the chairman of Thoms and Timpson.'

'That rings a bell, but not a very loud one. Who are they?'

'You must know: they're that conglomerate that started as some kind of mining company at the turn of the century and has been swallowing up smaller firms ever since.'

'And they're not in mining at all any more. Yes, I do remember. There was a big article about them in one of the Sundays recently, wasn't there?'

'Probably. Anyway, Mary-Jane wrote to me just after she took over the hospital appeal committee. She decided to get in touch with every professional woman who's ever had a particular reason to be grateful to the hospital and ask us all for money.'

Willow was surprised; as far as she knew Serena had always had enviably robust health.

'They were very good to my sister,' Serena said quietly, reminding Willow that Rob's mother had been in and out of the psychiatric wing of Dowting's for several years. 'I felt I owed them something for that and so I sent Mary-Jane a cheque. She wrote personally to thank me for it and added an invitation to a fundraising concert. I wasn't doing anything and, as I've been rather feeling the need of company these last three months or so, I decided to go. She took the trouble to seek me out.'

'It must have been some cheque.'

'It was fairly substantial,' Serena admitted before Willow could ask why she had been in such need of company recently. 'Anyway, I liked Mary-Jane and we got on well. She's sent me invitations to all her fundraising beanos since then and I've been to several.'

'I'm quite surprised that Ringstead went to any of them,' said Willow. 'He seems to have disliked the managers here so much that it's hard to believe he wanted to help raise money for them.'

Serena smiled, looking almost sly.

'I think it was more Mary-Jane than the financial crisis that got him involved.'

'Aha,' said Willow, at last remembering the cufflinks and the new, exotic silk ties Rob had heard about in the canteen. 'Were they er...an item?'

'I think so. He was clearly besotted and she seemed quite keen too.'

'But she's married.'

'So?' said Serena, looking obstinate.

'It just surprises me that a married woman should have paraded her lover at such public functions,' said Willow hastily, remembering that for some years Serena had been having an affair with a married Member of Parliament. 'I'd have thought that the wife of the important Sir George Roguely might have wanted to keep it all more discreet.'

Serena shrugged. 'I don't suppose George minded much. He's madly busy, always flying off around the world. I should think he was pleased she had the Friends of Dowting's to keep her happy and wouldn't have minded that she was indulging in a little romantic fling as well. He's pretty sophisticated.'

'Not the jealous sort, you mean?'

'No. And there's no need to look like that, Willow.'

Willow had not realised that her expression had changed or shown any of her instant suspicion.

'I know you and the way your mind works,' said Serena grimly. 'I also happen to know that George Roguely was out of the country on the night Ringstead died. He's a decent man as well as sophisticated.'

'How do you know? Not that I'm doubting you. I'm just curious.

'So I see. As it happens, I'd invited the Roguelys to dinner last Saturday and they declined because he had to be abroad.'

'Oh, so they do still go out together?'

'Good Lord, yes. They're very fond of each other. It's just that he's often busy. She's susceptible to charming, witty, lonely, high-achieving, sexy men and when her own one is otherwise occupied she finds a substitute.'

'Sounds like a marriage made in heaven,' said Willow, lying. She realised that she could not be at all emotionally sophisticated in Serena's terms and asked herself whether anyone, if he or she were honest, could really not be hurt by such a betrayal. 'Do they have children?'

'No. I'm not sure why not. Perhaps they couldn't.'

'Then d'you think Ringstead's work could have been part of his charm for her?'

'I think that's a bit far-fetched. After all, he wasn't short of more obvious sorts of charm.' Serena looked at her watch and said that she had to go and work on her brief for the following day's case.

'Before you go,' said Willow, 'where do they live, the Roguelys?'

'Kensington. One of those big white houses near the park. Why?'

'Oh, I was just curious.'

'He *was* in the States,' said Serena firmly, 'so it couldn't have been he who drowned Ringstead; and poor Mary-Jane adored him and so it couldn't possibly have been her either, even if she hasn't got an alibi. Don't go getting fantastic ideas about either of them. They're good people.'

'I'm glad to hear it. But do you happen to have any idea where she was that night?'

'I'd never realised that you, of all people, could look winsome. It's vile.'

'Sorry, Serena. Well?'

'No, I don't.'

'Pity.' Willow tried not to look either threatening or winsome. Winsome, she said to herself in disgust. Clearly maternity really was doing dreadful things to her old standards of self-control.

'I'd better be on my way.' Serena handed the shawl-wrapped baby back to her mother. 'Good to see you and the tadpole. I hope you'll feel better soon. I'm sure you will.'

'What?' Willow's eyes focused properly and she shook her head slightly, smiling at Serena. 'Thank you, and thank you for the lovely flowers. It was angelic of you.'

'Pure pleasure. And George Roguely is a thoroughly good chap. Don't forget that.'

'No, I won't,' Willow promised in farewell.

She was searching the ward for the telephone trolley ten minutes later when she looked back and saw Mrs Rusham standing at the foot of her bed, patiently waiting for her. There was yet another insulated picnic box at Mrs Rusham's feet and a tightly wrapped bunch of red carnations in her hand. Willow waved from the far end of the ward and walked back as quickly as her mending body would allow.

'Lucinda is looking well,' said Mrs Rusham.

'Isn't she? She has lost a bit of weight, but the midwife tells me it's normal.'

'She'll regain it within a few days,' said Mrs Rusham, sounding even more confident than the nurses. 'All babies lose some in their first week.' Remembering Mrs Rusham's experience and unassailable competence, Willow began to feel a little less nervous about the idea of taking Lucinda home.

'Come and sit down and have something from one of your wonderful picnics. They really have kept me going. I don't know what I'd have done without them.'

'I'm glad,' said Mrs Rusham gruffly.

'And Rob Fydgett has made great inroads whenever he comes. He says he's always hungry.'

'He's a good boy. I hope he's not working too hard.' Mrs Rusham's harsh face looked more cheerful, as it always did when she spoke about Rob.

'I don't think so,' said Willow. 'Whenever I worry that he's here too much, he reminds me that his exams aren't for more than a year.'

'Not much more than a year. And he was looking tired and worried when he came to the house yesterday.'

'Was he?' Willow felt guiltily that it was probably her mishandling of his attempt at illegal surveillance that had made him seem troubled.

'Yes. But Mr Tom soon sorted him out. He looked much better as I left. They were going out to have a pizza together for supper.'

'Oh, good,' said Willow and then, to her complete surprise, she told Mrs Rusham everything that had happened between her and Rob, what Tom had thought about it, and how bad she herself felt for having involved the boy. She also told her everything that she had discovered about the death of Alexander Ringstead.

Mrs Rusham listened in silence until Willow had finished and then she said: 'Robert didn't come to any harm, and, from what you say, it sounds as though he couldn't have heard anything germane even if he had used this scanning machine. I don't think you should start worrying about him. As far as I can see, you've done him nothing but good ever since he first came to the house.'

'Thank you, Mrs Rusham,' said Willow, feeling yet more unsheddable tears rising in her eyes. It's only the fluctuating hormones whizzing about in me, she said to herself and tried hard to believe it.

'In any case, it does sound as though someone ought to find out whether your obsetrician's suspicions of the ambulance-drivers were justified,' said Mrs Rusham. 'Do the police know about them?'

'I imagine they must, but I don't really know.'

'Because they do sound the likeliest of the suspects you've described. They're the only people who have been doing anything criminal at all. What does Mr Tom say?'

'"Leave it to the police".'

'Well, there you are.' Mrs Rusham brushed some invisible

crumbs from her skirt and stood up. 'He'll have dealt with it. After all, he'll know what's best to do in this situation.'

'Mrs Rusham, you're not going to go sexist on me at this late stage, are you?' said Willow, sounding shaken.

'Certainly not. But as a senior member of the Metropolitan Police Force, he can do far more than you to find out about these ambulance-drivers. And someone should do it quickly. It's outrageous that people being brought into hospital should have to fear burglary as well as ill health.'

'You're so sensible,' said Willow, smiling up at her. 'You do me good.'

Mrs Rusham reddened and started to pull the previous day's picnic box out from under Willow's bed.

'I expect by the next time I see you, you'll have settled the whole nasty business,' she said as she straightened up. 'You've done it often enough before, after all.'

'I'll do my best, but they're sending me home tomorrow and I probably won't have found out anything before then.'

'I'll make sure the house is ready for you and Lucinda then,' said Mrs Rusham before she left.

IT WAS NOT until the following morning that Willow managed to get hold of one of the telephone trolleys. Then, having pulled her curtains for privacy, she put in some money and dialled the number given for Mary-Jane Roguely in the fund-raising brochure. She thought that the least she could do to justify Mrs Rusham's faith in her was to remove a few of the unlikeliest suspects from her list. To her annoyance she was answered by a machine that said: 'This is the Friends of Dowting's Hospital. Please state your name, address and telephone number, the event you wish to attend, and the number of tickets you require. We will get back to you as soon as possible.'

Directory Enquiries were equally frustrating, telling her that the Roguelys' telephone number was unlisted. Later Willow asked for the number of Thoms and Timpson, which she was given with no trouble at all. She dialled it and asked to speak to George Roguely himself.

'I'll put you through,' said the telephonist, but it was a woman's voice that answered, an efficient but off-putting voice.

'Sir George Roguely's office. How may I help you?'

'I wondered if I could speak to him,' said Willow calmly. 'My name is King. Willow King.'

'He's extremely busy just at the moment, Mrs King. What is it in connection with?'

'It's a personal matter,' said Willow, feeling all the usual irritation at being cross-examined by a secretary. She knew that all efficient assistants have to learn to protect their employers from time-wasting calls, but, even so, it infuriated her. The fact that the secretary had assumed that she was married and using her husband's name did not annoy her nearly as much, even though she was mildly surprised not to be addressed with the much easier compromise of 'Ms'.

'I am his confidential personal assistant,' said the woman, sounding quite as irritated as Willow felt. 'If you will tell me what it is you want, then I'm sure that I shall be able to help you without bothering Sir George.'

'That's very kind of you,' said Willow, suppressing an inclination to slam down the receiver and swear, 'but I really wanted to talk to him personally about the fundraising for Dowting's Hospital.'

'Sir George has nothing to do with that,' said the secretary with a snap.

'In that case perhaps you could give me a telephone number where I could reach Lady Roguely. I understand that she has a considerable amount to do with it.'

The secretary smartly dictated the number that Willow recognised from the fundraising brochure.

'Ah, but I actually wanted to speak directly to someone,' said Willow. 'That number is answered only by a machine, which is why I thought I had better speak to Sir George himself.'

'I'm afraid that I cannot help you with that,' said the secretary, sounding as though she were managing to hang on to her patience with great difficulty. 'As I said, Sir George is a very busy man and he has no time to spare for his wife's charities. Goodbye.' She cut the connection without waiting for Willow to say anything more.

Her interest in the investigation gingered up by her frustration, Willow picked up the muddily photocopied list of fundraising activities that Mark Durdle had given her and looked for something she might be able to attend in the near future. The thought of evening activities was daunting; she knew that she would need to go to bed each night at almost the same time as Lucinda if she were to have any chance of retaining her sanity through the broken nights that lay in store.

There was a bridge lunch in five days' time. She thought she might be able to manage that, even if she did not last the whole afternoon. An early departure might be tiresome for the rest of her table, but Willow decided that all was fair in childbirth and detection.

She dialled the number of the fundraising office and left a message ordering a single ticket for the bridge lunch, dictated details of her Access card to pay for it and then gave her home address.

EIGHT

BACK IN her own house on the fringes of Belgravia, Willow was surprised to feel more rather than less confident than she had in hospital. Lucinda did not cry any more than usual; she woke no more often during her first night at home; and she continued to feed without difficulty.

'And,' said Willow to Tom as they finished their second breakfast together at the small round table by the window in their sunny bedroom, 'she hasn't sprouted green whiskers or anything like that.'

He laughed. 'Look, I'm going to have to go in a minute. You will ring me if you need me, won't you?'

'Yes, of course I will. But don't worry. The health visitor will be coming in later today—and Mrs Rusham knows about babies, so even if green whiskers do appear I won't have to face them on my own.'

'No,' agreed Tom cheerfully. 'There is that. Take care of yourself. I'll try and nip back for lunch to see how you are. And ring me if you need anything.'

'We'll be fine.'

'Can I get you anything before I go?'

'The newspapers?'

'Sure.'

He returned only a couple of minutes later with the three newspapers they regularly took and a couple of magazines.

'That should keep you busy. Oh, I sent a notice about Lucinda to *The Times*. It should be in today. I just said: "To Willow King and Tom Worth a daughter, Lucinda." I hope that was all right.'

Recognising how hard he was working to keep his normal

patriarchal—and domineering—instincts in check, Willow put
her hands on either side of his face and kissed him.

'"Willow King". Thank you, Tom. But you know, I
wouldn't have minded being Mrs Worth for that announcement...' She was about to add 'and we could have discussed
it,' but she did not want to spoil their peace.

'No,' he agreed and kissed her vigorously. 'At least, I didn't
think you would, but it seemed important just at this juncture
for you to be the independent kind of you. At one moment I
even thought of calling you Cressida Woodruffe, but then I
decided it would just be muddling and might upset fans, who'd
wonder what their favourite novelist is doing with some bloke
called Worth.'

'I think you were probably right about that. People get confused enough as it is about who I am and which combination
of names is the real one. Thank you, Tom.'

She did not think that there had been anything in her voice
but gratitude, but after a moment Tom said: 'Yes, I see that I
should have told you what I was thinking of doing.'

'Don't worry about it,' said Willow sincerely. 'We chose
her name together; the rest is just admin. I hadn't meant to
sound however I did sound.'

Tom's face lightened. 'Slightly detached. It's always a sign
that I've said something you don't like. Sometimes I can't
work out what it was at all; this time it was pretty obvious
once I'd started to think. I'm sorry, Will.'

She kissed him again, hoping that she put as much effort
into decoding his moods as he had just done for her.

'You'd better be off or you'll be late,' she said and watched
him go, with her trust in her feelings for him surfacing like a
dependably solid rock in the receding ocean of doubts that had
been threatening to drown her since Lucinda's birth.

IT WAS an enormous pleasure to fill the big bath and wallow
in her own hot water for as long as she liked without worrying
about anyone else wanting to use the bathroom. Lucinda's

routine, too, was more satisfying than it had ever been in hospital.

Willow had had a nursery made out of what had once been the spare bedroom and she was glad to discover that everything she needed was to hand and that the room seemed to suit the character that she sometimes thought Lucinda was beginning to reveal.

The walls were simply painted in a soft, powdery, darkish blue. The woodwork was white; the cot and curtains, a sunny yellow. A thick Spanish rug woven in blue, white and yellow softened the practical linoleum floor. Rob's mobile hung over the cot and another, which Willow had bought before Lucinda's birth, hung over the changing-table.

There was a big built-in basin to the left of the table, and on the other side were white-painted shelves with carefully chosen toys awaiting the moment when Lucinda was ready for them. An antique nursing-chair stood under the window, with a new loose cover of thick white cotton damask over its original upholstery. On the blue wall hung a painting of the sea. Willow knew that Lucinda would not be able to appreciate it for years to come, but she herself loved it for its peace and colour.

When the baby was washed, dried, powdered, changed and dressed in a fresh nightgown, Willow took her back into her own bed, which Mrs Rusham had already made up with clean linen sheets. Lucinda seemed quite happy to lie on her back, chewing wetly at her left thumb while Willow browsed through the newspapers. She and Tom took the *Independent* and *The Times,* and also the *Daily Mercury* because one of their friends, Jane Cleverholme, was its features editor.

Skimming through the news until she reached the pages for which Jane had responsibility, Willow paused at the gossip column and was intrigued to see a photograph of Mary-Jane Roguely in a glamorous long dress. She was standing beside a distinguished-looking man in white tie with some order or other suspended from a ribbon around his neck. The caption identified him as the Italian ambassador, the guest of honour at a gala performance of *Tosca* in aid of the Friends of Dowting's Hospital.

Lady Roguely looked, Willow thought, as though she might be in her late thirties, although it was hard to be certain. She could have been as young as twenty-seven or, with a rigorous fitness programme and a careful diet, as much as fifty. Her hair was blondish and plainly styled around an amused-looking, attractive face. Her dark dress was low cut, and with it she wore a magnificent triple-strand pearl choker with a diamond clasp in the front.

Staring at the photograph, Willow wished that she had asked Serena how long the Roguelys had been married. It would be useful to know whether they had grown up together or whether Mary-Jane was the kind of trophy-wife her clothes and looks suggested. If so, Roguely might genuinely not have minded what she did, provided she fulfilled her side of the bargain with glamour, visible sex-appeal, and good publicity.

Willow thought she could see exactly why a man like Alexander Ringstead, working with tired and anxious pregnant women, might have been attracted to Mary-Jane Roguely. It was less clear what she could have wanted from him. Remembering Serena's description of Mary-Jane's feelings for him, Willow thought they did not fit with the photograph, in which she looked dauntlessly cheerful.

Willow longed to ring up Jane Cleverholme and ask directly for everything she knew about both the Roguelys and Mr Ringstead, but Jane had been showing signs of resistance to being used as a private database, and Willow thought she would have to be a little more subtle than usual. It was possible that Jane might come to visit her, in which case all the questions could be slipped into an ordinary conversation quite discreetly.

'Would you like some juice or coffee or something?' said Mrs Rusham, pausing on her way to give Willow's writing room a thorough clean so that it would be ready whenever she felt like working again.

'I don't think I need anything at the moment,' said Willow, looking up from the paper. 'What do you think of this woman?'

Mrs Rusham took the *Daily Mercury* from her, put on her spectacles and looked at the photograph.

'It's hard to tell,' she said at last. 'She looks well dressed, pleasant, intelligent. Quite stylish, too. And that short upper lip somehow suggests a sense of humour.'

Mrs Rusham did not ask why Willow wanted her reactions, but she looked curiously at her as she handed back the newspaper.

'It's been suggested that she was involved somehow with the dead obstetrician.'

'Oh, I see.' Mrs Rusham looked over her shoulder at the photograph again, but she could not see anything else at all useful in it.

Willow flicked through the rest of the *Daily Mercury* until Lucinda began to whimper and then cry loudly. Willow dropped the newspaper, trying hard not to feel that she had been unfairly interrupted, picked Lucinda up and started to feed her. The telephone rang twice in quick succession but Willow ignored it.

Half an hour later Mrs Rusham returned, carrying a tray with a glass and a jug of fruit juice.

'I know you said you didn't want any, but I thought you might get thirsty later,' she said quietly, putting the tray down on Willow's bedside table.

'That was kind. It looks delectable. Who was it ringing up?'

'Your agent, wanting to know how you and Lucinda are and whether she could come and visit you, and Mr Crescent asking the same.'

'How nice of them! What did you say?'

'That I would ring them back when I had spoken to you. I didn't want to disturb you while you were feeding Lucinda.'

'Mrs Rusham, you are a jewel. I'd like to see them when-ever they can come. Well, perhaps not just after lunch; I'm getting very attached to the siesta habit. And the health visitor's due at three-thirty. But any other time. Can you fix with them so that they don't clash?'

'Certainly.'

'Oh, and would you ring Jane Cleverholme for me? She sent flowers to the hospital and I'll write in due course, but could you say I'm back and would love to see her if she's going to be anywhere near here in the next few days. I know, she sometimes is.'

Mrs Rusham glanced at the newspaper and then she smiled at Willow, nodding.

'I'M NOT SURE I'd ever have believed it,' said Richard Crescent when Mrs Rusham had ushered him into Willow's room at five o'clock, laid a lavish tea tray tenderly on the table near his chair, gazed at him with a severity that did not at all disguise her yearning, and left them alone. 'What's Tom Worth got that I didn't have?'

Willow looked at her erstwhile lover with more affection than she had ever been able to show in the old days.

'God knows,' she said with less than perfect frankness. 'But I somehow can't see you embroiled in nappies and sick.'

'Sick? How revolting! She's not going to throw up now is she?' Richard glanced at Lucinda out of the corner of his eyes, letting his mouth twist into a grimace of prim distaste.

'Possibly. Babies often do,' said Willow, feeling a quite unexpected superiority over the elegantly detached merchant banker. She had known him best in the days before she had properly come to terms with the idea of herself as a best-selling novelist, when his smoothness had sometimes made her feel as prickly as a teasel.

'But never mind that now, Richard. How are you? You look...worn out.'

'Knackered is probably the word you were looking for,' he

said with a short laugh. 'I'm all right. We've had a vile take-over battle, which we lost and so I'm marginally concerned about whether we're ever going to get our fees paid. It's bad enough working all night and killing oneself for loathsome clients when one wins and makes a decent profit, but this… Hateful. Luckily it doesn't happen very often.'

'Don't you ever get tired of it? The same struggle over and over again, always having to find new targets and new clients and then go through the same beastly rigmarole that always used to scare you witless?'

'Not exactly witless, dear girl, or I'd never have survived the various bloody culls that have decimated the bankers of this great city.'

'Only decimated? You've been lucky then. But don't you get sick of it, truly?'

'God, yes. I'm longing to retire. I reckon if I can stagger on for another five years, I can reasonably go then. I'll be fifty after all.'

'And you should have stashed away enough to live on one way and another,' said Willow much more lightly.

'I'm not sure one ever does that, but I can probably scale down my standard of living.'

Knowing that Richard had been earning an enormous salary and even more enormous bonuses for something over twenty years, Willow did not feel too worried about how he would keep himself from starvation.

'Won't you be bored if you retire completely?'

To her astonishment, he looked self-conscious, almost shifty, but he did not say anything. After a moment, she understood and laughed.

'A decade or so ago,' she said, 'I'd have asked whether you were planning to stand as an SDP parliamentary candidate, but those days are long gone. It's novels now, isn't it? What's it to be? A financial thriller or something in the more sensitive rite-of-passage line?'

'You always did know how to boost a chap's confidence in himself,' said Richard bitterly. 'How did you guess?'

'You just had that look about you, as though you've been thinking to yourself: well, if bloody Willow can do it, then I can't see why I shouldn't.'

At that Richard laughed too.

'Not so much bloody Willow as Bloody Some-Other-People. I thought I'd give it a go. In fact I have had a word with Eve Greville about it. She thought I ought to try. Shall you mind?'

'Only if your first advance is bigger than mine.' Catching a glimpse of his expression, she added: 'Selfish, I know, but it always is galling when all one's years of experience count for nothing and some new hotshot with a clever idea and a good agent gets a fortune for a book that turns out to be pretty ordinary.'

'And even more irritating,' said Richard, who still felt he knew her well, 'when it sells brilliantly, too.'

'Oh, absolutely. Makes one want to throw up. Or resort to murder,' she said, enjoying a renewed sense of herself as she had been before Lucinda's birth.

'Still you can hardly complain. There can't be all that many novelists who've consistently made as much as you have over the years.'

Richard looked round the beautifully furnished bedroom, with its glorious paintings and eighteenth-century furniture set against ivy-green walls that were lightened by the luxuriously pale carpets and curtains.

'Honestly, Willow, I'm not sure you should have the gall to object to anyone's luck. Here you are: an outrageously successful novelist, stunning house, perfect and loyal housekeeper, health, brains, love, Superintendent Worth to attend to your every whim and now a baby as well.'

'Put like that,' she said drily, 'it does sound like a pretty good score, doesn't it? Who'd have thought it in the old days?'

She had a sudden vivid memory of her life in the days

before she had even tried to write, when she had been living in a sad, damp first-floor flat in the unfashionable part of Clapham and working as a successful but isolated civil servant, so repressed that she did not even realise she was unhappy.

'Yes, I suppose you could have been said to have paid in advance with a fairly hellish start.'

'It wasn't that bad,' she said, suddenly ashamed of herself. 'I moaned and groaned when I was changing myself and my life, but...'

Richard brushed aside her protests, thinking much further back to the bleak unhappiness of the childhood Willow had once described in the most matter-of-fact way imaginable and the vulnerability that she still attempted to hide from everyone behind an angrily confident exterior.

'Now,' he said, deciding that it was time to change the subject, 'you'd better show me this infant of yours—so long as you can stop it being sick over me.'

'Her,' said Willow crossly and then felt even more cross with herself when she saw that he had been teasing her.

Richard held Lucinda confidently and admired all the right things about her before eventually giving her back to her mother and taking from his pocket a flat, dark-blue leather box.

'It won't be suitable for ages, but she may like it later,' he said casually, offering it to Willow.

Surprised, she took the box and opened it to find inside an enchanting Edwardian pearl pendant set in gold.

'Goodness, Richard, how absolutely lovely! And how incredibly generous! Thank you.'

'It was my mama's,' he said in the same deliberately off-hand way, 'and since it's pretty clear that I won't be having any daughters to give it to, I rather thought I'd like yours to have it.'

'Oh, Richard,' said Willow, gazing at him and wondering if she had actually ever known him at all. 'I really don't know quite what to say. It's beautiful, and you're...'

'No need to say anything, old girl. God forbid! You and I managed awfully well without talking about filthy things like feelings. Don't let's start now.'

'No,' she said, not sure whether she was more moved or amused. 'It's terribly kind of you, and, as soon as she's old enough, I'll give it to her and tell her all about you.'

'Good, and don't you go wearing it in the meantime. It's Lucinda's.'

'Yes, Richard. Very well. I promise. I won't take anything that belongs to my daughter.' Something inside Willow lurched with a kind of terror, which she tired to ignore.

'I should hope not. Now, enough of all that. What have you been up to recently. Did you finish the book before she was born?'

'Yes, I did, although I didn't quite crack the synopsis for the next one, which I had meant to get off to Eve before I went into labour. But now I come to think of it, you might be able to help me.'

'Oh, yes?' said Richard warily. 'What now?'

'Do you know a man called Roguely?'

'Sir George? No. Never had anything to do with him. Thoms and Timpson are clients of our biggest rival and they guard him like the proverbial goose. But what on earth has he got to do with your unwritten synopsis?'

'Nothing at all. I just wondered about him. I've been reading about his wife in the gossip column of Jane's paper, and I was curious. That's all.'

'I mistrust you when you sound artless like that, Willow. Are you getting yourself involved with another bunch of dangerous criminals?'

'Not exactly.'

'Oh, dear. What would the gallant superintendent say? He hated the last investigation you did even though you didn't come to any harm—or not very much.'

'He's hated them all, but I can't stop being myself and be bullied into being the little-woman-at-home just because he...'

Hearing a note of panic in her voice, Willow stopped, swallowed, smiled and finished: '…just because Tom doesn't like the idea of my getting involved in iffy detective work.'

'Willow, my darling, I don't think you need ever fear being anyone but yourself—or being bullied for that matter. You're about the toughest nut I ever tried to crack.'

'And have many of your nuts been tough, Richard? Funny thought, that. Your having tough nuts.'

'Oh, shut up!' he said, laughing in spite of himself. 'You always used to be a bit of a monster, but I thought you'd got over it. Poor Tom.'

She stuck out her tongue, thinking how much more she liked Richard as a friend than she ever had as a lover. He had been very convenient then—particularly in his refusal to let any connection but the most basic physical one come between them—and his attentions had given her a good deal of pleasure. But there had been no real honesty or freedom between them.

She was about to ask him if he would like to be Lucinda's second godfather when it struck her that Tom ought to be involved in the choice. To pre-empt any discussion about more godparents might make him think that she was taking some kind of revenge for his much smaller unilateral in action in sending his own version of the announcement to *The Times*.

'He's said to be pretty ruthless under the charm.'

'Who?' she said, completely at a loss.

'George Roguely. Although he's not quite such a psychopath as some of his rivals; I mean, he does have a sort of life beyond his work.'

'Yes,' said Willow, 'and a gorgeous wife, too, according to Jane's paper.'

Richard nodded. 'He's said to be utterly devoted to her, and his staff are believed to be equally devoted to him. They hardly ever leave, which speaks well of him. But he's ruined rivals without compunction and trampled over anyone who gets in his way. Does that help?'

'I'm not sure.'

As the front doorbell sounded, Richard got to his feet.

'Another of your admirers, I expect, Willow. I'd probably better be going in any case. I was teasing you, but it is actually rather good to see you looking so…satisfied.'

'Like a cat with its head in the cream jug?'

His grey eyes crinkled up as he smiled. 'Just like that. Goodbye, my dear. Don't lose touch.'

'Would I? I'm fearfully fond of you.'

'Ugh. Soppy. But I'm glad all the same. And I think the infant is s'blime.'

'Thanks, Richard. And thank you so much for the pendant. It's magnificent and Lucinda will treasure it. Goodbye.'

Surprisingly stirred up by Richard's visit, Willow rather wanted some time on her own so that she could sort herself out and even pretend that she was the old, secure, single, childless writer for a while. But she heard Mrs Rusham's voice downstairs, saying: 'Please go on up, and I'll follow you with the drinks. I know Mrs Worth has been hoping you would come.'

Then another voice, which Willow easily recognised as Jane Cleverholme's, said clearly: 'Great, terrific. Thanks, Mrs Rusham.'

Quickly looking down at her chest to make sure there were still no milk dribbles or unsightly glimpses of the armoured nursing-bra peeking out over the top of her embroidered nightdress, Willow got out of bed to welcome her friend.

'God, you look well!'

'And so do you,' said Willow sincerely.

Jane had always dressed flamboyantly, but that evening she had outdone herself. She was wearing a magnificent multicoloured Georgina von Etzdorf jacket over a pair of pencil-slim trousers.

'You look frightfully glamorous. What are you up to?'

'D'you think it's a bit over the top?' Jane examined herself in the cheval glass that stood in one corner of Willow's room.

'I love it and I'd been lusting after it for weeks, but I didn't think I could justify it until I was invited to a bash to be given by our esteemed proprietor tonight in his Eaton Square house. I went and bought it today. I want to be noticed.'

'You will be. But why?'

'Keep this under your hat, won't you? The editor's rumoured to be about to get the boot.'

'And you've got your eye on the job? Jane, that would be terrific. What a step!'

'I know. I don't suppose I'm even in the running, but I've never been asked to one of these dos before, and there must be a reason. Here's hoping.'

Willow laughed.

'A drink? Or would you rather keep your brain sharp for the big chief?'

'A drink would be great. Just a little one to get me going. You might not believe this, but I'm sweating with terror in my glamorous jacket.'

'Oh, I believe you, Jane.' Willow thought of some of her own odder mood swings. 'Mrs Rusham will bring up a bottle. Now, tell me everything that's been going on.'

'Me? You must be joking. You've been on the scene of the most dramatic thing that's happened in London all month. I want to know all about it.'

Jane had often been generously interested in the things her friends did, but Willow was surprised that she should be quite so excited by Lucinda's birth. Then she understood.

'You mean Alex Ringstead, don't you? Oh, Jane, for a minute I thought you were talking about Lucinda.'

Jane laughed.

'I should have been. How was it? How are you? Are you pleased you did it?'

'It was fairly awful. I'm absolutely fine except when I go a bit batty, which I do several times every day. And yes, I am, very pleased.'

'Completely?'

'Yes, of course. I do occasionally have my moments of doubt, but it's a bit like swapping jobs. I don't think it's reasonable even to think about whether it was a good decision for at least three months.'

'You always were a bit too revoltingly sensible,' said Jane, watching Willow with her head on one side. 'Oh, Mrs Rusham, that looks good.'

Mrs Rusham eased the cork out of a bottle of cold champagne, neatly collected the froth and poured out two glasses.

'Aren't you going to have one, Mrs R?' said Willow. 'Go on. Just for once. What is it they say? Wet the baby's head.'

Mrs Rusham decorously drank about two mouthfuls of the wine and then left the room, murmuring something about preparing dinner.

Jane forgot her splendid clothes and leaned comfortably back in the deep armchair in the window.

'So. What really happened to the gorgeous Alex Ringstead?' she said.

'You sound as though you knew him.'

'Not personally. But he's one of those chaps people talk about. I know lots of women who've had him for their babies. Everyone liked him.'

Willow did not think it would be sensible to list the people she had come across who had had reason to dislike—or even hate—him.

'He seemed pretty wonderful whenever I came across him,' she said. 'The last time must have been only about half an hour before it happened.'

'But what was it that happened? The dreadful thing is, it sounds funny, you know—"Obstetrician drowns in his own birthing pool". What a headline! And think of the photo.'

'I suppose it does,' said Willow after a pause. 'Perhaps if I hadn't known him, I could see the joke too.'

'I'm sorry. I know. I'm too flip. But what did happen?'

'I'm not sure. No one is yet, as far as I know. Tell me something, Jane?'

'Sure.'

'Is it true that he was having an affair with Lady Roguely?'

Jane raised her eyebrows as she nodded. Her eyes glittered and all the muscles in her face tightened slightly, lifting it.

'Interesting, isn't it? I confess I did a quick check about where her husband was that night.'

'The States, I'm told,' said Willow.

Jane nodded once again. 'Isn't it annoying? So you're as curious as I am. I thought you would be. What have you found out?'

'Not much. The police must have discovered something by now, but they're playing their cards very close to their chests and I haven't been in a fit state to go finding things out for myself.'

'But doesn't your equally gorgeous husband tell you about what they've found?'

'You must be joking, Jane. Tom never told me anything even in the days when he was involved with investigations, which he isn't any more. I get more from your newspaper than I ever have from him. Listen, there he is now. You can ask him yourself and see if you get any further than I have.'

'Goody,' said Jane, 'although I can't stay long or I'll miss my chance of wowing the proprietor. Hello, Tom! How wonderful all this is. I think the new arrival is a paragon of brains and beauty.'

Willow was silently amused at Jane's rehearsal of her wowing technique. Since she had not even glanced at Lucinda, her compliments were more than absurd. Tom knew Jane pretty well by then and took them at their real value.

'It looks to me as though she's been fast asleep for a while. Have you actually had a chance to assess her brains?'

'You know me—razor-sharp intuitions from fifty feet.'

Tom laughed and came to kiss Willow.

'How are you?'

'Wonderful. Quite myself again. And this bubbly you laid in is delectable.'

'Good. So why are you looking so smart, Jane?'

'Off to a don in Eaton Square. I say, Tom, how's the Ring-stead murder hunt going?'

'God knows. I'm stuck at the Yard these days, arguing about policy. I don't get to hear about operational details of other people's cases.' He pulled down the knot of his tie and undid the top button of his striped shirt. 'That's better.'

'D'you want a swig out of my glass?' asked Willow.

'No, don't worry. I'll go and get one out of Mrs R.' He turned round so that he could wink at Willow without being seen by Jane.

'I'd better go or I'll miss all the movers and shakers at the party,' said Jane, standing up and showing off her long legs. 'I'll walk down with you, Tom.'

When he came back five minutes later he was laughing.

'Your friends, my love! I don't know whether she thinks I'm susceptible to such gross buttering-up or whether she was just teasing me about my job.'

'She's a lot brighter than she lets herself seem.'

'Yes, I know. But I was damned if I was going to give her anything. Now she's gone, I can tell you that the principal suspect for the murder has just been released.'

'Who?'

'A man whose wife had had a baby at Dowting's a month or two back. There was some problem with the delivery and the baby was seriously damaged. The parents seem to have blamed Ringstead for it and the father was heard to make some pretty violent threats. That wasn't enough in itself to justify an arrest, but I gather that Boscombe and the team collected a bit more and they were interviewing him for most of yesterday. Unfortunately they've had to let him go.'

For a moment Willow could not say anything. She was so full of gratitude for Tom's taking the trouble to find out what she wanted to know and trusting her with it that she could only look at him. He stretched out a hand and she took it between both of hers.

Suddenly she knew the answer to Richard's question. He had always been just as frightened of intimacy as she had been, but Tom had been brave enough to risk it; and he never gave up. There had been many times since their first meeting when he and Willow had fallen out, when it would have been much easier to part, or at least drift into a state of polite neutrality, and yet Tom had always been prepared to try again.

'Was it lack of evidence?' she asked eventually, wrenching her mind back to the investigation.

'Not so much that, I gather, as an unbreakable alibi. He didn't come across with it at first, but once he was actually charged and heard the text of the new caution, he decided to produce it.'

'Pity. He was one of my likelier suspects, too.'

'Was he? Sorry about that. You're right about this champagne. It is good, isn't it?'

'Tom, since we're talking about poor Alex Ringstead, do they yet know how he was tripped into the pool? I mean, it would have taken someone about ten feet tall actually to overpower him. Were there any marks on his shins that could suggest a trip-wire? Or on the back of his knees? I suppose he could have been felled with a blow there from a baseball bat or something.'

'Apparently not. The only marks I've heard about were the bruises on his neck.'

'Damn! I don't see how it was done then. It would have taken someone of quite incredible strength to force him down on to the floor and push his head into the water.'

'I understand,' said Tom, showing the first signs of reluctance to discuss the murder with her that evening, 'that the current theory is that he must have been asked to look at something or fish it out of the pool so that he was already kneeling down when he was assaulted.'

'Evidence?'

'Some. His right sleeves were pushed a long way up his forearm. That's the white coat, the jacket of his suit and his shirt sleeve. And his right arm was in the pool when he was found, even though the left was hanging down outside it.'

'Ah, I see. Yes, good. That does make sense. One other thing: have you managed to find anything out about the ambulancemen?'

Tom sighed. Catching sight of Willow's face, he produced a faint smile.

'I passed on a hint of what you suspected to Inspector Boscombe. I'm sure she'll have looked into it. But that's enough of that, Will. How's my daughter been today?'

'Not bad at all,' said Willow, wishing that Tom would stick to the point. There was still a great deal that she wanted to know.

Lucinda suddenly started to cry with short, urgent, angry bursts of noise. Willow forgot her frustrated investigation as she flung back the duvet and embarked on a long and increasingly frightening exploration of the baby's distress. Her nappy was clean and dry. There was nothing sticking into her. She was not hungry. She did not want to be rocked. Singing did not help. She just cried and cried until two hours later when, as suddenly as the frenzy had begun, it stopped.

Tom, who was holding her at the time, walking up and down their bedroom, stopped moving. Hardly daring to breathe, Willow watched him begin to walk again very slowly and then lay Lucinda down in her cot with infinite care. Nothing happened. He looked over his shoulder at Willow and pointed towards the door.

Together they crept out of the room and downstairs to where Mrs Rusham had laid out their dinner before she had left for the day. Willow sat at the dining-room table, feeling more exhausted than she would have imagined possible. She put both elbows on the table and laid her aching head on her clasped hands.

'We'd better eat,' said Tom after a while. 'This sort of thing may go on for months. We'll need food.'

Dragging up her head, which felt as though it were six times heavier than usual, Willow looked at him.

'D'you think we'll ever make it?'

'We've got to.'

She looked at him and thought: yes you can't stop half-way through a parachute jump. You either make it or die.

NINE

THAT NIGHT Lucinda woke for her usual midnight feed and then again at six-thirty, but in between she slept. Willow did not do as well, waking every hour or so to check that the baby was still breathing. She seemed none the worse for her tantrum and, when Willow changed and washed her after the early-morning feed, she could not find any sign of anything wrong at all.

Both she and Tom were appalled at the memory of Lucinda's unassuageable distress and still afraid of what it might mean. They practically grabbed Mrs Rusham when she arrived.

She listened to their account of the previous evening and said that she thought the crying fit sounded more like the result of over-stimulation than anything else and suggested that no visitors should be received in Lucinda's presence after five o'clock in future, that the light should be kept dim after that and all sounds should be carefully controlled.

'As simple as that,' said Tom, leaning forwards almost as though he were about to kiss her. 'Mrs Rusham, you're magnificent. I'll be off then. Take care, Will. And if you need me, ring the Yard. I've got an eight o'clock meeting, but I should be in my own office from about ten-thirty.'

'Fine,' said Willow, still unable to let herself stop worrying. When he had gone she went back to bed and managed to get another forty minutes' sleep until Lucinda woke again, crotchety but not nearly as bad as she had been the previous evening.

When Mrs Rusham brought Willow's breakfast tray upstairs at nine o'clock, she said: 'You asked me to remind you about the bridge lunch. Do you feel up to it or would you rather I telephoned to cancel?'

Willow decided to go. Tired though she was, she thought that getting out of the house and seeing other people might help to remind her that there was a world beyond Lucinda's terrifying fragility and unknown needs.

Having tried painfully to express some milk, Willow eventually succumbed to Mrs Rusham's suggestion that she should make up a bottle of formula milk for whenever Lucinda showed signs of hunger. At last, feeling guilty but determined to get away for a while, Willow dressed in a loose but reasonably stylish linen jacket and skirt and set off by taxi for the Roguelys' house to the west of Kensington Gardens.

Half-way there, she asked the cabbie to take her first to a small jeweller, from whom she had bought several things in the past. The need for Lucinda to have something blue to ward off the evil eye seemed urgent after her screaming fit. Willow knew that she was being absurd, but she was prepared to indulge herself.

Ten minutes later she was standing in the cool of the jeweller's shop, looking at a collection of turquoise necklaces, brooches, bracelets and pendants. The owner of the shop seemed quite unsurprised by Willow's explanation of what she wanted to buy and he waited quietly for her to make her choice.

Eventually she picked a plain necklace of turquoise beads, which could be hung on the wall of Lucinda's bedroom until she was old enough to wear them. They were a particularly good, clear colour and their matt texture was pleasing. Willow, who usually negotiated fiercely when she was buying any piece of jewellery, paid the asking price without complaint, took her package and left the shop, feeling that she had done everything she could to protect her daughter.

TWELVE BRIDGE TABLES had been set up on the ground floor of the Roguelys' big house in Kensington. There were two in the square hall, four in each part of the double drawing-room and two in the conservatory. When Willow arrived she found that there were already several women standing on the doorstep chatting to each other. Their hostess, easily recognisable from the newspaper photograph, opened the front door and greeted most of them by name. When she saw Willow, she held out her right hand, saying: 'How do you do. I'm Mary-Jane Roguely.'

'Willow Worth.'

'Of course. You asked for a ticket only the other day, didn't you? It's so good of you to be helping us out like this.' She shut the door behind the last arrival, kissed her, and then turned back to Willow, saying: 'Come on into the drawing-room and meet the others. How did you hear about us?'

'In Dowting's itself, actually. I was there having a baby, my first in fact, and someone gave me a list of all your functions.' Willow smiled, but she suddenly felt surprisingly weak. 'I didn't feel up to an evening do, but the thought of getting away from the crying for a while was marvellous.'

Mary-Jane pulled forward a chair and made Willow sit down. 'You look awfully pale. Was it very recent, the birth?'

'Well, it was nearly two weeks ago,' said Willow. 'I'm not sure why I'm quite so wobbly because I'm perfectly fine, except the last night was a bit tricky.'

'You're mad to have come out so soon. I'll get you something to drink. What would you like? There's coffee made or some of the wine we'll be having with lunch or fizzy water, juice, anything.'

'Fizzy water, please.'

Mary-Jane went to speak to one of the chattering women, who nodded and then came over to where Willow was sitting. The woman was slim and pretty with strikingly glossy black hair tucked behind a padded velvet hairband. Big gold earrings and efficient makeup stopped her looking too much like a schoolgirl.

'Isn't it ghastly?' she said with a cheerful smile. 'I don't blame you for needing to get out of the house for a while. I always do. It really does seem like a prison sentence, doesn't it, however much one loves the little darlings. We'll start playing soon and then you'll feel better.'

'If I can remember anything about the game,' said Willow, feeling idiotically pathetic and hating it.

She reminded herself bracingly that she was lucky to have anyone as reliable as Mrs Rusham to take over Lucinda's care. Plenty of new mothers had no chance of getting away from their babies for important matters, let alone something as frivolous as bridge—or uninvited detection.

'Have you played much bridge, Mrs Worth?'

'Off and on since I was at university,' said Willow, 'but I haven't played regularly for years. I'm very rusty.'

'You sound as though you know much more than any of us. Most of us only started a couple of years or so ago.'

'D'you all know each other then?'

'Lots of us do. Mary-Jane and I were at school together, along with Susie over there and Pippa; and a lot of the others live round about so we know them too.' The woman waved her heavily ringed left hand towards the group. Willow, mesmerised by the size of the solitaire diamond on her wedding finger, could not identify any of the people she was talking about, but it did not seem to matter.

Mary-Jane returned with a tall glass of mineral water with ice and lemon floating in it.

'That looks wonderful,' said Willow. 'Thank you very much. I'm so so sorry to be causing so much trouble.'

'You're not. Look Jinx, why don't you take Mrs Worth into the conservatory and I'll send you two others and you can start playing straight away. There's no reason to wait for the whole lot.' She whirled away to answer the front doorbell.

'It's not a bad idea,' said the woman, hoisting the chain of her Chanel handbag higher up her shoulder. 'By the way, I'm Camilla Chaldon. Mary-Jane should have introduced us but she's a bit preoccupied just at the moment.'

'Why did she call you Jinx then?'

'At school they always said that I put a jinx on things,' she said over her shoulder as she led Willow through the back drawing-room to the conservatory. 'If I was involved in any escapade we'd always get caught. Any car I was in would get puncture. Any train would be late. Jinxed by me.'

'Poor you! That's awful.'

'I didn't mind,' she said with a warm giggle. 'It wasn't half as bad as a lot of the things the others were called. Stinky and Fatty and that sort of thing. And I always think Jinx sounds rather jolly now; you know: young and frivolous. I should sit there. It's much the most comfortable chair.'

Willow sat down in the shade of a large palm tree and felt the softness of down-filled cushions all round her. She did not normally like conservatories because of the glare and stuffiness, but the Roguelys' was a haven of cool greenery, with efficient blinds covering the entire glass roof, several open windows, and an octagonal pool floored in green glazed tiles and continually refreshed with water from a spout in the wall above it.

'It's wonderful. You are kind.'

'Not at all. Now, can I grab you for my partner before the others find out how long you've been playing or do you think we ought to be honest and cut for partners?'

'I'll fit in with whatever you decide. But before they come,' said Willow, deciding to seize her opportunity, 'tell me about Lady Roguely. Is she all right? I wanted to say something helpful, but she seemed so in control that I didn't dare risk it.'

Jinx's face was absolutely but politely blank.

'About Alex Ringstead,' whispered Willow. 'He told me how he adored her and ever since I heard what had happened to him, I've been so worried about her.'

'I didn't realise you'd known him that well,' said Jinx, her smile returning. 'It's so awful for her not really being able to let go. I mean, George didn't mind at all that she was seeing Alex, obviously, or she'd never have done it, but he'd be pretty upset if she went into some kind of mourning now, and so she's got to pretend not to mind. She's awfully fond of George and wouldn't do anything to hurt him.'

'Did he really not mind? I know Alex found it hard to believe.' Suddenly Willow, who had never minded lying before, felt ashamed of exploiting the immediate friendliness of Jinx Chaldon.

'I honestly don't think he did. Anyway, he's so busy always that he hasn't got time to do much with Mary-Jane and he knows she gets lonely when he has to be on these trips to the States and places. In the past she's kind of brooded about not having any children; it's been suggested that not minding about people like Alex was George's reparation for the low sperm count.'

Jinx suddenly looked almost embarrassed and quickly added: 'Besides, look at her; she's so gorgeous, George would forgive her anything. And he's always known she'd never leave him.'

'Even for Alex?'

'She might have fantasised about it sometimes, but she wouldn't have done it. George is far too important to her,' said Jinx definitely. 'Here are the others. Mrs Worth, this is Susie Hall and Pippa Browning. Girls, this is Willow Worth. She's just had a baby and she was a friend of poor Alex.'

'Wasn't it ghastly?' said Pippa at once. She brushed the front of her dress and Willow saw that she was about seven or eight months pregnant. 'I don't know what I'm going to do. I know that sounds selfish when he's actually dead, but he's done me both times before and he knew all about me and my foibles. I'm appalled at the prospect of going through it all without him.'

'His registrar is pretty good, too,' said Willow. 'Not as immediately attractive, but...'

'Registrar?' Pippa looked puzzled. 'Who's that?'

'He's called Kimmeridge,' said Willow, suddenly realising that Pippa must have been a private patient. She added: 'I had mine on the NHS.'

'That was fearfully brave,' said Pippa.

Willow watched her exchange glances with her two friends. They all looked so surprised that Willow was tempted to laugh and remind them that most women in the United Kingdom still had their babies in National Health Service hospitals. Before she could say anything, four more women appeared in the doorway to the conservatory and eventually, having cut for partners, sat themselves down at the other table.

'We'd better get going,' said Jinx. 'Willow and I are going to be partners. We can cut to see who ought to deal.'

Willow's concern about her lack of practice soon dwindled. She discovered that her fellow players were almost as interested in gossip as in playing cards and did not seem to have any competitive spirit at all. Whenever they were in any kind of dilemma they would ask each other's advice, wanting to know what they should be bidding when they had a lot of points and a seven-card suit, or whether their teacher had told them that leading a low card promised a high honour or announced a shortage in the suit. Several times they asked, halfway through a game, which suit was trumps.

But Willow found to her surprise that she liked them. Their gossip was never cruel, even though they clearly enjoyed passing on stories of the dreadful things that were happening to their friends, and their attitude to bridge was refreshingly unusual. They were wholly unconcerned with etiquette, and bridge jargon sent them all into fits of giggles. They could never remember what they were supposed to do; they changed their minds about cards they had actually played and, provided a card had not been covered, they felt they could pick it up and substitute another; and they never stopped talking.

By the time Willow had bid and made a small slam in the third game, which provoked squeals of glee from the delighted Jinx and open-mouthed admiration from the other two, she felt well enough established with them to raise the subject of Alexander Ringstead again.

'D'you know when Alex's funeral is going to be?' she

asked. 'I've been scouring *The Times* every day, but I haven't seen anything, and it's days and days now since it happened.'

Jinx leaned forwards right across the table, making a face.

'Apparently the police can't release the body until they know what happened.'

'Don't his family mind that?'

'Well, his ex-wife certainly doesn't, although their boys may,'

'How old are the boys? He never mentioned them to me.' That at least was true.

'Twenties?'

'Not as much, Susie, surely. He was only forty-eight.'

'Well they could be easily in their twenties then if he married at, say, twenty-four. Some people do.'

'Yes, I suppose so. Not many doctors, though. Funny, he's the same sort of age as George, but I've always thought of him as much younger,' said Pippa. 'But no, Willow, I don't suppose the boys would worry that much about a funeral. One's in the States and the other's in Australia, I think, with their mother. I can't see them agitating for a service, and Alex's own mother's in a nursing home somewhere up in Scotland. I don't think there's anyone except Mary-Jane and she can hardly organise his funeral.'

'Isn't it sad?' said Jinx. 'Although obviously he had friends. Well, like you, Willow.'

Feeling guilty all over again for pretending to have known him well, Willow shrugged.

'We weren't exactly close,' she said. 'But I'd come to depend on him, and I owe him a lot. It was frightening having a first baby at forty-four...'

'You're not,' said Susie, open mouthed again.

'I am and you've all been making me feel my years today.'

'We're not that much younger,' said Pippa, looking mockingly at Susie. 'In fact we were all forty last year. And in spite of what everyone said would happen we're all still pretty sane.'

'Oh, I don't know,' said Jinx. 'You got pregnant again, Mary-Jane kicked over the traces with Alex, and I...'

'Yes, Jinxy, come on, out with it. I dare you.'

Blushing furiously, she shook her head. Willow, intensely curious, thought that she would soon be told. From what she had already heard, it was clear that these women positively longed to tell anything they knew about anyone—even themselves. Sure enough, after a little more teasing, Jinx admitted that she had started an Open University course in computing.

'Good for you!' said Willow, amused that the only thing that had made any of them blush was an attempt to get a degree.

'Great! Here's lunch,' said Jinx, obviously glad to be distracted from her particular form of mid-life madness. 'Willow, it's only sandwiches, buns and a bottle of wine. We generally eat it here and then carry on playing for another hour or so.'

'That sounds great, but the fountain is making my stretched bladder...'

'Poor old you,' said Pippa at once. Heaving herself up from her chair, she went on: 'I'll take you up to Mary-Jane's bathroom. I wouldn't mind a pee myself.'

By the time they returned, the cards had been removed and a plain white tablecloth laid over the green baize. An oval salver of sandwiches sat in the middle of the table. Willow thought they looked quite as good as any of Mrs Rusham's. As she was sitting back in her comfortable chair, Mary-Jane Roguely appeared with two bottles of white wine and eight glasses.

'Any problems?' she asked from the doorway.

'None at all,' said Jinx, getting up to take one bottle and some of the glasses. Willow noticed that the women at the other table were still playing. Mary-Jane put their bottle and glasses on the deep shelf that ran about two feet from the ground all round the conservatory. Pots of flowering plants were grouped at intervals along it, but there was plenty of space for the wine.

'They seem very keen.'

'They do, don't they?' Pippa peered over her shoulder and then hissed at Willow: 'Perhaps they're just better than us. I don't think I've seen any of them before. That one on the far side looks pretty terrifying, don't you think?'

She certainly stood out from the other three, who looked as though they, too, might have been at school with Mary-Jane Roguely. Probably nearer sixty than forty, she was a big woman, handsome and well-dressed, but sharing none of the gaiety of Willow's table. In fact she looked thoroughly discontented and sighed audibly as her partner led what she clearly considered to be the wrong card.

'I'm glad we haven't got her here,' Pippa said. 'She looks positively ferocious.'

'Doesn't she just? Who is she?'

Pippa shrugged. 'God knows. Oh, I know. I'll just get us some water,' she said, standing up again. 'I don't want my child to be born with foetal alcohol syndrome.'

'I think you need rather more than a glass of wine for that,' Willow said, but Pippa had already gone.

The others had started their sandwiches by the time she came back with a bottle of Badoit and she announced that if they had eaten all the smoked salmon she would be seriously angry. They had not and she chattered away about sandwich fillings until the other table finished their game. In the clatter of chairs being pushed back and plates being laid, she whispered to Willow that Mary-Jane had said the irritable older woman was a recently retired member of George Rouguely's staff called Petra Cunningon. She was trying to build some kind of social life for her retirement and finding it hard, having done almost nothing but work since she was eighteen. George had asked his wife to include her in as many events as possible and she was doing her best, but it was hard to make the woman enjoy anything and Mary-Jane was beginning to lose patience with her.

Willow let the others talk while she watched Petra over

Jinx's head. Her tightened lips and air of barely controlled fury made it clear that she thought not only her partner but also their opponents too stupid for words. Eventually she managed to exchange civilities of a sort over the sandwiches and wine, but it was not until she pushed back her chair, saying loudly that she was going to wash, that the rest of her table relaxed. As soon as she had gone, two of them started to laugh and the noise level rose significantly.

Willow waited a little while and then, full of curiosity, followed her back upstairs to Mary-Jane's bedroom. To Willow's delight she found that there was a queue for the lavatory. Sitting down on the enormous double bed beside Petra Cunningon, Willow was surprised to notice that she was wearing an exotically heavy scent. It seemed unsuitable both for the time of day and for such a sensible-looking woman.

Willow smiled politely at her and, fanning herself with her hand, murmured something about the unseasonable heat.

'The conservatory is cool enough,' said Petra Cunningon.

'I know. Marvellous, isn't it? And so wonderfully planted; I do think Lady Roguely is brilliant. Most glasshouses are deserts of dullness and discomfort. Hers is paradise. What sort of standard is your table?'

'Childish.'

'Oh, dear. But I gather none of them here have been playing for very long.'

As the bathroom door opened and the woman at the head of the queue moved forwards, Petra Cunningon said: 'You can learn a great deal in a short time if you concentrate. Unfortunately none of the these women seems able to keep her mind on anything at all for more than a few minutes at a time. I can't think why not, since none of them has anything else to do. They haven't any idea of the most fundamental principles of the game, let alone the conventions. When my partner bid four no-trumps, naturally I assumed she was calling for aces. I bid five clubs and she passed. We hadn't even got six clubs between us. Afterwards, when I asked what she thought she'd been doing, she said she'd forgotten that you only need three no-trumps for game and thought she ought to be in game because she had two aces. I ask you! And then she actually blushed and said: "Oh, I know what you mean; you thought I was doing rolling gerbils."'

'"Gerbils"? Oh, I see; Rolling Gerber. And four no-trumps is Blackwood anyway. How irritating for you,' said Willow, unable to suppress a smile. 'What a good thing we're not playing for money.'

Petra Cunningon blew like a spouting whale and then laughed, looking friendly for the first time.

'What an appalling idea! I hadn't thought anything could be worse than this morning, but now I see that I just lack imagination.'

'Or perhaps you're an optimist,' suggested Willow.

'Hardly that,' she answered, looking bleak rather than disapproving. 'If I ever was, what's happened recently has cured me for good and all. I wish we'd been playing together, although I suppose we would have wiped the floor with the rest of them.'

'Perhaps. Tell me: how do you come to be here? Are you connected with Dowting's in some way?'

'No. I'm an old friend of George Roguely's—we used to work together—and when he heard that I had time hanging heavily on my hands since I retired he suggested that I should give his wife a little help with her charities. And you?'

'I had a baby in Dowting's and was so grateful to them that I felt I ought to contribute in some way. This seemed an attractive way of helping the fundraising effort. I must say that I'm enjoying myself.'

'Lucky you.'

'Oh, dear. Is it really that bad?'

'Almost,' said Petra with another gleam of humour. 'I don't think George can have had any idea of what he was letting me in for. I feel as though I've been sent back to the nursery.'

The last woman in the queue before Petra took her turn in the bathroom, leaving them alone.

'Well,' said Willow, smiling as she tried to build on the suggestion of complicity between them. 'I don't suppose he's ever around in the daytime to see the circles his wife moves in.'

'Exactly. Poor man.'

'In what way? He sounds remarkably fortunate from all I've heard.'

Petra grimaced. 'I think it's always difficult for a very clever man who falls in love with a silly woman; and when he's both rich and busy it's even worse. George adores Mary-Jane as much as he did twenty years ago, and yet they have virtually nothing in common. He gives her everything she could possibly want to make her happy and then has to face the fact that she's still discontented. To be quite frank, I think he gives her too much.' Her fleshy face took on an expression of considerable harshness. 'She'd be better for a dose of reality and then she might treat him decently.'

The sound of the bathroom door opening made Petra clamp her lips together. Willow looked at her face, settling back into its familiar lines, and said gently: 'Perhaps his busyness explains both her discontent and his continuing generosity. He might be trying to make up for not being able to give her the kind of ordinary companionship less preoccupied spouses can offer.'

Petra heaved herself to her feet without saying anything and Willow watched her walk over the thick, silky carpet towards the bathroom, leaving heavy footprints in its sheen. Willow could not help wishing that she had had slightly longer to break down the other woman's reserve and pump her for information about Sir George and his ideas about his wife. It crossed Willow's mind that he might have sent Petra to the bridge lunch as a kind of spy, but then she regretfully dropped the idea. No spy was going to make herself as conspicuous as Petra's bad temper had done.

Reaching the bathroom, she looked back and nodded to Willow.

'You could be right at that. If he'd had more time with her he might have seen her for what she is and been disillusioned. He might have been happier, too. Some of us tried to tell him how badly they were suited, but he's always been stubborn.'

She went on into the bathroom and locked the door. Willow stared at its blank white panels, wondering about Petra's partisanship of Sir George Roguely. Willow had always detested the assumption that every single woman over the age of about twenty-five must be suffering from unrequited love for some man who had barely noticed her existence, but the bitterness of Petra's contempt for Mary-Jane suggested that her feelings for Sir George were pretty intense.

The telephone beside the bed started to ring. Certain that it must be Mrs Rusham at the other end, Willow picked it up without even remembering that she was in someone else's house.

'Hello?' she said. 'Mrs Rusham, is that you? What's happened?'

'This is Sir George Roguely's secretary here,' said a voice Willow recognised all too easily. 'To whom am I speaking?'

'My name's King,' said Willow as crisply as possible, feeling thoroughly ashamed of herself. 'Shall I fetch Lady Roguely?'

'Thank you, Mrs King.'

Much embarrassed Willow went in search of her hostess, who covered her surprise efficiently.

'I'm so sorry,' said Willow very directly. 'I can't imagine what came over me to answer your telephone. I think it's just that I'm so worried about my baby that I assumed the call was for me.'

'Don't fret about it,' said Mary-Jane, putting a hand on Willow's arm. 'This won't take long. Come with me and you can ring your nanny as soon as I've finished.'

Together they went back upstairs. There was no sign of

Petra and the bathroom door was open. Mary-Jane picked up the telephone receiver.

'Yes, Miss Wilmingson?'

There was a pause, during which Willow saw an expression of supreme fury distort Mary-Jane's attractive face. But when she spoke her voice sounded distantly polite:

'It is quite unnecessary for you to have bothered, Miss Wilmingson. My husband has already told me that he will be back on this evening's Concorde. Goodbye.'

She banged down the receiver, hissing through clenched teeth.

'What cheek! ''Just calling to make sure that you've remembered Sir George is due home tonight. He'll be very tired when he gets in and probably hungry. You know he doesn't like eating during a flight.'' What does she expect? That I'll starve him or haul him off to an all-night discothèque? Sour, stupid, interfering…I am sorry, but what a woman!'

'Goodness!' said Willow. 'She sounds absolutely awful.'

'Not really.' Mary-Jane was beginning to calm down. 'I shouldn't have got so angry. Do please forget it, won't you? She's worked for him for years and is a wonderful secretary for a busy man. This is merely part of her technique of smoothing his path around the world and making sure he has everything he needs without having to ask. The fact that I'm his wife rather than a hotel receptionist doesn't seem to have occurred to her.'

'Poor you.'

'Not really.' Mary-Jane gave Willow a dazzling smile. 'Now, your baby. That's much more important than my husband's secretary. You'd better ring home straight away. I'll see you downstairs later.'

When Willow reached Mrs Rusham, she sounded uncharacteristically harassed and admitted that Lucinda was awake and crying much more than usual. She had also refused the formula milk and was probably hungry. Willow promised to come straight home, put the telephone down and ran down-stairs.

'There's trouble at home. I'll have to go back,' she said as soon as she saw Mary-Jane. 'Will you…? I'm sorry. It'll ruin the numbers and Jinx and Co. won't be able to play.'

'Don't you worry. We can shuffle the tables about and al-ways get other tables' dummies to bid your hand if necessary. You go on. Don't worry about us. I hope your baby'll be all right.'

'Yes. I'm sure she will be. Thank you for today. I've en-joyed it.'

'Me, too. I hope you'll come to another of our lunches.'

'Yes, I'd love to.' Willow could not think of anything ex-cept Lucinda and did not want to waste any more time in politeness, but she did say as she hurried towards the front door: 'Would you say goodbye to Jinx, Pippa and Susie for me? I liked them all so much.'

'Good. Did you come by car?'

'No, but I'll get a taxi in no time.'

'You might not at this time of day. They can be infuriatingly scarce. I'll get Jinx to drive you. Hang on.'

Before Willow could protest, Mary-Jane had disappeared and when she came back with the unfortunate Jinx neither of them would listen to Willow's protests. They escorted her down the steps to where Jinx's gleaming Volvo was parked in the forecourt and eased her into the front passenger seat.

'I really am sorry to be dragging you away like this,' said Willow. 'I wouldn't have dreamed of asking for a lift. I could easily…'

'It's fine. Honestly.'

Willow shut her eyes and lay back in her seat, trying not to think of all the things that might be wrong with Lucinda. The car stopped at traffic lights every now and then, but Jinx had her home in fifteen minutes.

'Would you like to come in?' said Willow, hanging on to

her manners with difficulty. Jinx seemed to understand. She shook her head.

'You don't want visitors at a time like this and I'd better go back and rescue the others. I'll ring you later, if I may.'

'You're so kind,' said Willow. 'But, really, there's no need for that.'

She heard the front door opening behind her and whirled round to see Mrs Rusham with the howling baby in her arms.

'I'm sorry,' she said, 'but I can't quiet her and I don't think it's good for her to cry like this.'

Willow flung herself down on the drawing-room sofa, wrenching off her jacket and unbuttoning her shirt. Lucinda arched her little back and screamed even more loudly as Willow took her from Mrs Rusham.

'Don't worry,' said Mrs Rusham. 'She'll recognise the scent of your milk in a moment.'

Miraculously she was proved right and in a very little time Lucinda was pulling at Willow's nipple. Her breathing caught heartrendingly every so often and twice she choked, but she grew progressively calmer and was eventually relaxed enough to fall asleep against Willow's breast. Willow leaned back against the sofa and let the waves of panic die down.

TEN

WHEN LUCINDA WAS properly asleep, with the turquoise necklace hanging at the end of her cot, Willow changed out of her clothes into a thin, yellow kimono and lay down to recover her composure. But she was too restless and worried to sleep. Eventually she got up, took another look at Lucinda, made sure that the baby alarm was switched on and went down the passage to her writing-room.

The typescripts of her earlier novels neatly arranged on the shelves above her computer ought to have reassured her. But they did not. They just sat there confirming her fears that her old life had gone for ever. She opened the bottom drawer of the filing-cabinet to pull out a folder of her reviews. Rereading them was usually a good specific against looming depression.

That did not work either. The tagged pages seemed to fall apart naturally at the bad reviews, the ones where her intentions had been misunderstood or the piece written by someone who sounded like either a disappointed novelist or a person with a bad attack of indigestion.

'Bad mother; bad novelist,' she said to herself. 'Bad wife. Useless investigator. Damn it! I must find out who killed Alex Ringstead.'

Reaching for a lump of discarded typescript, which she used as scribbling paper, she upset her box of paperclips and silently cursed her own clumsiness. She could not remember what she had done with the list of questions she had written in hospital and realised she would have to start the whole process over again. The idea that she had once been a competent, indeed high-flying, civil servant seemed ludicrous. Reminding herself that she had drafted White Papers, influenced important legislation, had innumerable private meetings with ministers, even prime ministers, that she had organised large groups of distinguished, acrimonious men and women, and kept a sizeable staff in order, she picked up a felt-tipped pen and tried to make herself think usefully.

'That's the pool,' she muttered, having drawn a circle in the middle of the paper and tried to remember the layout of the obstetrics unit.

Eventually she had completed what looked like a reasonable plan of the whole area and realised that the killer had not been taking too much of a risk in luring Alex Ringstead to his death. Only if someone had happened to be going in or out of one of the other delivery suites along the corridor at the exact moment when Ringstead was persuaded into the birthing-pool room could there have been a witness to what had happened.

Willow herself had been delivered in the last room of the row, overlooking the front of the hospital; there had been four between her and the one with the pool and then two on the far side of that. The police must already have established that no one had heard or seen anything that would give a clue to the identity of the killer or they would already have made an arrest.

Setting her imagination to work, Willow recreated the scene in her mind. Whoever the murderer was, he had had to get from the lifts to the birthing-pool room without arousing suspicion and then somehow persuade Ringstead to join him there. Once the door was shut on them both, the killer had persuaded Ringstead to bend over the pool and then pushed his head down into the water and held it there until he was dead. Six minutes.

There must have been a great deal of splashing, and possibly some shouting, but even that did not help. Willow sighed. On that floor splashings and shoutings were not at all unknown. And with porters, doctors in white coats and doctors not in white coats, nurses, friends and attending fathers wearing everything from torn jeans to city suits, not to speak of demonstrating feminists from WOMB, almost no one would have looked out of place.

The only way to get anywhere, Willow decided, would be to approach the problem from the other side and concentrate on the people who might have had reason to want Ringstead dead. She wrote them all down, however silly their motives seemed, and then immediately put a line through the parents of the brain-damaged baby (because the police had already released the father) and Sir George Roguely (because he had been in the United States). She was left with: Durdle or another manager; the suspect ambulance crews; the nurse who had been Ringstead's girlfriend before Mary-Jane; Mary-Jane herself; and Doctor Kimmeridge. It seemed a pathetic list.

After a moment she put a line through Mary-Jane's name as well. When she had shaken hands with Willow in the hall of her house she had had long, impeccably manicured nails. Anyone whose neck she had gripped would have had marks from those nails; and some of them would undoubtedly have broken.

'Haven't you ever heard of false nails?' said Willow crossly putting a dotted line under Mary-Jane's name and writing 'stet' beside it. Then she concentrated hard and was almost certain that the varnish on Mary-Jane's nails had been clear. No false nails could be convincing without a thick layer of coloured varnish over them. And in any case, would she have been strong enough to force Alex Ringstead's head under the water, even if he had allowed her to entice him into an empty delivery room? Reaching for the Tippex, Willow blotted out her dotted line.

Before she could do anything else, she heard a sound from the baby alarm beside her and dropped everything before running along the passage to the nursery. Lucinda's eyes were open and she was coughing. When she saw Willow's face, hanging down over the edge of the cot, she started licking her lower lip and then almost smiled. It was not a proper smile, Willow admitted to herself as she smiled back, but it was a definite movement of the lips and it seemed to express pleasure. Lucinda raised her arms and waved her fists about like a conductor bringing in sections of her orchestra. In her neat blue-and-white baby-gro, she looked very appealing, especially now that her face was skin-coloured rather than red.

Willow laughed and put her hand down. Lucinda grabbed one of her fingers and held tight.

'Oh, Lucinda, you darling.'

The baby gurgled and Willow forgave her everything. She put her other hand out to make Rob's mobile move and watched her daughter's eyes catch the movement and look towards it.

When Tom got home he found Willow asleep on the floor beside the cot with one hand pushed through the bars and resting on the mattress. Lucinda was asleep, too, flat on her back with her thumb in her mouth. Feeling horribly excluded, Tom backed out of the room as quietly as possible, and went downstairs to the kitchen to find out from Mrs Rusham what had been happening during the day.

Later, when he discovered that Willow was still asleep, he fetched a rug to lay over her and went exploring. He never usually entered her writing-room without an invitation, but he felt the need to be connected to one part of her life at least. Besides, the door was wide open and he knew that she was not in the middle of a book. He told himself that she could not possibly object and went in.

The first thing he saw was the scribbled plan on top of the neat heaps of paper on her desk with the circle labelled 'POOL' in the middle of it.

'Oh, Willow,' he said, sighing, and reached for the telephone.

Five minutes later he had reached the incident room for the Ringstead murder and asked to speak to Superintendent Darnley, who was in charge of the investigation. When the man came on the line, Tom identified himself and explained his interest in the case.

'I can't tell you much,' said Darnley, but he said it quite pleasantly.

'Pity. Are you close to an arrest?'

'I can't say yet. But don't let your wife worry. According to the interview reports, she neither heard nor saw anything at all. Even the most paranoid scrote isn't going to think she can identify him. She's not at risk.'

'No,' said Tom, not wanting to explain that it was not Willow's fear of the murderer's trying to silence her that was worrying him but her apparent determination to pre-empt the enquiry. 'Is there really nothing I can tell her?'

'Fraid not. Sorry. Between you and me, it's a bugger of a case. No useful evidence from the forensic scientists. No eyewitness statements of any use at all. People milling around in and out of all those rooms all the time. Lots of them know each other, but lots don't. No one can remember seeing anyone particularly out of place. But then they were all busy or terrified. There was another, worse, emergency than your wife's haemorrhage, and they were all rushing about like blue-arsed flies. The last identified sighting of the victim was in the delivery room next to your wife's, switching off his bleeper.'

'D'you know who called him?' said Tom at once.

'Unfortunately no. There's no record. The switchboard operators answer calls all the time and bleep whichever doctor's needed. They can't remember this particular call and they don't tape them, so we've no idea whether it was a man or a woman, an internal caller or an external. We're stuffed as far as that goes.'

'Lines of enquiry?'

'Several,' said Darnley, sounding irritable for the first time. 'Look, I can appreciate your interest, Worth, but there is nothing I can tell you.'

Admitting to himself that he, too, would have been reluctant to tell any of his colleagues about the progress of one of his enquiries, particularly if it had not been going well, Tom thanked Darnley and put down the telephone. He wanted to tear up the notes Willow had made, but he knew she would hate that and feel, if not say, that he was trying to confine her into some fantasy of his own of what his wife ought to do.

She still seemed unable to grasp that his only concern was for her safety. She was not equipped to chase murderers; the police were. Tom could not understand her dangerous and infuriating obsession with tracking down violent criminals. He had hoped that their increasingly serene life together and the appearance of Lucinda might change her, but it looked as though she were hanging on to her old ways.

'What does she want?' he muttered aloud in desperation and then flinched as he felt her hands on his back.

'Only peace, Tom,' she said from behind him. He turned in her chair and laid his head against her still-swollen abdomen. She hugged him and stroked his hair. 'I can't help it. I just panic at the thought that I'm losing myself. Thinking about who killed Ringstead is holding me together.'

He kept his face pressed against her kimono, wanting to say all kinds of completely unsayable things like, 'Aren't I enough for you? What more do you want? And when am I going to get you back anyway? You've been off limits for months. I hate it. It's not fair.'

'I don't do it to torment you,' she said at last. He looked up at her and was half resentful and half relieved that she had no idea what he wanted.

'I just wish I could understand why you take such risks,' he said after a while.

She pulled away.

'Tom, scribbling down ideas about who might have hated Ringstead enough to drown him is hardly taking risks.'

'But it isn't only that, is it?' Tom was quite pleased to have something to which he could legitimately object and said angrily: 'You've been after his mistress today.'

'How the hell do you know that?' she asked, moving backwards. 'Have you been spying on me?'

'No, of course I haven't been spying on you,' Tom said,

feeling ashamed of himself and sounding tired. 'I just asked Mrs Rusham how you'd been today. She told me you'd been out to play bridge—and then she told me where. Willow, it's dangerous.'

'Why? Do you think Mary-Jane Roguely drowned her lover? Have you seen her? Relatively small, slight, and with impeccable, long-nailed hands.'

Tom covered his face with his hands for a moment.

'No, I don't suspect her. Not least because, like you, I have no evidence of who killed him and no way of getting any. I have no part in this enquiry. The woman you saw today probably had nothing to do with it. But if you go around asking questions of people involved with any murder victim you risk stumbling on someone who knows something and needs to protect himself.'

Tom waited for Willow to give in, trying to pull himself together and forget that part of him wanted her to prove he was more important to her than anything else at all—even their daughter.

'I'm not trying to be a tyrant. I'm just begging you to take care.'

'For Lucinda's sake.' Willow was horrified to hear a bitter edge to her voice and hastily covered it with a question about Tom's early meeting, adding: 'You must be fearfully tired after last night. I've had a sleep, after all, and I still feel pretty weedy.'

'So I saw,' he said, also making an effort to sound unemotional. Then he smiled. 'You looked very sweet curled up on the floor. How are you feeling?'

'Not too bad. Weaker than I expected. I think going out today was a mistake for all sorts of reasons.'

Tom leaned forwards again and laid his face against her, no longer exuding anger and despair. They stayed together until they heard Mrs Rusham's tread on the stairs. Tom went out to ask what she wanted. When he came back it was to say that she had asked whether Willow would like her dinner in bed or laid in the dining-room as usual.

'In bed would be bliss,' she said, 'unless you loathe the idea?'

And so they dined on crab soufflés, salad and cheese, with Willow lying in bed and Tom sitting at the table in the window. She gave Lucinda a final feed, changed her and settled her for the night, before retreating to bed with her nearest rival's new novel. Tom joined her at ten and they switched off their lights half an hour later.

THAT NIGHT there were four interruptions from Lucinda. In the morning Willow woke even before the first cries came through the alarm and felt very much stronger than she had the previous day. Full of confidence that she would be able to find out who had killed Alex Ringstead in spite of Tom's disapproval, she slipped out of bed to get her maternal duties over as quickly as possible.

Lucinda accepted her feed serenely and allowed herself to be laid back in her cot without any fuss at all, leaving Willow and Tom to eat their breakfast in peace. Mrs Rusham surpassed herself, providing them with sliced mangoes, small freshly made brioches filled with wild mushrooms and topped with bacon crisped in the oven, and perfect coffee.

Willow even had time to drink a second cup of coffee before the baby alarm disturbed them. She stood up when she heard the first gulping cries and brushed Tom's head as she passed his chair. He reached up to touch her hand and smiled at her. Neither of them said anything about what she might be planning to do that day.

By the time she had quietened Lucinda once more, Tom had had to leave for work. Willow took a third cup of coffee into her writing-room and set about deciding how best to find out what she needed to know to identify Alex Ringstead's murderer.

She was distracted almost at once by the sight of her half-written synopsis, which was lying on the desk under her plan of Dowting's obstetrics unit. She picked up the fifteen pages of typescript, guiltily asking herself how she could even contemplate trying to beat the police at their own job when she had plenty of work of her own in addition to everything she had to do for Lucinda.

Skimming through the synopsis, she decided that it was puerile and boring, too, which was worse. She could not think how to improve it and wasted a lot of time picking up bits of paper and putting them down again, trying to tell herself that the novel would be all the better if she did a little successful detection first, but unable to let herself ignore it.

Eventually she rang up her agent for some bracing advice. Eve Greville listened carefully to everything she had to say about the synopsis, interrupting only to ask a pertinent question here and there. At the end of Willow's despairing account of her 'useless idea', Eve said: 'I think it's simply that you're trying to do too much too soon.'

'Don't you tell me to concentrate on maternity, please,' said Willow with deep feeling. 'I was relying on you to say that having a baby need make no difference at all and to lash me on to finish the damn' synopsis and get a move on with the book itself.'

Eve laughed. 'Don't sound so cross. And don't be silly. It's perfectly obvious that something as dramatic as having a baby is going to take time to absorb properly. It'll probably add a useful dimension to your work if you let it. Most serious and difficult things do.'

Willow sighed in relief. She was not quite sure whether it was Eve's understanding that the whole business of Lucinda's existence was difficult or the possibility that it might prove fruitful for her work that was making her feel better, but something was. She heard the front doorbell ringing, but ignored it since she knew that Mrs Rusham would deal with whoever was outside.

'Besides,' said Eve, 'you did start the synopsis a bit too

soon after finishing the last novel. I know why you did it, but I think you ought to take some more time to let the new idea bubble up of its own accord instead of forcing it. Ignore it for the time. Concentrate on something else: knitting or something like that. You'll find that the novel will be all the better for a bit of a delay, and probably so will you.'

'Thank you, Eve,' said Willow fervently. Since she had never done any knitting in her life and never intended to do any, she felt as though Eve had given her permission to apply all her spare energies to the investigation. She put down the receiver.

Almost at once Mrs Rusham pushed open the door to say: 'Lady Roguely is downstairs. She called to enquire about your health and Lucinda's and she's anxious to see you if you're not too busy.'

'Oh, good! No, I'm not too busy at all, Mrs Rusham, would you be very kind and give her whatever's suitable to drink at this time of day while I tidy myself up a bit? I'll be down in the drawing-room as soon as I can.'

When her housekeeper had gone, Willow ran along the passage in her bare feet to exchange the bright-yellow kimono for one of her most discreet maternity dresses. Made of heavy dark-blue linen, it fell in severe but unsewn pleats from her shoulders and it was extremely comfortable. Mascara and some discreet brown shadow on her eyelids, a dusting of peach-coloured blusher and a little terracotta lipstick made her face fit to be seen, and she vigorously brushed her chin-length hair. She had washed it several times since getting out of hospital but it was out of shape and badly needed cutting.

Shrugging at her unsatisfactory reflection, she pulled out a pair of navy-leather espadrilles and put them on her bare feet. In her own house she thought she could get away without wearing tights.

When she reached the drawing-room, she regretted both her bare legs and her unkempt hair. Mary-Jane Roguely was looking impeccable, and not at all overdressed, in a beige Armani trouser-suit with a cream-coloured silk T-shirt and a short string of remarkably fat-looking pearls. Her blonde hair was artlessly arranged, but so shiny that it was clear she had only recently emerged from her hairdresser's, and her face was so well made up that it looked almost natural. She was standing looking out at the small garden, but she turned at the sound of Willow's greeting, smiled and held out a large bunch of freesias.

'Hello. How are you? I was so worried about you yesterday. I had to come and see you.'

'How sweet of you! I'm fine now. But what about you? You don't look well at all.' Willow looked more closely and saw the lines beneath the pristine makeup, the shadows under the large grey eyes, and the dryness of the lips under their translucent raspberry colour.

'I didn't sleep much last night,' said Mary-Jane. 'But that's nothing. I quite often don't these days, and since I don't approve of sleeping-pills there's nothing for it but to stagger through the day as best as I can, knowing that I'll get a better night next time as a result.'

'That's brave,' said Willow. 'I do occasionally succumb to pills. Do sit down. Is Mrs Rusham getting you a drink?'

'Well, yes, actually. I let her tempt me with the idea of iced coffee. I don't think I've had any since I last had tea in Derry and Tom's roof garden with my mother some time in the sixties.'

Willow laughed. Of all memories of the 1960s that was the most incongruous she had ever heard. Clearly all the psychedelia, raves, happenings and demos of swinging London had passed her by unnoticed.

'What?' said Mary-Jane, sounding less gracious as she settled herself in Tom's chair on the window side of the Adam chimneypiece.

'Oh, I was just remembering Jinx and the others yesterday,' said Willow, not completely untruthful. They probably had not noticed the youth cults of the sixties either. 'I liked them a lot and was very sorry to mess up their bridge.'

Mrs Rusham appeared with the iced coffee in two tall glasses topped with whipped cream sprinkled with chopped toasted hazelnuts. There was also a plate of her most delectable biscuits, flavoured with a mixture of white chocolate and macadamia nuts. When she had gone, taking the flowers to put in water, Willow urged Mary-Jane to have a biscuit.

'I shouldn't, but perhaps… You are lucky to have a housekeeper like her. She seems marvellous.'

'She is. She's been with me for nearly ten years now.'

Mary-Jane looked puzzled. Willow could not imagine why.

'You're such an amazing mixture,' said Mary-Jane at last. She was frowning but she spoke tentatively. 'A house like this, a long-term housekeeper, a husband in the police force, having your baby on the NHS, a friend of Alex Ringstead's. It doesn't sort of add up, if you don't mind my saying so.'

Willow leaned back against the arm of the sofa and swung her legs up on the seat cushions.

'That's better.' Willow tried not to feel outraged, which was hard, and to remember that if she wanted to ask questions it would ill behove her to be obstructive of someone else's. Speaking as politely as possible, she added: 'It's not really all that odd. A lot of people do have their babies on the National Health Service, even nowadays and even when they could afford to go private.'

'I'm sorry,' said Mary-Jane at once. 'I must have sounded awfully rude.'

'No.' Willow, who had once guarded her privacy like the most damaging of state secrets, decided to punish her a little. 'Just surprisingly curious and perhaps a little unaware of life beyond the security of inherited money.'

Mary-Jane blushed.

'To satisfy the rest of your curiosity perhaps I'd better add that my husband's been a policeman ever since he left the army. Although I have made a certain amount of money for myself, I had my baby at Dowting's because I believe passionately in the NHS and I share the original idea that if it ceases to be a universal service and dwindles into not much more than a charity for the poor, standards will sink. It seems to me that we're moving horribly fast towards that point. With all the talk of rationing, waiting lists and so on, more and more people who can afford it are taking out private health insurance. But I don't know why I'm telling you all this. You must have heard it all many times before.'

'Not quite like that.' Mary-Jane had recovered her complexion. 'Although I do know that Alex was appalled by what was being done to the Health Service.'

'So I gather. He'd had a run-in with the managers over rationing and budget cuts, hadn't he?'

'Several. They drove him mad, you know. The worst was a little pipsqueak who knew nothing about medicine but had been given an absurd amount of power. Alex couldn't get him to see that the things he was doing just caused friction within the hospital and didn't help the patients one bit.'

'What sort of things was he doing?'

'Oh, silly things mainly. Like pinching the consultants' carparking slots. He told Alex they would have to rent themselves space in a commercial carpark. That might not have mattered but the wretched little man went on parking his own car at the hospital.'

'How infuriating! Who on earth is he?'

'A man called Durdle, Mark Durdle, I think. But the carparking row was almost irrelevant. The worst thing he tried to do was ration anaesthetics for women in labour.'

'That's outrageous,' said Willow, forgetting everything else.

'Just what Alex said. Apparently Durdle told him that women had done perfectly well with gas-and-air before epidurals were invented and he thought they should go back to that. It would be much cheaper because it doesn't involve an anaesthetist.'

Seeing that Willow could not speak for fury, Mary-Jane smiled and nodded.

'I know. Alex was boiling with rage when we met for lunch after the meeting when all that cropped up. He told Durdle that when he'd been through a full labour he could talk about rationing anaesthesia for pregnant women and not until then.'

'Good for him!' Willow expected Mary-Jane to smile at her fervent approval, but she did not. Instead she sat in silence for a while and then said carefully: 'Mrs Worth, how well did you know Alex? He never mentioned you to me, but Jinx was telling me yesterday that you were a friend of his.'

Willow, who had been trying to remember whether anyone had mentioned seeing Durdle in the obstetrics unit on the night of Ringstead's death, looked up and saw that Mary-Jane had a most painful expression in her eyes. There was unhappiness in it but there was suspicion as well and a hint of anger.

'I hardly knew him at all,' Willow said at once. 'I was his patient; that was really all it was.'

'Then I don't understand.' Mary-Jane put her coffee glass down rather too sharply on the table beside her chair, but the glass did not crack. 'Why were you asking questions about him? I thought you must…he must…I thought he hadn't told me about you because you were more than a friend.'

'Nothing like that. Oh dear, this is awful.' Willow saw that there were tears overflowing Mary-Jane's carefully made-up eyes. Her lashes must have been dyed rather than coloured with mascara because the streaks that appeared on her cheeks were colourless.

'I was his patient and I liked him,' Willow went on. 'He was killed while I was giving birth and I felt I had to find out more about him.'

'You mean you were spying on me yesterday?'

'No, not spying. I wanted to make sense of it all, to find out what had happened and why anyone should have wanted to drown a man like him. I'd heard that you and he were friends and I thought I might be able to talk to you and find out more about him. It was silly, I suppose, but I just wanted to talk about him.'

At that Mary-Jane's back crumpled and she bent over her beige knees sobbing into her hands. Even then Willow could not stop herself noticing that Mary-Jane's nail varnish was indeed colourless and the nails themselves perfect and quite long. Those hands, however well-protected by gloves, could not have gripped the back of Alex Ringstead's neck without leaving marks in the skin.

'I'm sorry,' Willow said, hoping that her voice was as full of pity as her mind.

'Could I go somewhere and wash my face?' said Mary-Jane eventually, not looking at Willow.

'Yes, of course. Come on upstairs.' Willow led the way up to the spare bathroom, which was as immaculate as every room for which Mrs Rusham was responsible, and left Mary-Jane to reapply her makeup.

'I am sorry to be so silly,' she said when she returned to the drawing-room some time later. Willow could see that the whites of her eyes were slightly red, but that was the only sign of grief left on her face.

'You weren't. It must be hell for you to have to do your grieving so secretly.'

Mary-Jane smiled with difficulty and bowed her head.

'I don't know how much you know about me and Alex, but you clearly know that we were close. I hoped…It's even sillier, but although I wanted to find out whether you and he…I just wanted to talk about him too.'

With a silent apology to the absent Tom, Willow took the opportunity that lay in front of her begging to be used.

'He and I were truly no more than doctor and patient. What made you think we might know each other better than that?'

Mary-Jane's cheeks coloured again and she looked up at the ceiling as though determined not to let any more tears seep out of her eyes.

'It's just,' she said, still gazing upwards, 'that when we fell

in love he had to extricate himself from another relationship.
And the awful thing was that the woman still loved him and
couldn't bear to let him go. He hated having to do it, but he
had no option, honestly. I remember pitying her then and admiring the way she handled it. She was very dignified and I
found myself once hoping that I'd be able to behave as well
as she did when it was my turn to be supplanted. I just hadn't
thought that my turn might come quite so quickly.'

'Well, you don't need to worry about that any more because
it hadn't,' said Willow. 'But it was generous of you to admire
her in those circumstances. Who was she?'

'A nurse at Dowting's. A nice woman, intelligent and attractive. I felt sorry for her, but they'd run out of what was
good between them and it had turned into no more than duty.
In a way it was ruining both their lives. That probably sounds
horribly cruel, but it's true. It had been wonderful and she'd
been very good to him after his divorce, but...'

'He'd got bored with her,' suggested Willow brutally.

'Yes.'

Willow respected Mary-Jane Roguely for that simple assent.
It would have been so easy to make excuses for Alex Ringstead.

'Have you see her since? Do you know what's happened to
her?'

'I haven't seen her, but I know she's working at that new
private hospital out at Chiswick. Alex got her the job. At least
he arranged for her to be head-hunted by them. He's an old
friend of one of the owners. He thought it was the least he
could do once she'd decided she had to resign from Dowting's. She's earning much more at Chiswick than she did in
the Health Service and she'll get over him. I'm sure she will.'

'What's her name?'

'Why do you want to know?'

Willow shrugged and waited.

'Marigold, if you can believe it,' said Mary-Jane with the
first suggestion of antagonism to her predecessor. 'Marigold

Corfe. He called her Goldilocks.' Tears gathered in her eyes again and she looked at Willow as though she were begging for something.

'What did he call you?' she asked, trying to provide it.

'Just Mary-Jane.' The tears fell and she sobbed once and caught her breath. 'He said that this was too important to water down with silly nicknames.'

'I'm sure it was,' said Willow. 'He must have loved you very much.'

At that Mary-Jane gave in to such a storm of tears that Willow felt she needed help and went to fetch Mrs Rusham, who seemed quite capable of doing everything that was necessary. Willow herself, hearing Lucinda crying, ran upstairs to rescue her.

The maternity dress had not been designed with feeding in mind and Willow had to undo the long zip at the back and pull the dress down round her waist while Lucinda lay in her cot, crying with ever-increasing frenzy. When she was sucking strongly, Willow stroked her soft, fuzzy hair, which to her great relief still looked more brown than red, and thought about what Mary-Jane Roguely had told her.

ELEVEN

WHEN MARY-JANE had left, well enough soothed by Mrs Rusham to remember to ask to see Lucinda and say all the right things about her, Willow telephoned the glossy new private hospital in Chiswick. A beautifully spoken receptionist answered and Willow asked to speak to Marigold Corfe adding: 'Unless she's still on night duty.'

'Are you certain it's Sister Corfe you want? She has never been on night duty since she started working here.'

'Hasn't she?' said Willow. 'I thought someone said she had been doing nights for the last three weeks.'

'No, you must be thinking of someone else. Hold on a moment.' Within a very sort time the receptionist was saying: 'Could it possibly be Nurse Curtis you were thinking of? She's certainly been working nights.'

'No, I don't think so,' said Willow, wondering how to get out of the mess she had made of her attempt to establish an easy alibi for Marigold Corfe. 'It really is Sister Corfe I want. Marigold Corfe.'

'Very well. Hold on a moment and I'll see if she's available.'

Willow waited, rehearsing her opening remarks, but it was the same efficient, attractive voice that eventually said: 'I am afraid she is tied up just now, but she should be free within ten or fifteen minutes. Would you like to leave your name and number so that she can get back to you?'

Willow gave her name as King and dictated her telephone number. As she sat waiting for the call, it struck her that Marigold Corfe must be one of the very few people who would have had trouble escaping notice in the obstetrics unit of Dowting's Hospital. Anyone who still worked there could move in and out of the various rooms and wards without worrying about being conspicuous, and any stranger would be assumed to be a relative of one of the women giving birth. But a nurse who had once worked in the hospital and then resigned would be bound to cause comment. Someone would have recognised her and wondered what she was up to. The telephone rang under Willow's hand and she picked up the receiver at once, saying merely: 'Hello?'

'Hello?' said a slightly irritated voice. 'Am I speaking to Ms King?'

'Yes, indeed,' said Willow. 'Is that Marigold Corfe?'

'Yes. May I ask who you are?'

'A patient of the late Mr Ringstead,' said Willow, who had invented and rejected several different excuses for her call as she waited.

'Oh, yes?' The voice was even more irritated. 'And just exactly what do you think I can do for you?'

'I wondered whether I might come and see you.'

'Why?'

'I've been asked to write a...a sort of appreciation of him for a newspaper.'

'What? An obituary?'

'That kind of thing.'

'For which newspaper?'

'You sound very suspicious.' Willow laughed lightly and decided to rely on Jane Cleverholme. 'It's for the women's page of the *Daily Mercury,* actually.'

'And why should you want to talk to me?'

'I gather that you had worked with him for years at Dowting's. I just thought that perhaps someone who...'

'Oh, come off it and tell me what you really want. He died almost two weeks ago. Any obituary that was going to appear would have been written by now. Stop wasting my time and tell me: just who exactly are you?'

'Oh, dear,' said Willow, quickly deciding to take a gamble on the basis that she did not in fact have anything at all serious to lose, except face. 'Perhaps I really have given birth to my brains as well as my baby. To tell you the truth, I am trying to find out who could have killed him, and I thought…'

'That it was me? Is that it? You and the police both. I've just seen them off, and now I'm faced with a bungling amateur. God preserve me! Just who the hell do you think you are ringing me like this?'

'I am really sorry,' said Willow, cursing herself and her bad timing. 'I do not think it was you who killed him, not least because as an ex-member of the Dowting's Obstetrics Unit, you are one of the few people whose presence there that night would have been noticed.'

'Well, I suppose that shows a modicum more intelligence than the police offered.'

'Thank you.' Willow thought it would not be in her interest to suggest that the police had probably been seeking background information from Sister Corfe rather than interviewing her as a suspect. 'You obviously knew him very well, and I thought you might be able to give me some insight into what kind of man he was.'

'I could do that all right,' said Sister Corfe, sounding contemptuous. 'Where exactly would you like me to start?'

'Could we meet? I mean, it would be so much easier to talk face to face. Do you live in Chiswick?'

'No.'

Reminding herself that she, too, would have been obstructive if she had been cross-examined about an ex-lover by an unknown female over the telephone, Willow tried to sound placatory.

'I was just trying to think where would be the most useful place for us to meet. I live fairly near Sloane Square. If you'd rather I didn't come out to Chiswick, what about the coffee shop in Peter Jones? It's nice and neutral and it's late-night shopping there tonight, but if you live in the opposite direction I'd hate to drag you all the way into the middle of London.'

There was a short gasp of half-suppressed laughter, which

made Willow think that either her own frankness or Sister Corfe's feelings about Alex Ringstead might make her cooperate after all.

'Well, I suppose I could come to Sloane Square. As it happens I've got to be in Leicester Square at six-thirty this evening.'

'Brilliant,' said Willow, not wanting to give her a chance to withdraw again. 'What time would suit you?'

'I suppose I could be at PJ's by five.'

'Perfect,' said Willow at once. 'How will I know you?'

'I'm five-seven, blonde, shortish hair with a fringe, and I'll be wearing a Burberry over jeans.'

'And carrying a copy of the *Financial Times*,' said Willow laughing.

'More likely the *Evening Standard*.' Sister Corfe sounded less angry and Willow began to hope that she might actually turn up. 'And you?'

'Three inches taller. Red haired. Not sure what I'll be wearing. I'll find you, and the coffee's on me.'

'Too right. Sticky buns as well. Lots of the most expensive of them.' There was a click and then silence at the end of the telephone.

Smiling, Willow put her receiver down and looked forward to meeting the feisty Marigold, who sounded rather more her type of woman than Mary-Jane Roguely.

WHEN WILLOW CAME face to face with Marigold Corfe over a pile of Iranian prayer rugs in the carpet department of Peter Jones just outside the fifth-floor coffee shop, she was disconcerted to see how much like Mary-Jane she looked. There were the same big grey eyes and the same thick blonde hair, although Marigold's was a lot less sleekly arranged than her supplanter's. They also had very similar figures. But there was no appealing friendliness in Marigold's expression. Instead there was defiance, anger, endurance and a suggestion of curiosity that gave Willow hope.

'So you're Ms King,' she said, neither smiling nor attempting to shake hands. 'Well, we'd better get down to it.'

They collected trays and queued up for their coffee and cakes, exchanging meaningless remarks about the weather as though they were old but distant acquaintances. There were not many other people in the coffee shop; the usual day-time shoppers were at home overseeing their children or cooking, and the people likely to take advantage of the late opening were still in their offices. Willow led the way to one of the desirable tables in the window, which had proper chairs instead of stools.

'All right, what do you want to know?' said Marigold as she stirred the foam into her cappuccino.

'Who you think might have killed Alex Ringstead.'

'I haven't a clue, but I can assure you it wasn't me.'

Willow could not stop herself looking down at Marigold's nails, which were cut very short indeed. Seeing the direction of Willow's glance, Marigold spread her strong-looking hands out on the edge of the table.

'What do you think? Could these hands have forced Alex's head into the water and held him there until his lungs filled with water and he stopped breathing?'

Refusing to be embarrassed, Willow nodded. 'I can't see any reason why the hands couldn't have done it,' she said. 'I'm not so sure about the mind, though.'

'Why?'

'Why don't you tell me?' said Willow like the most irritating kind of teacher.

'We were lovers for three years. However much I hated what he did, how could I have killed him?'

Willow looked at Marigold's face and shook her head.

'I have to say that it seems unlikely.'

'Good. Because, as I explained to Inspector Plod and her mates, the only person I have ever wanted to slaughter is that rich bitch who trailed herself in front of him just because she's bored with her own husband and wanted distraction. Alex and

I could have had a life together—in fact we'd had a really good one until she spoiled it—whereas she only wanted him to play titillating games with. If she'd been the victim, you'd have good reason to suspect me. I could have held her wretched head under water with the greatest possible pleasure.'

'Except that you're far too intelligent ever to kill anyone,' said Willow, rather enjoying Marigold's energy and undisguised rage. 'Murder is such a stupid crime. No one like you would ever imagine that it could solve anything.'

There was a distinct slackening of tension in the woman opposite Willow. After a moment Marigold smiled and shook her head.

'You've found the joint in my armour there,' she said, sighing. 'I've always been a sucker for people who thought I was clever. What makes you…?'

'It's written all over you.'

'That's how Alex got to me, you know.' Marigold sipped her coffee and then licked some foam off her upper lip. She was looking less ferocious and as she talked her lips began to curve and her eyes softened. 'I was experienced enough to see most seduction techniques coming. Some male doctors try it on as a matter of course, as though they have to test their vitality on any woman who's in charge of anything. But that time I was the complete sucker. He used to ask my opinion about women on the ward or about new ideas in obstetrics, and one day he actually said: "I can't think why you've stuck with midwifery; you'd make the most marvellous doctor."'

Willow was framing a question about what sort of man Alex had really been when Marigold tightened her spine again and said more harshly: 'It wasn't until later—much, much later— that I began to realise he was as much of a Don Juan as all the rest and just had a cleverer line in flattery. Pretty slick, eh? I don't suppose he tells the lovely Lady Roguely that she's clever. I wonder what her secret dreams are?'

'Perhaps,' said Willow, more concerned to keep the conversation flowing between them than because it was what she really thought, 'to be pursued by a man who demonstrably wanted to spend time with her rather than with his work as her husband does.'

'I doubt it,' said Marigold through a mouthful of pecan-and-date ring. She swallowed. 'D'you know what my secret fantasy has been even since she made Alex dump me?'

Willow shook her head.

'That I would be around to gloat when he sacked her and moved on to someone else. To be perfectly frank, it's that rather than any hidden intelligence that's the reason why I'd never have wanted him dead. And it would have happened, you know.' She sighed as though she were feeling an almost physical pleasure. Willow raised her eyebrows. Marigold grinned like a naughty child found stealing sweets.

'It's wonderful to be able to say all this. I wasn't sure why I'd been mad enough to agree to meet you, but it's worth it for this alone.'

'Haven't you been able to talk to anyone else?'

'Not like this to anyone I know.' Marigold took another mouthful of coffee. 'I felt so humiliated at the time that I couldn't bear anyone at Dowting's to know that I even minded what Alex had done. And at Chiswick no one knows we were close.'

'What makes you...? I mean, I'm sure you're right, but what makes you certain that Alex wouldn't have stayed faithful to the Roguely woman?'

Marigold laughed.

'At the beginning of their fling I told myself that he was only pursuing her at all because of the dry rot. If the fruiting bodies hadn't been found in the basement, the trust wouldn't have needed to try to cut Alex's budgets and he would never have felt challenged into trying to prove that he could raise far more money than their proposed cuts would have saved them. He wouldn't have had anything to do with the fundraisers or seen Mary-Jane Roguely or needed to motivate her to work on his behalf.'

'Are you saying that he only pretended to fall for her to try to make her work harder for the appeal?' asked Willow. 'Could he have been that cynical?'

Marigold sat with her lips tightly closed.

'Could you ever have loved anyone who could be as cruel as that?' Willow said. 'As you say, you and he had built up a life together.'

'There are some men,' said Marigold coldly, 'whose position as alpha male of the band, tribe, troop, what-have-you, is so important to them that any other consideration fades before it. For that even more than the other reasons Alex would not have been able to bear being beaten by Mark Durdle. Everything else would have had to give way. It's possible that once he'd won their battle, he would have come back to me.'

'Perhaps,' said Willow, but she could not forget what Mary-Jane had said about Alex Ringstead's boredom with Marigold. It was probably too much to expect either woman to see the other without the distortions of jealousy or defensiveness, but Mary-Jane's diagnosis of his state had sounded convincing.

'Why exactly was Alex so badly at loggerheads with Mr Durdle?' Willow asked.

Marigold shrugged and ate another piece of her bun.

'They got across each other almost as soon as Durdle was appointed.'

'I know there was trouble over the car-parking,' said Willow.

'That was a pinprick compared with some other things.'

'Such as?'

'Oh, they had a terrific row over outpatients.'

'What? I don't understand.'

'We're going to need more coffee if I'm to regale you with the whole dreary history,' said Marigold. 'I'll get them. Espresso again for you?'

'Thanks.'

Willow watched her walk briskly back to the counter and return only a few moments later with two more cups of coffee.

'You probably know about the Patient's Charter,' Marigold began. Willow nodded. 'Well, outpatients are supposed to be seen within thirty minutes of their appointment time. On a busy day, when a consultant has a whole string of difficult cases, he or she may overrun that, but Durdle could never accept it. He used to time Alex's clinics with a stopwatch.'

'Then that must have been where I'd seen him before,' Willow exclaimed.

She had been wondering at intervals whether she could have caught sight of him on the night Lucinda was born, which would have pushed him right to the top of the list of suspects.

'I knew he looked familiar, but I just couldn't place him. Thank you. One mystery solved.'

'Not a very interesting one, I'd have thought.'

'No. But I'm glad to have it sorted. So tell me more about their war over the outpatients.'

'Durdle used to draw up a report, a sort of chart thing, at the end of each week and berate Alex for his slackness at the clinics. You see, for Durdle, clinical necessity is not as important as meeting government targets. Alex once said that Durdle behaved as though he'd rather symptoms of pre-eclampsia were missed in one woman than that another should have to wait ten minutes extra for her consultation.'

'Durdle couldn't think that,' Willow protested. 'No one could.'

'No, of course he didn't really. That was just one of Alex's jibes. But, you see, Durdle's responsibilities do not include the actual treatment of patients. His job is to make sure the money is there and spent to its best advantage, and that there's a steady stream of patients coming into the hospital. If Dowting's loses out to St Thomas's, Guy's or St George's, it'll be closed down. Durdle is there to make sure that doesn't happen, and it's a tough job. But Alex couldn't let himself see things that way. All he could see was that he was being told what to do by ''an arrogant little shit'' half his age who knew nothing whatever about medicine.'

Willow watched Marigold as she spoke, intrigued to notice how warmly she was speaking up for Durdle. No one else in any way connected with the hospital had done that.

'But I can see why that would have irritated any doctor,' Willow said, hoping to find out why Marigold should have felt such sympathy for the hated manager. 'I think in Alex's place I might have felt like throttling Durdle—or banging his head against the floor—but it wasn't Durdle who was killed.'

As Marigold's big eyes filled with tears, Willow felt furiously guilty.

'I'm sorry,' she said directly.

Marigold shook her head. 'Alex had other ways of getting back at people who'd annoyed him, and he did get back at Durdle.'

'So I've heard. There was the grand humiliation at the budgeting meeting. But could any reasonably intelligent man have got seriously upset by Alex's joke about women in labour having to cross their legs and hold on until Durdle could afford to let them have their babies?'

'I suspect that when you feel yourself as beleaguered as many of the managers do these days,' said Marigold slowly, 'any mockery from the medical staff can burn like acid. And you mustn't forget that Alex had a big following in the hospital. Almost every woman there adored him, and most of the men thought he was the bee's knees. If all I heard about that meeting was true, he got the whole lot of them, including most of the other managers, laughing at Durdle. It would take gigantic self-confidence to ignore something like that and poor Mark had never been giantlike in any department, least of all self-confidence.'

'I see. Then do you think he could have been upset enough to want Alex dead in revenge?'

'No, I do not. He might have gone so far as to fantasise about how wonderful it would be if a divine thunderbolt were to strike Alex down, but I can't see him laying hands on anyone. And he doesn't exactly look strong enough to do what must have been done that night.'

Willow just nodded. It was a thought that had occurred to her more than once.

'Have you talked to the perfect Lady Roguely yet?' asked Marigold. 'I'd have thought she'd be able to tell you a thing or two.'

'Really? My discussions with her haven't been exactly fruitful.'

'So you have met her. Do *you* think he'd have stayed with her?'

'I'm not sure,' said Willow, picking up her coffee cup.

'I genuinely don't think he would have,' said Marigold, shaking her head. 'A man who's left one woman as easily as Alex left me is always going to have it in mind as a possibility. And when he does see someone he wants more than her he won't think twice about giving himself the treat. However difficult the first time is, the second must be a doddle.'

'As they say about murder.'

'Do they? Look, why are you doing this? Alex's death is none of your business and you have no personal connection with him. It'll infuriate the police when they hear what you're up to, and I can't see it doing you much good either.'

'Probably not,' said Willow and then reluctantly sketched in some of her recent mental turmoil. She was disconcerted to see the woman opposite her shake with laughter.

'I'm sorry,' Marigold said, wiping her eyes. 'But this is the first time I've ever come across a woman dealing with postpartum depression by tracking down a murderer. You must admit it sounds ludicrous.'

'I'm damned if I'm going to admit any such thing,' said Willow, but she laughed, too, and felt much better. 'Come on, there must be something useful you can tell me. Did Alex make many enemies—apart from Durdle, I mean?'

'Not really except the rest of the people who'd annoyed

him. He always had a neat way of humiliating them. It was the other side of the coin from his skill in making one feel spectacularly wonderful. Seeing people's fears and weaknesses as easily as he did, he was able to go either way with them.'

'So which of them do you think it could have been? Durdle hated him but doesn't seem a likely killer to you, and you must have known him quite well. Could one of the other managers have done it?'

'Committed murder? I shouldn't have thought so. After all, it's not as though Alex was killed by someone hitting out in a blind rage. This was planned—and quite cleverly, too. Besides, didn't it happen at night? You'd never catch a manager in hospital outside nine-to-five.'

'Wouldn't you? Then who? You must have some idea who could have hated him that much.' Willow heard her voice sounding both petulant and shrill, and she modified it. 'What about other doctors? They have to take life-and-death decisions all the time. It might be easier for one of them to kill someone who got in his way.'

'I think that's naive, if you don't mind my saying so. I suppose oncologists and geriatric specialists might find it easier than most to help someone to die, but only in the sort of case where the line between pain-relief and poison is so thin it's hardly there. It wouldn't apply to Alex.'

Willow drank some more of her espresso and then, remembering Kimmeridge's views about the cruelty of forcing very premature or very damaged babies to live, said: 'Although obstetricians do sometimes take the law into their own hands, don't they?'

'I suppose some of them do, but only out of the strictest need to prevent suffering.' Marigold looked serious and slightly withdrawn. 'And a great many of them are like Alex and go to any lengths to make sure any viable child is given every possible chance of survival. Who are you suspecting now? Not John Kimmeridge, surely?'

Willow shrugged, for the first time wondering how Kimmeridge squared his views about the cruelty of resuscitating very premature babies with his Roman Catholicism. Unaware of the turn Willow's thoughts had taken, Marigold leaned forwards a little in her eagerness to say: 'You'd be mad to suspect Kimmeridge. Under his sarcasm, he's the gentlest thing in the world. And intelligent, too, if that's really a contraindication murder.'

'Then what about the ambulance crews and their rage over Alex's allegations?' Willow knew that she was flailing around, but she wanted to try out all her possible suspects on the woman who must have known Alex Ringstead better than anyone else.

'What? I don't know anything about that. What allegations?'

'Alex is said to have thought some of them were running a burglars' information service,' said Willow drily. 'Apparently he was trying to get them sacked and some of them were resisting and talking about industrial action at least.'

'That must have been since my time. I don't know anything about it.' Marigold looked down at her watch. 'I'll be late if I don't go soon. Look, is there anything specific that you want to ask me? If there is I'll do my best to answer, but now's your chance. I've quite enjoyed letting off steam, but I'm not going to be amenable to any more questions after this evening. And I don't want you ringing Chiswick again. Is that clearly understood?'

'It sounds fair enough,' said Willow. 'All right. Do you think that any of your other friends, suitors, supporters, what-have-you, might have misunderstood your choice of revenge for what Alex did to you and killed him out of some kind of misplaced loyalty to you?'

For the first time Marigold looked worried. The blood receded from her cheeks as she shook her head.

'Certainly not. What a completely stupid idea!' She even sounded shaken.

Willow was shocked but at the same time extremely inter-

ested that her idle suggestion had produced such a strong reaction. Marigold stood up, belted her Burberry firmly around
her waist and picked up her large handbag.

'Thank you for the coffee. I understand why you feel the
need to do something useful, but, believe me, this is not it.
You'll only cause trouble and get nowhere. Concentrate on
your baby and on controlling your feelings and you'll use your
energies to much better effect. Goodbye.'

Willow stood up and held out her hand. After a moment's
hesitation, Marigold shook it briefly. Having liked her, Willow
found that she did not want to part without some kindness
between them.

'It's none of my business,' she said quietly, 'but quite
frankly I can't imagine what he saw in Mary-Jane Roguely
after knowing a woman like you.'

Marigold bit her lip and turned away. She did not look back
as she walked fast between the pale wood tables and their red-
seated stools.

Willow was left with her mind buzzing. If there was one
thing clear to her it was that she would have to get back to
Dowting's and question the nurses about who might have
loved Marigold enough to want to take revenge on her behalf
for the way Alex Ringstead had treated her.

WHEN WILLOW got back to the mews house she was completely distracted from the investigation by the sound of voices
coming from the drawing-room. As she dropped her keys on
to the pewter plate on the hall table, Mrs Rusham emerged
from the drawing-room with an empty tray in her hands. Her
face lightened as she saw Willow.

'Oh, I am glad you're back. Robert's here on his way home
from school and also Miss Gnatche.'

'Gnatche?' said Willow in complete surprise. 'Emma
Gnatche?'

Mrs Rusham nodded.

'Good heavens. How nice!'

Willow had not seen Emma for nearly three years, not from her own choice but because Emma had withdrawn herself after a short affair with Richard Crescent had gone badly wrong. Willow had missed her guilelessly entertaining company but had not wanted to cause any trouble or make what had obviously been a painful episode any worse. At first she had simply waited for Emma to contact her when she had recovered her usual high spirits. Later Willow had become so taken up with her marriage to Tom and then her pregnancy that she had almost forgotten Emma and their old friendship.

'I haven't let them go up to the nursery, although they both wanted to see Lucinda,' Mrs Rusham was saying. 'She's asleep at the moment and I don't think she should be disturbed.'

'Very wise. I'll go in and see them.'

Remembering Emma's debutante girlishness, Willow was slightly surprised to hear that she and Rob were deep in a lively conversation. Tempted to eavesdrop and find out what they could possibly be talking about so animatedly, Willow made herself behave properly and pushed open the drawing-room door. Both her visitors stopped talking at once and got to their feet. Waving at Rob, Willow went to kiss Emma.

'What a lovely and unexpected treat! It's been ages. How are you and what's been happening to you?'

Emma, who had returned the kiss with warmth, said: 'I'm absolutely blooming, thanks, in spite of having finals in four weeks' time. I hope you don't mind my coming, but when I saw the notice about Lucinda in *The Times* I just couldn't stay away. I think it's the most glorious piece of news I've heard in years.'

Willow found herself laughing in delight. She had forgotten Emma's warmth and instant affection, which had been distorted the last time they met by her guilt over the break-up with Richard Crescent.

'Finals already?' said Willow with admiration. 'Goodness

me, it's been a long time. Have you been enjoying university? I must say that you look terrific on it.'

'Thank you,' said Emma, sitting down again.

Willow noticed that Emma's familiar velvet hairband and pearls had gone and with them the self-satisfied drawl that she must have picked up from her family. She looked much older than the three years' absence warranted and, to Willow's eyes, more attractive. Her fair hair had been cut short around her head, showing off the good bones of her face, and she looked much more alive than she ever had in the old days. There was a new maturity about her blue eyes, too, as though she had seen and understood a great deal that had escaped her in the past.

Remembering Rob at last, Willow turned to explain to him how she had come to know Emma.

'I know,' he said before she had got very far. 'She's been telling me all about it. You met her when the minister of your department was murdered on Clapham Common and you didn't stop her helping with your enquiries then, even though she was only a year older than I am now.'

'Was she?' Willow was astonished when she remembered that Emma had already worked for the minister as a temporary secretary not long before he was murdered. 'Yes, I suppose she was.'

'And you let her help again on some of your other cases.'

'So I did,' said Willow, remembering how well they had got on in spite of her suppressed jealousy at the easiness of Emma's life. Willow had been irritated, too, by many of Emma's inherited assumptions and by her cheerful conviction that she had the freedom of Willow's flat whenever she wanted it. No one had ever had that in those days. Looking back, Willow was surprised—and retrospectively grateful—that Emma had continued to be so affectionate in the face of several rebuffs.

'But girls mature much earlier than boys do,' Emma was

saying as she grinned at Rob. He laughed back at her with a cheerfulness that surprised Willow.

'I can see I'll have to keep an eye on Lucinda in that case to stop her getting too big for her boots,' said Rob. 'How is she, Willow?'

'Very well, but getting to be a bit noisy at night. She's got a way to go yet, Rob. Although she's already noticing and liking your mobile. It was an inspired present.'

Turning to explain the mobile to Emma, Willow felt frustrated. Fond of both of them, she would have enjoyed talking to either, but the mixture was difficult.

As though she understood, Emma said: 'I'm going to have to go soon, alas. I've promised to meet my tutor to explain why my last three essays have been below the standard she thinks I ought to reach.' She made a face and shuddered. 'I'd better get on, but I couldn't resist dropping in to see if you were here. Finding Mrs Rusham was such fun. May I come again? I don't want to lose you for a second time.'

'That would be nice. Shall we fix a time?' They agreed that Emma would return the next day just after lunch. Willow escorted her out into the hall and thanked her for coming, adding: 'Are you really meeting your tutor?'

'In fact, yes, but I'd have gone anyway,' Emma said in a low voice. 'It was silly of me to come without warning. I hadn't somehow thought that you might be entertaining a schoolboy.'

Willow laughed. 'I've changed almost as much as you clearly have.'

'Yes. Ironic really, isn't it?'

'Why?'

'You sent me away to university to turn me into a real person, didn't you?'

'Did I really? It was remarkably arrogant if I did. I'm sorry, Emma.'

'Don't be.' Emma touched Willow's wrist. 'It's the best

thing that could've happened to me. I'll tell you all about it when I come back. What about you? Are you happy?'

At that impossible question, Willow stood in silence. She saw consternation in Emma's big eyes and tried to answer.

'In most ways,' she said. 'But I am a bit up and down at the moment. I don't quite know...'

'It was a silly thing to ask, particularly when you must still be rather fragile after the birth and all that. I'm sorry.' Emma swung her scratched leather shoulder bag over her arm. 'See you tomorrow. 'Bye.'

''Bye.' Willow shut the front door and leaned against it, wishing she had not been faced with that particular question. It seemed almost as threatening as Lucinda's existence. Then she went back to Rob, who stayed for dinner and tried to pump Tom for more news of the ambulance crews and what they might or might not have done to protect their alleged racket from Mr Ringstead's interference. Tom parried his questions with jokes and drove him back to his aunt's house in Stockwell as soon as they had all finished eating.

TWELVE

TRAPPED IN a nightmare, Willow felt as though her life was being sucked out of her. Someone was holding Lucinda out of her reach, dangling her over a deep chasm. Willow was too weak to help, but she knew that if she did not make a proper effort Lucinda would be dropped in the chasm and die. There was danger all around. Willow could not move.

Fighting her way out from under the duvet to rescue her baby, Willow felt only air. She opened her eyes. A stripe of moonlight split the curtains, letting her see the familiar shapes and patterns of her own bedroom. For a moment all she could feel was relief that the horror had been nothing more than a nightmare.

Then she realised that the sheet underneath her was wet. She flung back the duvet and saw blood, a lot of it. When she got out of bed her legs wouldn't hold her up and, dizzy and faint, she fell heavily on to the floor.

'What is it?' said Tom roughly. He sat up, pushing both hands through his hair. Then he saw the bed. 'Will? Where are you?'

She pulled herself up from the floor, pressing down on the edge of the bed as she tried to kneel upright.

'I'm sorry, Tom, I...'

'Don't waste your energy, Will,' he said, flinging himself out of bed and stubbing his toe agonisingly against the table. He gasped and then said as calmly as possible: 'Don't worry. I'll get you straight back to Dowting's.'

'No ambulance.' Willow could not waste the strength she needed to explain that she did not want a Dowting's ambulance-driver to know that their house would be empty.

'No,' agreed Tom, who was thinking of other things. 'At this time of night it'll only take ten minutes by car.'

He was pulling a pair of jeans and a loose cotton sweater over his pyjamas as he spoke. When he had tied the laces of his trainers in double knots, he lifted Willow gently up from her slumped position by the bed and wrapped her dressing-gown around her shoulders.

'We'll have to take Lucinda,' she said, feeling so ill and frightened that everything seemed too difficult for her. 'But I don't think I can walk on my own.'

'Don't worry. I'll get you down to the car and then come back for her. Hang on.'

Tom took her downstairs and left her lying on the back seat of the car with all the doors firmly locked, before running back into the house to fetch Lucinda. She screamed as he picked her out of her cot and dumped her unceremoniously in the Moses basket that stood waiting on the changing table. Grabbing a blanket, he tucked it round her and took the basket downstairs as quickly as he could. He ignored the burglar alarm but he did take the time to double-lock the front door behind him. He swung the basket into the back of the Volvo, locked the hatchback, and ran round to the driving-seat.

There was no traffic, and no pedestrians appeared to make him slow down. He averaged sixty miles an hour throughout the short drive across the river to Dowting's and squealed to a halt in the empty carpark.

'I'll have to leave her in the back for a minute or two,' he said, looking down at Willow's face, which was as white and tense as his own. 'But she'll be safe. I'm sure she will.'

'Hurry, though.'

Tom got Willow into the hospital foyer, saw a nurse striding along looking down at a clipboard, and shouted at her. Seeing Willow collapsing at his side, the nurse ran towards them. Three short questions elicited enough of the relevant facts for her to send Tom back to the car to fetch Lucinda.

It was only ten minutes before the nurse had Willow lying

on a trolley with Doctor Kimmeridge examining her and a
night nurse she did not know standing by to carry out his
instructions.

'I thought we'd seen the last of you,' Kimmeridge said
cheerfully as he shone a bright light between her legs.

'Sorry.'

'Don't worry. This is easily dealt with. It's a little bit of
retained placenta.'

He saw that Willow was looking confused and added
kindly: 'The afterbirth did not separate completely from your
womb. The bit that got left behind has now come away, and
it's left a raw patch on the lining of your womb, which is
bleeding. It's not dangerous now you're here. We'll deal with
it and you'll soon be comfortable again.' He turned aside to
give some orders to the nurse and then stayed with Willow,
talking cheerfully until the nurse returned.

The sharp sting of a needle in her arm made Willow feel
better. All the weakness was still there and much of the pain,
but there was less fear. She knew that she was in the safest
place she could possibly be, and she had no responsibility any
longer, not even for Lucinda. Lying back with her muscles
slackening, Willow smiled up at Doctor Kimmeridge.

'Better?' he said.

'Much. Is there any sign of my husband?'

'I'm here,' Tom said from behind her. He came forwards
and touched her arm. 'That was awful.'

'I know. I'm sorry. How is Lucinda?'

'She's fine. One of the nurses has got her and when they
find you a bed they'll wheel her cot in. She wasn't even crying
when they took her away. Oh, Will.'

'I'll leave you to it,' said Kimmeridge kindly, 'and chase
up the bed. Don't worry, either of you. Everything's going to
be fine.'

BY NINE O'CLOCK the next morning, Willow had still not been
given a bed. She was quite happy on her trolley, but Tom was

pacing up and down the corridor, looking both ill and angry. He knew perfectly well that neither Kimmeridge nor any of the nurses could help; he also knew that Willow was safe where she was and that Lucinda was in good hands. But he could not bring himself to leave for Scotland Yard until they were together in one of the proper wards.

Willow, who knew that he had a series of important meetings that morning, urged him to leave her. His anxiety was difficult for her to absorb and yet there was nothing she could do to soothe it. He stood at her side, looking down, biting his lips.

'Don't worry so, Tom. Some new mothers are bound to be let out this morning and then I'll get a bed. I'm fine here. It doesn't hurt any more. Kimmeridge has done everything that needed to be done. I'm not going to roll off the trolley or anything like that. You go to work. We'll be fine.'

'I can't leave you like this. What's the time?'

'Just after nine. You're going to be terribly late.'

'Blast. Look, that business manager you mentioned must be here now, even if he is a clock-watcher. I'll have a word with him.'

He had gone before Willow could protest, and so she lay back, wishing that one of the nurses would bring Lucinda for her feed. Willow's breasts were heavy with milk and becoming painful.

Tom came back, looking better, ten minutes later.

'You should get a bed quite quickly now, my love,' he said, leaning down to kiss her forehead.

'Why? What did he say?'

'Say?' Tom grinned. 'He didn't get a chance to say very much. I gave him a good strong lecture about what his hospital had done to you, what sort of state you were in last night, how dangerous it had been for you that they had been careless enough to leave half your placenta behind...'

'It doesn't work quite like that, Tom,' Willow said, but he hushed her.

'That doesn't matter. Durdle was impressed—or scared—enough to assure me that you would get the first available bed this morning. I'll be off now, but I'll drop back as soon as I can. Okay?'

'Fine, Tom. Thank you. You've done brilliantly.'

'Not so bad,' he said, looking remarkably pleased with himself. He turned at the end of the corridor and waved. Willow waved back and wished she had asked him to bring her a book.

She was allocated a bed just before lunch and was wheeled into one of the bays in the maternity unit in time to eat a hospital cheese salad and a bowl of tinned fruit. Lucinda's cot was pushed into place beside her bed.

The library trolley was brought into the ward just after Lucinda had finished her feed and Willow browsed contentedly among the romances and detective stories until she found one that appealed to her. She was glad to see that there were several of her 'Cressida Woodruffe' novels and that they looked well used. One of the other women in the ward chose one and Willow watched her covertly as she returned to her bed and started to read.

When Willow was satisfied that the woman was not going to throw the novel on to the floor in disgust, she opened the one she herself had chosen and was well into the second chapter before the first few visitors appeared in the ward. Not expecting anyone herself, since only Tom and Mrs Rusham knew where she was, Willow went on reading until she was disturbed by Emma Gnatche's voice, saying: 'I went to the mews and Mrs Rusham told me you were here. How are you? It sounds as though it was all quite terrifying.'

'Emma! How lovely to see you!'

'You sound remarkably cheerful. Wasn't it awful?'

'For a time; but it's over now. Don't let's talk about it. It's really good of you to have come. How did it go with your tutor?'

'I think I'm beginning to recover from her savaging,' said Emma cheerfully as she sat down and crossed her bare, slender legs. 'But it'll take a day or two more, I suspect, before I don't sweat at the thought of meeting her again.'

'Was it really as bad as that?'

'Almost. I know she only does it for my own good, but I do sometimes feel flayed by the things she says to me. You see I've been accepted for a post-graduate course, but if I don't get a good enough degree that'll be a washout. She's as anxious for me to make it as I am.'

'Postgraduate? Emma, you continue to surprise me. What's your speciality going to be?'

To Willow's amusement, Emma's eyes slid sideways as they had done in the old days whenever she was embarrassed, and she even pushed her fingers behind her ears as she had so often done when her blonde hair was long enough to scoop back.

'Criminology, in fact,' she muttered.

'Oh, good for you! Emma, that's terrific news. I should think it'd be fascinating. Why are you looking so coy about it?'

'Well, it's such a change from the sort of life I always assumed I'd live that I feel a bit of an imposter. And also...' She broke off and pushed her non-existent hair behind her ears again. 'In a way I felt as though I was sort of copying you, if you see what I mean. I hoped you wouldn't mind. I...'

'Emma, Emma, stop it.' Willow touched her hand for a second. 'You're not like that any more: sweet and desperate to please. You are yourself with a right to your own ideas. But tell me: what made you choose criminology?'

'I suppose it was partly because I had a kind of...' She broke off, laughed at herself and started to look less childish.

'I admired you so much after you found out who killed poor Algy Endlesham all those years ago that I began to read everything I came across that had to do with crime and the law. And I couldn't help noticing that there are a lot of cases in which the police appear to know exactly who committed the crime—as do all the lawyers involved—but the evidence isn't admissible or not enough to persuade a jury to disbelieve an ingenious defence. I really hate that, but it didn't occur to me for ages that I might actually do anything relevant. Then I heard about this postgraduate course and thought I'd have to have a bash at it, see where it takes me.'

'I think it's wonderful news.'

'You're almost the first person who's said anything like that,' said Emma with a wide, grateful smile. 'As you can imagine, my brother was appalled when I told him.'

'Criminology not being a suitable interest for a nice girl?'

'Pretty much, and I think he feels that I'll become somehow contaminated and a bit disgusting if I so much as think about crimes, let alone encounter any criminals. He probably has visions of me walking the streets around King's Cross and getting picked up and murdered—or worse.'

Amused by Emma's doomy voice, Willow thought about her first meeting with the pompous, self-satisfied Anthony Gnatche. He had only recently left the army then and still seemed to be locked into the conventions he had learned from his brother officers. From what Emma had just said, it sounded as though he had not changed much.

He was a lot older than she and had always done his best to take the place of their father, who had died during Emma's last year at school. Anthony's motives for telling her what she might and might not do had probably been thoroughly admirable, but he had known so little of what went on beyond the tight world of his class and smart regiment that she would have been severely limited if she had obeyed all his orders.

'You've done well to stand up to all his prejudices, Emma,' said Willow. 'I think you'll be a great success.'

'I haven't done anything yet and I may discover that I'm useless or that criminology and I don't mix, in which case I'll have to think again.'

'I don't think you need worry,' said Willow, realising that Emma might be in a position to help her with her own investigation. 'Listen, I've got a problem at the moment. I can't talk to Tom about it because he's being even more protective than usual and I need to talk in order to sort out my ideas. They're in a complete muddle at the moment and whenever I'm on the point of getting somewhere Lucinda wakes up and distracts me. See what you can see in it all, and tell me if I'm being particularly obtuse about some obvious solution.'

'I don't suppose I'll see anything you haven't,' said Emma frankly, 'but I'd love to hear all about it.'

And so Willow described yet again everything she knew of what had happened to Alex Ringstead, what she had discovered about his life within the hospital and beyond it, and which inhabitants of his various worlds might have hated him enough to kill him. It amounted to pitifully little.

'So have you discovered who might be so devoted to this Marigold woman that he could have committed murder on her behalf?' asked Emma when Willow had finished.

Willow shook her head. 'I haven't found out anything at all since I saw her. I've been hoping that the student nurse— Susan Worbarrow—will appear so that I can ask her. She's always been much the chattiest of them all and clearly loves to gossip.'

'But would she know much about this? It sounds as though she's very young and can't have been here long.'

'Emma, you are wonderful. I knew talking to you would help. That hadn't even occurred to me, but of course you're right. I'd better set my sights on Sister Lulworth. She's been here for years and is occasionally prepared to tell me things. Although, you know, devotion to Marigold does seem to be about the least convincing motive for murdering someone as admirable as Alex Ringstead.'

Sensing disagreement in Emma, Willow looked at her and after a moment said warily: 'Am I making a clot of myself again? You're looking rather critical. What have I missed in the Marigold saga?'

'It's not that,' said Emma with a sweet smile. 'I was just

thinking that from everything you've said, he doesn't actually sound all that admirable.'

'In that case I can't have described him properly,' said Willow. 'He was charm personified, an extremely good doctor, and funny, too.'

'Yes, I know. I got all that from what you said. But you also said that he was a rake whose relationships kept failing: first his marriage; then what sounds like a long-term affair with Marigold. He took pleasure in the public humiliation of people like Mark Durdle who'd annoyed him. He pursued vendettas over trivial things like the carpark space. He went to extraordinary lengths to resuscitate babies whose chances of living a full or healthy life were so low that other doctors would have allowed them a merciful death without interference. He wouldn't listen to anyone who disagreed with his ideas. He may even have blocked the chances of another doctor's promotion by giving him unfairly bad references. Honestly, you know Willow, he sounds deeply unattractive to me, however charming and charismatic he might have been to meet.'

'I suppose so,' said Willow as her eyebrows twitched together. 'But although different people have alleged things like that, they don't give a fair picture of the whole man. They really don't. No one could have been as kind to his patients as Ringstead was if he'd been the selfish villain you just described.'

'Although,' said Emma, watching Willow with a surprising depth of compassion, 'there are men—and women, too—who find it much easier to be impersonally kind to people who pass through their lives, stopping only briefly, than to those with whom they have to live in any kind of intimacy. Perhaps it was his inability to empathise with people in any long-term way that both ruined his relationships and made him able to ignore the costs of saving the lives of the very ill babies. After all it was a cost that would not have been paid by him but by the child and its parents for years and years and years.'

'True, but...'

Before she could finish her sentence Willow saw Sister Chesil coming down the ward towards them. She stopped at the foot of the bed.

'Mrs Worth.'

Willow, who had forgotten both the harshness of her voice and the intensity of her angry personality, tried to look welcoming.

'Hello, Sister. I'm surprised to see you in the daytime.'

'My night duty ended last week.' Sister Chesil picked the chart up from where it hung at the foot of Willow's bed and clicked her tongue. 'I need to talk to you.'

She turned to look at Emma with a frown that carried an unmistakable order with it. Emma smiled back blandly and waited.

'Oh, this is Emma Gnatche,' said Willow, impressed with her young friend's surprising coolness. 'Emma, this is Sister Chesil, who saw me through the whole business of Lucinda's birth. She was wonderfully unflapped when things began to go wrong and no one could find poor Mr Ringstead.'

'How do you do?' said Emma. 'Do you need to have some time alone with Willow?'

'I do need to examine her,' said the midwife in a slightly more conciliatory tone.

Willow shook her head, but Emma was not looking at her. She was watching Sister Chesil with as much directness as her innate good manners would allow.

'I'll nip down to the visitors' canteen, have a cup of coffee, and come back a bit later,' said Emma at last. 'We've still got lots to talk about.'

Before Willow could protest, Emma had picked up her shoulder bag and walked away, leaving Willow with Sister Chesil's anger and her own anxiety.

'Now, what can I do for you?' Willow said as politely as possible.

Sister Chesil pulled the curtains shut around the bed before saying in a furious undertone: 'I would like to ask what you think you've been doing.'

'Nothing that could have given rise to the bleeding. It just happened. Doctor Kimmeridge did say it wasn't my fault.' Willow detested the pathetic sound of whining apology in her voice.

'I am not talking about your health,' said Sister Chesil impatiently. 'You have been interfering in a police investigation. Does Inspector Boscombe know what you've been doing? I have a good mind to talk to her myself and have you stopped before you do any more damage.'

'I haven't been doing anything illegal,' said Willow firmly. She was relieved that she had managed not to encourage Rob to bug the ambulance-drivers' telephone calls after all. 'The police might resent my asking questions about what happened to Mr Ringstead, but this is still—just—a free country. They can't stop me.'

'Perhaps. But freedom entails responsibility. Don't you think you should have considered the feelings of a woman you had no business even talking to at a time when she's maximally vulnerable?'

'Ah,' said Willow, realising that she might be being presented with the answer to one of the questions Emma had just asked. She could not help looking at Sister Chesil's strong hands with their neat, short nails. 'You mean Marigold Corfe?'

'Precisely. Don't you think that she might have suffered enough without your self-indulgent curiosity? A man she thought was going to be her husband throws her over with no warning whatsoever because he likes the idea of a rich mistress who isn't going to ask anything of him that he doesn't want to give. She's then forced out of the job she loves and loses the friends she's worked with for twenty years. That same man, whom she still cares about in spite of his hideous behaviour, is found dead. Murdered. She's badgered by the police, who assume that hell knows no fury like a woman scorned, but she survives it. And then she comes face to face with yet another woman who thinks her own amusement is more important than other people's lives.'

'When you put it like that,' said Willow, determined not to let herself look away from her accuser, 'it does sound inconsiderate. But it wasn't like that. There was no amusement in it for me. And your friend did tell me that she was glad of the opportunity to talk about Mr Ringstead.'

'I'm not surprised. She's a generous-minded woman.'

'You must care about her a lot.' Willow thought that there was no point reminding the furious midwife that Marigold was quite tough enough to have refused to say anything at all. Having no official status, Willow could never have forced anyone to talk to her. After all, even the police found that pretty difficult with the sanctions of the Police and Criminal Evidence Act hanging over them.

'Enough to want to protect her from people like you,' said Sister Chesil. 'I've met prying voyeurs before and I know that you won't stop asking questions and ferreting out things that are none of your business, but I don't want her worried again. If you must ask questions, ask me. At least I'm not emotionally involved.'

Willow blinked. The offer was far too good to refuse, but, coming unexpectedly like that, it was difficult to take up. Thinking that she might have discovered the source of Sister Chesil's continuing anger, she asked the easiest question of all: 'All right. Then who do you think killed Alex Ringstead?'

'I have no idea, but I've always thought that the likeliest explanation is that it was a patient of the hospital's long-stay psychiatric wing.'

'Really?'

'Yes. The wing's recently been closed and we've had some of the patients wandering into the hospital ever since then in search of somewhere safe and warm to sleep. I suspect what happened that evening was that one of them saw a man in a white coat and was paranoid or deluded enough to believe that he represented a threat. Mr Ringstead may even have said something that frightened the patient. Very few people who suffer from mental illness are violent, but sometimes, when they haven't taken their medication and are confused or frightened enough, they can kill.'

'I wonder if that's the answer. I suppose it's possible,' said Willow, thinking about it.

'Possible or not, it's the only solution I can think of and so I told the police.'

'Were they convinced?'

'I have no idea and very little interest. It's their business. Not mine and certainly not yours.'

'I don't see how that can be true,' said Willow slowly, watching her heavy face with interest. 'You're far too conscientious a nurse to believe that it's not your business if there's a deluded and violent person wandering about these wards. The protection of the killer, let alone that of your own patients and their babies, would worry you a lot.'

'Of course it would matter,' said Sister Chesil sharply. 'But the police know everything I know and it is their responsibility, not mine.'

'I wonder what it is you really believe.'

'I have told you. If you're not convinced, there's nothing I can do to persuade you. And if you're about to ask whether I murdered him myself, I can assure you I did not.'

'It never crossed my mind that you might have killed him,' said Willow truthfully, an instant before she was seized by an attack of queasiness brought on by the recognition of just how easy it would have been for Sister Chesil to have done it.

Always more interested in people's motives for wanting someone dead than in the opportunity and means they might have had, Willow silently admitted that she had been ignoring one of Tom's most important dicta on the subject of murder investigation:

'Motive may be useful in building a case against a suspect, provided you first have some real evidence of his involvement, but it is rarely more than that. Once you start to use motive as a way of identifying possible suspects, you are landing yourself in trouble and aeons of wasted time.'

Sister Chesil had been in and out of the delivery suites all night; she was one of the few people with the authority to summon Doctor Ringstead to the birthing pool. For her, he might well have knelt down to investigate something she could have put in the water for the purpose. She knew where all the clean, dry overalls were kept. And she, alone of the people Willow had interviewed, had felt the need to produce a plausible explanation of the killing.

Trying not to show any sign of what she was thinking, Willow looked at the midwife and noticed the breadth of her shoulders and the strength of her spatulate fingers. She thought about the anger that had always hung about the woman like a miasma and began to long for the curtains to be opened again.

'Since I'm here, I'd better have a look at you,' said Sister Chesil.

Startled out of her thoughts, Willow clutched the sheet that covered her. A surge of fear rose in her brain as she thought about the two severe haemorrhages she had suffered since Lucinda's birth and tried to assess the possibility that they could have been the result of something someone had done to her when Lucinda was born. Sister Chesil would have had more opportunity than most for that as well. Perhaps she really had murdered Alex Ringstead and, afraid that Willow might have seen or heard something that would have given her away, decided that Willow, too, must die.

Trying to sound perfectly cool and as confident as Emma, Willow explained that Doctor Kimmeridge had already examined her. Sister Chesil listened and nodded.

'Yes, I know he had a look at you. I was briefed when I came on duty. Nevertheless I must do my job.' She looked down at Willow with an indefinable expression before producing a small, cold smile and saying with audible sarcasm: 'You are quite safe here, you know. And in any case there are plenty of people within earshot if you need them.'

Half ashamed of her melodramatic fears, and yet still afraid, Willow closed her eyes, pushed down her bedclothes and let Sister Chesil get on with what she had to do. The examination was painless and over quite quickly.

Sister Chesil stripped off her gloves with a sharp snapping sound, disposed of them and wrote some more notes on the chart. She then suggested that Willow stop wasting time fantasising in her unhealthy way about Mr Ringstead's death and concentrate on her responsibilities to her child.

Willow was left feeling a fool and still tingling from the adrenaline left by her access of fear. Before it had completely dissipated, Emma returned and her intelligent interest in the murder helped restore Willow's emotional balance. Emma had plenty of questions to ask and as they talked Willow felt as though she were discovering a remarkable person.

Eventually Emma said quietly: 'You know, I can see that Chesil has the strength to have drowned Ringstead, plenty of opportunity, the anger necessary to cloud her judgment, and possibly even a slight motive, but she doesn't convince me as a murderer. And if she had done it, wouldn't she have been heavily splashed with water when she came back to deal with your haemorrhage? Surely you would have noticed that, even in those circumstances.'

'I might not have because they were all wearing voluminous overalls at that stage. She could easily have put a dry one on over her wet uniform. They must have stacks of them somewhere.'

'Even so, I can't see it, Willow. Angry she undoubtedly was at the way Ringstead had treated Marigold, but she must have known that murdering him would hardly help restore her friend to happiness. I'd have thought this Durdle man a much better bet. From everything you've told me, he sounds the likeliest apart from Sir George Roguely, and you say that his alibi is watertight. Oh dear, how unfortunate! Unbreakable, I mean.'

Willow acknowledged Emma's unintended slip with a slight smile.

'But Durdle's so smooth. I can easily accept that he might have wanted to get his own back on Ringstead and even resorted to every possible kind of petty bureaucratic revenge, but physical action seems way outside his capabilities. It really does.'

'I'll have to take your word for that. After all, I've never met him. But you said at one moment that you thought you'd seen him before. Are you absolutely convinced that it could only have been at a clinic?'

'Well, it's much the likeliest, Emma. Marigold said that he used to attend the clinics with a stopwatch... No.' Willow almost shouted and sat up much straighter. 'Emma, you are brilliant. You're right: it wasn't at a clinic. I did see him on the night Ringstead was killed.'

'Aha!' said Emma with manifest satisfaction. 'Where?'

'There was a man in a grey suit standing under the canopy rioting. I'm sure it was Durdle. I couldn't see him all that clearly at first, but he did come out into the light for a second. I'm sure it was him. The figure I saw had all his dapperness and was about the right height.'

'But didn't Marigold tell you that no manager is ever to be found in the hospital outside office hours?' said Emma, playing devil's advocate for once.

'Yes, she did. But that doesn't mean much. It's the sort of thing the medical staff might well say. All the nurses seem to have been up in arms about something Durdle had tried to do to control them. If it was him...I wonder.'

'So do I,' said Emma.

'And just what exactly are the two of you wondering about?'

Willow and Emma both looked up, startled, to see Tom walking towards them, carrying a bundle of newspapers.

'This and that,' said Willow, holding out her hand. Tom took it between both of his, letting the newspapers slither on to the bed. 'My mind doesn't work at all well these days. It used to be so precise and analytical. Now all it does is wander fruitlessly round and round questions and wonder about the answers.'

'Does it?' he said drily. 'Never mind. You're looking much better than you were this morning, and the brains will sharpen up again soon.'

He kissed his wife and then turned to shake hands with Emma, adding: 'Will told me you were back in our lives, Emma, and I've been looking forward to this. It's really good to see you. How are you?'

She stayed with them for long enough to hear about Tom's new job at Scotland Yard and tell him about her plans for the course in criminology. He was more enthusiastic about that than Willow would have expected and talked about two of his colleagues who had done the course and found it helpful.

'I'm glad. I'll pass that on to my dear brother the next time he starts pontificating about the waste of time he's sure it'll prove to be. He has a great respect for law'n'order.'

'Even so, he'd die of chagrin if he thought you might join the police,' said Willow. Emma let out a ringing peal of laughter and when she could talk again said: 'On that note, I'd better go. It was bliss to see you both. I'll be in touch.'

'Goodbye, Emma.' Tom stood up to kiss her cheek. When she had left the ward, he turned back to Willow. 'I'm glad she's back. I suspect you've missed her.'

'D'you know, I think I may have. It hadn't occurred to me before. Now, d'you want a turn with Lucinda? She's been behaving beautifully.'

'Has she? She's a good little baggage, isn't she? No, you stay there. I'll get her.'

He cradled Lucinda in his left arm, using his right forefinger to stroke her as he crooned endearments. Willow looked at them askance, hating herself for not being more pleased that Tom was so much at ease with their daughter. As though she could understand everything that her mother was feeling, Lucinda started to cry.

'Don't worry, Tom,' said Willow with entirely false brightness. 'She's probably just hungry. Hand her over and I'll feed her.'

'Okay. Look, I ought to be getting back in any case. Don't flog your brain too hard, Will,' said Tom, bending down to place Lucinda in Willow's arms. 'Boscombe and her team are good at their job, and it *is* their job. I know you can't forget Ringstead or stop thinking about who killed him, but try not to tear yourself apart over it.'

Willow looked up at him, glad that he understood so much and was not trying to make her ignore the murder.

'And make sure you get plenty of sleep tonight,' he went on. 'If the baggage makes a row give her to one of the nurses for soothing and turn over and go to sleep again. It's what they're paid for.'

'All right.' Willow put up her free hand to hold Tom's cheek for a moment. He kissed her hand with a flourish and then disappeared, missing the arrival of Mrs Rusham by a bare five minutes.

'I'm sorry to interrupt,' Mrs Rusham said as she put the box down. 'Shall I come back later when you've finished feeding her?'

'No, don't. It's lovely to see you.' Willow was surprised by quite how much she disliked the idea of being left alone in the hospital. She kept telling herself that she could not really be frightened, but what she was feeling did seem disturbingly like fear whenever she let herself think about it.

'How are you, Mrs Rusham?'

'Well, thank you. I've brought you another picnic basket as well as the mail and all your messages. I wasn't sure how long you would be in this time, and so there isn't all that much food.'

'I hope they're going to let me out again tomorrow,' said Willow devoutly and then tried to cover her fervour by adding casually: 'I'm awfully sorry about the mess I must have left at home.'

'No, that's fine. Don't worry about it. The washing machine is dealing with the sheets at the moment, and I think the mattress will come up quite well. Are you in much pain?'

'Not a great deal now and they're generous with their pills.'

'Excellent.' Mrs Rusham bent down to open her heavy-looking shopping-bag and brought out a tied bundle of envelopes. 'Here's the post. Several more deliveries of flowers have come: a huge arrangement from your American publishers and several bouquets and plants. There's a list of the senders here. Oh, yes. A Miss Wilmingson called round in person.'

'Miss Who?'

'Wilmingson. Noel Wilmingson? She said that she was secretary to Sir George Roguely and she had come in search of a scarf his wife had left behind when she visited you. Miss Wilmingson said it was a Hermès scarf, which Lady Roguely particularly treasured because her husband had given it to her. I said that I had not seen anything like that but that I would ask you about it.'

'Thank you.' Willow frowned. 'I don't remember seeing a scarf at all when she arrived, and I certainly didn't notice one hanging about after she'd gone. What about you?'

'I simply didn't look to see what she was wearing at all. I do apologise.'

'Good heavens! It's not your fault, Mrs Rusham. Mary-Jane probably left it in her car or something. I'll give her a ring and sort it out. Thank you for bringing all these.'

'It was a pleasure. I'd better get back to the washing.'

'Fine. I'll probably see you at home some time tomorrow.'

'Very well. Goodbye.'

THIRTEEN

WILLOW IGNORED her letters and messages, determined to let Lucinda take her time feeding. Tom was right: she could not stop thinking about Alex Ringstead. The all-too-horrible probability that his murderer was somewhere quite close to her was beginning to take over her mind. She did her best to think about Lucinda, but she was not very successful. When the baby had given up bothering to suck at all, Willow gently withdrew her breast, wiped Lucinda's minute mouth and propped her up against her shoulder, patted her once or twice and thought of something else that might keep her mind away from murder. She began to open her post around Lucinda's back.

The first envelope was a stout brown one, out of which fell a clutter of press cuttings. There was a short note attached to the first in Richard Crescent's spiky black handwriting:

Willow, here's all I could find about George Roguely. You seemed very interested in him. I hope this helps in whatever it is that you are up to. I also hope the infant has stopped being sick and that you're recovering from all the beastliness. Although I must say, for someone who'd just been through all that, you looked magnificent. Let me know when you're up and about again. I'd like to fix a celebration dinner for you and Tom.

Love, Richard.

Lucinda produced a satisfactory bubble of wind just then and so Willow laid her back in her cot. She herself sat down in one of the visitors' chairs to read through the cuttings. They went back several years and consisted mainly of short paragraphs about takeover battles George Roguely had won, acquisitions he had made, or announcements about his enormous—and apparently ever-increasing—annual salary package, but there was also a long interview with him from one of the main Saturday broadsheets.

Willow read through it with interest, intrigued to see how much the interviewer had admired George Roguely. Among his other attributes was apparently a deep loyalty to his staff, which was surprising in view of what Richard had said about his ruthlessness. Willow stared at the transparent side of Lucinda's cot, seeing nothing as her brain began to add up all the separate bits and pieces of information she had been given. Eventually, arriving at no useful sum, she shrugged and went back to the cutting.

The journalist went on to comment on Roguely's superb management, his legendary drive, and his breadth of interests. At the end of the remarkably laudatory article came the interviewer's final question:

> 'And what, Sir John, would you say was the secret of your extraordinary success?'
> 'Luck.'
> 'That sounds very modest.'
> 'Is it? It's true, though. I have had the luck of being born optimistic, which has meant that I am not crippled by fear at times when I need all my energy for whatever project is underway. I have had the luck to be married to the perfect wife, who has given me everything a man could want including undeviating loyalty, which I can never sufficiently repay. And I have had the luck to work with excellent colleagues, who have all become friends and without whom I could never have achieved a tenth of what I have.'

Re-reading the last paragraph, Willow had to remind herself that Roguely had been in the States on the night Lucinda was born. If it had not been for that, as Emma had said, he would have been the ideal suspect: a ruthless, efficient man, who was still in love with his faithless wife, and who must have known at least something about the hospital for which she was working so hard.

Willow went so far as to consider whether it would have been possible for Roguely to sneak back to London, perhaps on Concorde, drown Ringstead and fly back to New York in time to be seen there at breakfast time the following morning.

'Don't be a fool,' she told herself silently as she saw through her longing to discover that the culprit had nothing to do with the hospital in which she was imprisoned for another night at least. 'If the police got as far as Marigold Corfe, they'll certainly have checked something as obvious as Roguely's alibi.'

Looking again at the last few lines of the interview, Willow tried to imagine what it was that Roguely had done to require so much loyalty from Mary-Jane that he had to mention it in public. She also wondered how he had managed to go on believing in his wife's loyalty once he had become aware of her affair with Alex Ringstead. The date on the cutting showed that the interview was only a week old, which meant that it must have been written well after Roguely had learned about the liaison, indeed possibly after Alex Ringstead's death. Perhaps Serena Fydgett had been right about Roguely's 'emotional sophistication'.

'Hello!' said a cheerful voice. 'You're looking very stern.'

'Am I?' said Willow, surprised by the salutation from an apparently strange woman. It took her a moment to identify her visitor. 'Goodness, Ros! I hardly recognised you.'

The strawberry leggings, heavy black hiking-boots and sagging cotton sweater of the WOMB demonstrator had been replaced by a short-skirted black linen suit, cream camisole and matt-black tights. They could have been worn by anyone in advertising, public relations, publishing or journalism. Ros's face was beautifully made up, too, and her hair gleamed with conditioner and careful blow-drying.

'You're looking remarkably smart,' said Willow, noticing that it was not just Ros's clothes that were different. There was something about her glowing skin and ecstatic expression that suggested the sleekness of a woman well and truly stroked. 'Have you been promoting WOMB on telly or something?'

'No. I had an information-gathering lunch in that new restaurant Nine-Nine-Nine,' Ros said, tossing back her hair. She wriggled. 'Amazingly good though it was, I'm not sure it was worth dressing up like this. I can't wait to get back into leggings; I hate skirts and high heels. But I thought I'd drop in and see you first and find out whether we couldn't perhaps do each other a bit of good.'

'Really? I can't imagine why. And how did you know I was back here?'

Ros's beautiful face took on a self-conscious smirk.

'I heard that you'd had another haemorrhage, and I thought you might need some help from us.'

'Who told you that?' Willow had an unpleasant sensation of people whispering about her behind her back and reporting on her to other people who had no right to know anything about her at all. She glared at Ros, who did not seem to notice her antagonism.

'Just someone I was having lunch with. May I sit down? We ate such a lot that I'm feeling quite exhausted.'

'But who was it? Not Doctor Kimmeridge, surely? He at least would keep his patients' affairs confidential.'

'Of course it wasn't him. None of the doctors here talk to us; they loathe us.'

'So do the managers,' said Willow, watching Ros closely. Her eyes were sparkling but her lips were tightly closed. 'Was it one of the nurses? Surely not. You seem much too glamorously done up for lunch with a nurse.'

Besides, Willow thought, could any of the nurses be powerful enough to risk being seen in a local restaurant with an anti-hospital demonstrator who had had to be forcibly removed from hospital property during the riot?

'Not all the managers hate us,' said Ros slyly. 'Some of them have better taste than that.'

'Oh, I see. You've got one of them to fall at your feet in adoration, have you? How very useful!'

Ros laughed, shaking her head. Willow decided to believe the laugh rather than the gesture, but she was puzzled.

'And it was a manager, was it, who told you I was back? I wonder why any of them should have been interested enough to remember my name.'

Ros shrugged and went through her familiar hair-tossing performance. Willow tried to think of Ros as though she were writing her into a novel, working out her motives and her weak points as well as the inconsistencies in her story. Thinking that she had found one that might be fruitful, Willow said casually: 'You know, ever since we last talked I've been wondering how you heard about that unfortunate brain-damaged baby, given that even his parents didn't know exactly what had happened to him until your lawyer told them. Did the news come from this same manager?'

Ros began to look a little less sly and pleased with herself. She even stopped playing with her magnificent hair.

'Besotted as he is, he's been feeding you information, hasn't he?' said Willow, staring at her. 'Does he know what he's doing or are you extracting it so subtly that he hasn't twigged yet?'

Ros's face began to flush, but she said nothing.

'Do you think you're being quite fair to him?' Willow went on, trying to needle her into saying something useful. 'Dressing up to the nines like that and letting the poor sap think he's going to get somewhere with you? Do campaigning feminists really behave like fictional sirens these days? They didn't when I was young. *Eheu fugaces!*'

Ros, who was beginning to look positively sulky as well as red-faced, shrugged.

'So what? If he's prepared to be exploited, why shouldn't I use him? There's nothing unfeminist about that. After all, men have been using us for years. It may not be fair to flirt with him to get information, but whoever said life was supposed to be fair? At least it's in a good cause.'

'And the ends justify the means, do they?' Willow heard herself sounding derisive and was glad of it. She was coming to dislike Ros. 'Well, I suppose the means are useful too. At least you get a jolly good lunch and plenty of compliments. I should think those are more than welcome after the boredom of hanging about out there handing out leaflets and shouting slogans. Did he fall in love with you by chance or did the others send you in to seduce him because you're the only pretty one?'

Ros got to her feet. Willow saw that her hands were clenched into fists. But she was not quite as manipulable as Willow had begun to assume.

'Any tactic is fair when you're fighting a war as serious as the one we've got on our hands,' said Ros, refusing to swallow the bait.

'You may be right.' Offensiveness not having produced what she wanted, Willow let herself sound more placatory, privately admitting that she was using some pretty dirty weapons herself. 'Which of them is he, Ros? Come on. Tell me that much at least.'

'His name isn't important. But your condition is. I can't think why you're so calm about it. Aren't you furious with the doctors for having left a bit of the placenta inside you? Don't you want some kind of compensation?'

'No. They didn't exactly leave it; it got stuck.' Willow had no intention of sharing her fear that the haemorrhages might have been the result of something Sister Chesil had done to her. Equally unsayable was the rather different thought that had been hovering at the edge of her mind ever since she had woken in the night bleeding. She had always expected disaster to follow the arrival of her baby. In comparison with the possible consequences, what had actually happened seemed trivial.

As though the memory of the previous night had shocked her brain into working again, Willow realised at last who the mysterious escort must have been. The only manager likely to have heard anything about her reappearance in the hospital was the one who had been savaged by Tom that morning.

'It was Mark Durdle who took you out to lunch, wasn't it?' she said abruptly, hoping to bounce Ros into an admission.

Ros gave an infinitesimal nod and then shook her head much more vigorously. 'It really isn't any of your business who he is.'

'I can't think why you're being so secretive. This place is such a gossip factory that it won't take me very long to get his name. Someone must have seen you together and been surprised enough to remember it. But if you didn't come up here to talk about him, tell me what it is you want.'

'There's no need to be so hostile. I told you: I came because I thought you might like to add your experience to our campaign and let us do something to try to get compensation—or at least an apology—for you.' Ros sounded hurt. 'After all, you had the senior consultant attending you for part of the birth, with all the interventionist machinery and drugs at his disposal, and yet here you are back in hospital with complications that might have been very dangerous. I'd have thought you'd want to make some kind of protest.'

'I see. No thank you.' Willow could hear the coldness in her voice but she did not care. 'By the way, what is happening to the parents of the brain-damaged baby?'

'Haven't you heard about that? The father was arrested for the murder of Mr Ringstead, as though he hadn't already suffered enough at the hands of the doctors here.'

'Yes, I knew that. But he was released, wasn't he? Lack of evidence or something.'

'An unbreakable alibi,' said Ros, looking pleased. 'His wife didn't have one at all, but at least they didn't suspect her. Even the police could see that she's far too small and fragile to have overpowered a man that size. They're all right, or as near all right as they'll ever be until their poor child dies. Look, are you going to join WOMB or not? Did you read the stuff I left you?'

'Yes, I read it,' said Willow, looking at Ros's long, well-muscled arms, and her surprisingly badly bitten fingernails. 'But I don't think I am actually going to join you.'

'Oh? Why not?'

Willow considered fudging her response with trouble-saving politeness but then decided to be frank.

'Mainly because of your ambulance-chasing tendencies. What happened to me is a known complication of pregnancy and no one's fault, as you must know if you're as well-informed about childbirth as you've claimed. Yet, in spite of its relative ordinariness, you came up here to do to me what your colleagues did to that unfortunate couple: whip up my anger against the hospital—or rather the doctors—to serve your own ends. I don't admire that at all.'

Willow suddenly remembered all the boxes in Durdle's office and the flash of bright yellow she had seen in one of them, the same bright yellow of the WOMB leaflets. She also remembered the surprising professionalism of the design and printing of the leaflets. There was no evidence that Durdle had provided the design expertise or recommended his own printer to WOMB, but Willow was beginning to think it quite likely. She wondered whether it had ever occurred to Ros that the exploitation in her relationship with Durdle might not be as straightforward or one-way as she had suggested.

'That's absurd.' Ros stood up. 'I heard you were back. I'd liked you the first time we met. You seemed to share our aims. I thought I'd come to see how you were and find out whether you wanted our help.'

'Bollocks!' said Willow, waking Lucinda, who started to

whimper. For once Willow ignored her daughter's appeal. 'I'm not sure whether your organisation genuinely exists to promote the interests of women or whether it was set up by one or more of the managers of this hospital in their efforts to persuade the doctors to use cheaper techniques on their patients.'

'Don't be ridiculous,' said Ros. Her face hardened until it no longer looked at all beautiful. 'It is, of course, your privilege to believe whatever nonsense you choose. But women will never get anywhere until they learn to trust each other.'

'Trust,' said Willow in a sadder voice. 'Now there's a dangerous concept. You need to know a lot before you start trusting anyone. Tell me, when exactly was WOMB set up?'

'If you're not going to join us you can have no more interest in the organisation. If you ever change your mind, you'll know where to find us. Goodbye.'

'Was it before or after the dry rot was found in the basement here?'

'What is all this?'

'Just curiosity,' said Willow, deciding that there was little point in asking Ros anything else. 'But I mustn't detain you from your next noisy demonstration or whatever else you're planning to entertain us with this evening.'

Willow watched Ros walking away with strides much too long for her tight skirt and wished that she could believe in WOMB. Its aims were so admirable that it was horrible to think that it might have been no more than a front for Mark Durdle's war against Alex Ringstead. She was sad to think of the women outside being used so cynically. At least some of them must have been sincere.

Trying to decide whether the conspiracy between WOMB and Mark Durdle was a sideshow or part of the main circus she was trying to understand, Willow was distracted by renewed protests from Lucinda and got out of bed to soothe her. When the baby had eventually hiccupped into quiet again, Willow put her back to sleep, pulled on a clean yellow kimono and went to find out whether Susan Worbarrow was on duty.

Willow found her trying to teach one very recently delivered mother about nappy-changing. The poor young mother was struggling to rationalise her terror of damaging the baby with the need to get the nappy tight enough around his minute and wrinkled red body. Willow watched in sympathy and waited until the fretful woman and her equally fretful baby were settled back in bed.

Nurse Worbarrow smiled at them both, said something encouraging to the mother, and turned to leave the ward, sweeping Willow up with her.

'I was sorry to hear that you'd had to come back in. How are you feeling?' she asked as the doors swung behind them.

'I'm fine now. Pining to get back home. But listen, I've got just one more question I need to ask you.'

'Fire away.'

'When was the meeting when Mr Ringstead made a mockery of Mark Durdle's demands that he cut the obstetrics budgets?'

'I don't understand.'

'Come on, Susan. Don't let me down. When was the meeting you told me about at which Mr Ringstead pretended to be offering to tell women to cross their legs and wait until the hospital could afford for them to have their babies and everyone laughed at Durdle?'

'Oh that one! About two months ago, I think. Why?'

'I just wondered. Thanks.'

Wishing that she had made a timetable of everything she had heard about the war between Durdle and Ringstead, Willow decided that she would have to talk to the manager again. She had not been able to accept Emma's suspicions of him when she first heard them, but they were beginning to seem rather more convincing.

It was possible, as Willow herself had suggested to Ros, that Durdle was an unwilling dupe of the WOMB activists, but the more she thought about that the less likely it seemed. A much more credible explanation was that he himself had played a part in setting up the organisation, helped to arrange the printing of the leaflets, and provided information about mistakes made by the doctors in the obstetrics unit for WOMB to use as ammunition in their campaign. It was also possible that he had persuaded them to start a riot so that he would have cover for the noise of Alex Ringstead's terrible death.

At one time Willow had not thought Durdle capable of physically harming anyone, but that was before she had known of his relationship with Ros. He would not have been the first man to push himself to behave in a tougher, more aggressive way than usual in order to impress a beautiful woman. And Ros was very beautiful.

Willow herself had seen Durdle, or so she believed, watching the demonstration just before Ringstead had come to examine her for the last time. Perhaps Durdle, satisfied that his dupes were making enough noise, had then slipped up to the obstetrics unit, summoned Ringstead to an impromptu meeting and tricked him into bending over the pool.

Or perhaps, thought Willow, not all the rioters were dupes. Durdle and Ros could have plotted the murder together. They might have psyched each other up, exaggerating their loathing of Ringstead for each other until they had persuaded themselves that it would be better for everyone—even for the hospital and its patients—if he were to die.

'Now, how are you feeling this evening?' asked a man's voice, making Willow jump.

She tried to control her hammering heart as she looked up to see that Doctor Kimmeridge was talking to the woman in the next bed.

'Curtains, Nurse,' he said sharply. A moment later Willow saw Brigid O'Mara's bright face before her view was blocked by the familiar blue-and-green checked curtains.

She turned over in her mind everything she had heard and seen, but she could not retrieve any single piece of evidence that would prove anything about Durdle or Ros and what they might have done to Alex Ringstead. If they were guilty she would just have to trick one of them into admitting it.

Kimmeridge finished with the woman in the next bed and came to stand at the foot of Willow's in silence, reading the notes Sister Chesil had added to her chart. Then he looked up and his thin lips widened briefly into a smile.

'Good evening, Mrs Worth.'

'Hello, I'm sorry I was rubbernecking a minute ago. It was thoughtless staring rather than curiosity.'

'I know. You were miles away, weren't you?' he said, smiling more naturally.

She thought that he looked younger and more carefree than she had ever seen him. He gestured to Brigid, who pulled Willow's curtains between them and the rest of the ward.

'Now, let's have another look at you.'

Willow resigned herself, kicked off the bedclothes and pulled up her nightdress. Pollyanna-like, she told herself that at least Kimmeridge did not have a troop of gawping students with him for once.

'That's fine.' He removed his gloves and went to drop them in the nearest bin before washing his hands in the basin beside the ward door.

'Why is he looking so cheerful?' Willow whispered to Brigid O'Mara as he elbowed on the gushing taps.

'He's been told he's got a very good chance of getting the job.'

'Mr Ringstead's job?'

'Not the clinical directorship, of course, but it does sound as though he may be a full-blown consultant here at last.'

'But what about the Freemasonry? He hasn't gone and joined them just to get the job, has he?' Willow was surprised by the unmistakable sound of outrage in her own voice. She had not realised that she cared enough about Doctor Kimmeridge to mind what he did.

'I don't know anything about any Freemasons,' Nurse

O'Mara said repressively. 'But Doctor Kimmeridge couldn't possibly be one. Not for any reason.'

She blushed as he came back and smiled at him. He smiled back, looking both gentle and extraordinarily alive. After a second he turned to Willow again and looked perfectly ordinary as he said: 'Now, Mrs Worth, we won't need to trouble you much longer. Your husband may come and collect you any time he likes tomorrow morning.'

'He's a bit busy for errands like that,' said Willow, not averse to showing herself as well as Tom that she was still capable of running her own life, 'but look, if I'm not at risk of any more bleeding, couldn't I take Lucinda home again tonight? We could get a taxi and be out of here in no time at all.'

'Better not. Have one more night with us just to be on the safe side.'

Willow wanted to say that she no longer felt at all safe within the hospital, but her suspicions were still too nebulous and unfocused for that and she did not want to make a fool of herself. She tried to believe that her fears were no more than the irrational products of her fluctuating hormones.

FOURTEEN

WILLOW TOOK one look at the food on the hospital's supper tray and declined it, turning instead to Mrs Rusham's typically lavish picnic basket. Later, she telephoned Tom to say that she and Lucinda would be home again the following morning and then went back to bed with the book she had borrowed from the hospital's library trolley, trying to keep her mind off her anxieties.

The knowledge that both Durdle and Sister Chesil must have left the hospital some hours earlier ought to have helped her to feel safe, but it did not seem to have changed anything. Eventually she found enough self-control to concentrate on the novel and pretend she was not frightened any longer. Whenever she stopped reading the anxiety came back and so she did not stop. The other inhabitants of the ward all got themselves ready to sleep and one by one turned off their reading-lights. Willow, kept hers on.

A nurse she did not know looked into the bay just after half-past eleven and, seeing that she was still awake, came quietly across the ward.

'Can't you sleep?' she asked.

'My mind seems much too active.'

'Then you must try to relax it. You certainly shouldn't be reading as late as this. You need all the sleep you can get.'

'I know that,' said Willow, remembering her broken nights at home and the feebleness they had left behind them. 'But reading is better than lying awake worrying about not sleeping.'

'That's true, but you must be very tired. I'll look in again in half an hour or so and I bet you'll be asleep. Good night.'

'Good night,' said Willow frostily.

She read on for a little while but her concentration had been broken and the book could no longer hold her thoughts at bay. She reached up to turn off her light and lay listening to babies snuffling, women turning in their sleep and occasionally letting out a soft, bubbling snore. A late boat on the Thames outside hooted once and she could just hear the traffic on the far side of the river.

Some two hours later she woke to feel a hand on her shoulder, shaking her lightly. A female Scottish-accented voice was whispering: 'Mrs King, Mrs King, wake up.'

Willow opened her eyes with great difficulty, about to say that she was not 'Mrs King', and saw a grey-haired doctor standing by her bed.

'Come along, Mrs King. It's important. Wake up.'

Pulling herself out of the depths of heavy sleep was agony, but the urgency of the doctor's hand shaking her shoulder was too much to ignore.

'I'm not Mrs King,' she said loudly, licking her lips and wishing that her tongue did not feel so thick and woolly. 'What do you want?'

'Shh. We mustn't wake the others. Aren't you Willow King? It says so on your chart.'

'Yes, I'm Willow King,' she said, still too sleepy to explain. Her heavy eyelids threatened to close again.

'I thought so. You're half asleep. Come along. We've got to get you and your baby downstairs as soon as possible. Get up now.'

At the mention of Lucinda, Willow opened her eyes. She saw the middle-aged doctor put both hands on the edge of Lucinda's cot and start to push it towards the door. Willow sat up at once and fought her way out of the bedclothes.

'Where are you taking her?'

'Shh,' said the doctor again as she stopped. She beckoned to Willow, adding very quietly: 'You must try not to wake the others. I have to take her downstairs for one last procedure before you leave. We've had the results of the tests and there's just one more that we need to do. It's urgent. Hurry up.'

Without waiting any longer, the doctor set off with Lucinda's cot. Willow hesitated no longer. Her mind was too soggy with sleep to work properly, but she was not going to let anyone take her baby anywhere without her. She groped for her kimono in the dim light and did not even think about waiting to find her slippers. The sash caught on the edge of the bed and she wrenched it away with a muttered curse.

Dragging the thin dressing-gown round her shoulders, she stumbled off after the doctor, who was already beyond the swing doors. Rushing after her through the heavy doors and along the passage past the empty nurses' station, Willow was afraid that there must be something terribly wrong with Lucinda.

She was crying. The sound forced Willow on, even though she could feel her stitches pull painfully with every stride. When she caught up with the doctor in the lobby where the lifts were, Willow stopped beside the cot and put her hand down beside Lucinda's face. When she had got her breathing under control, she started to murmur soothing endearments. Eventually, as Lucinda grew a little calmer and her cries turned to soft, syncopated gulps, Willow turned to the doctor to say: 'What is it that's wrong with her? Please tell me.'

'Probably nothing. This is just a precaution,' said the doctor soothingly. She sounded very Scottish as she pressed the lift buttons again.

Beginning to wake up properly, Willow thought that something about the doctor seemed vaguely familiar, although she could not remember ever having seen her before. She looked reassuringly competent with her old-fashioned, permed grey hair and stocky figure and she smiled as she added: 'But we need to make certain. I'm sure you can understand that.'

'No, I don't. I don't understand any of this. Doctor Kimmeridge didn't say anything about Lucinda having something wrong with her. He said we were both doing fine and that we could go home in the morning.'

'That's exactly why we've got to get these tests done to-night. The radiographers have stayed late especially,' said the doctor impatiently. 'Do try to keep calm. You're only upsetting the baby.'

It was true that Lucinda's cries were sharpening again. Willow turned away to gaze down at her devastatingly vulnerable child.

'Don't cry,' she said, even though she knew that Lucinda could not understand a word of what she was saying. She felt her eyes filling with tears and she tried to smile, leaning forwards so that Lucinda would be able to sense her familiar presence. 'Whatever it is, they'll deal with it.'

The doctor pressed the lift button again, cursing under her breath. Surprised at the crudity of some of the words she was using, Willow stared at her in sudden suspicion. She still looked competent and she was dressed like all the other doctors in an unbuttoned white coat with a stethoscope hanging around her neck. But there was no name badge on the left breast of her coat.

For a moment Willow stood absolutely still. All the terror she had been at such pains to rationalise away shot back through her body. Until then it had not even occurred to her that the doctor might be an imposter, but in that moment she was convinced of it. She opened her mouth to shout for help.

A sharp memory of Sister Chesil's theory stopped her before she had made any sound at all. The midwife had said that Alexander Ringstead's murderer must have been a past patient of the long-stay psychiatric wing of the hospital who had been frightened into violence by something he did or said.

The woman in front of Willow might be entirely sane and have had nothing to do with Mr Ringstead's death, but if there were even the slightest possibility that she had already killed and might kill again, Willow could not take any risks at all.

Whatever she did, she would have to avoid frightening the

woman or showing her any kind of threat. If she was danger-
ously volatile, even a shout or a sudden movement might be
enough to tip her over the edge into violence.

Willow felt sick and very cold indeed. Her bones ached and
she knew she had been wickedly stupid in not having insisted
on seeing some identification or checking the woman's *bona
fides* with one of the nurses before she let her take Lucinda
anywhere.

'Who are you?' she asked as calmly as possible, edging
closer towards Lucinda's cot.

'Doctor W-Wilson,' said the woman with the first hint of a
stammer. 'Paediatrics.'

She still sounded perfectly sane and looked it too. But her
muttered swearing at the dilatory lift had been unlike anything
Willow had heard from any other doctor. She did not know
what to believe, but she could not risk making a mistake.

As the lift arrived at last and the doors swished open, Willow looked around for help and then wished she had not as
Doctor Wilson seized Lucinda's cot and pushed it inside.
There was no one else anywhere near them. The night nurses
were well out of earshot. There were some public telephones
only a few feet away, but Willow could not bear to leave
Lucinda alone for a minute. She knew that there was no one
but her to protect the child and that she must do something
quickly.

She caught sight of a fire-extinguisher in a stand bolted to
the wall beside the lift, but it looked far too heavy for her to
lift, and it would probably have made a dreadful noise, clang-
ing against its iron stand.

Willow, whose breathing was quickening as her fear grew,
tried to keep herself calm, knowing that somehow she had to
make the woman feel unthreatened for long enough to get
Lucinda safely out of her clutches. Casually, as quickly as
possible, Willow tried to find something else she might use as
a weapon. The only possible object within reach was a tall

ashtray that stood on a plastic pillar under a minatory no-smoking notice.

'Mrs King, hurry up,' said the doctor from inside the lift. 'We're wasting time and it's essential that we get your baby to X-ray as soon as possible.'

Without another thought, Willow pretended to stumble into the ashtray and in the legitimate clatter picked up the top part, realising with despair as she felt its insignificant weight that it must be made of aluminium. It would be a pathetic weapon, but it was all she had. She held it behind her back and tried to smile calmly as she walked between the lift doors, hoping that she could deal with whatever was to come and protect Lucinda from any kind of harm.

The lift was about seven feet by five, big enough to take a full-sized bed and at least two porters. Willow stood with her back to Lucinda's cot and pushed it unobtrusively towards the back of the lift. The woman who had called herself Doctor Wilson pressed one of the buttons on the control panel and the lift doors closed.

X-ray, Willow repeated silently. Surely they don't give babies X-rays. And why does she keep calling me Mrs King? Nobody calls me that. Who is she? Is she mad? Am I mad to be so afraid?

She stood between Doctor Wilson and Lucinda and waited, gripping the edge of the aluminium ashtray behind her back.

'Where are we going?' she asked as quietly as possible.

'The basement, of course.'

'But the X-ray department is on the first floor,' said Willow, who had been there several times during her pregnancy for ultrasound scans.

The doctor pressed the red 'stop' button on the lift wall. The whole closed room juddered to a halt. Ignoring subtlety, Willow pushed the wheeled cradle hard towards the back of the lift and heard it clatter against the metal wall. Lucinda started wailing at once and her cries soon rose to panic-stricken screams.

Willow risked looking away from the doctor for a second to glance at Lucinda. It was a bad mistake. Even though she was half-expecting it, the first blow shocked her as it landed hard in her stomach. She doubled up, gasping in pain. Terrified for Lucinda, she lashed out with her pathetic aluminium ashtray as she went down, and caught the woman's shins.

Grunting in surprise, the doctor pitched forwards against the cot as Willow twisted away from her. Panting, still clutching her stomach with her left arm, Willow straightened up. The cot itself was rocking from the impact of Doctor Wilson's fall, but it had not tipped over. Lucinda was still screaming, but Willow did not dare risk even looking at her.

'Bitch,' shouted Doctor Wilson, who was on her feet again. Her face was contorted with fury. Her hands were clenched into fists and she was shaking.

Willow stood with the ashtray in her right hand and her left held out as a pathetic defence, trying to work out where the next blow would land. She knew that there was blood on the edge of the ashtray, but she did not care. All that mattered was keeping the woman away from Lucinda.

The doctor was pouring out a stream of insults that Willow hardly heard. She did not even notice that the voice no longer sounded at all Scottish.

'Bitch. Slut. Interfering cow. Someone's got to stop you. Slut. Bitch.'

Lurching forwards as she shouted more and more loudly, Doctor Wilson hit out at Willow, who dodged. The doctor fell heavily against the side of the cot again. Lucinda's screams rose in a crescendo of terror.

Desperate, without any doubts at all about what she was doing, Willow brought down the ashtray as hard as possible on the back of the woman's grey head. The aluminium buckled but it had little effect on the doctor.

Willow raised it again and whacked it down once more, fumbling with her free hand for soft, sensitive bits of the woman's head, face and body. She pushed her away from the cot and felt only triumph when she heard the doctor scream in pain and shock and saw her trip over her own feet to fall heavily, banging her head against the side of the lift. Willow followed her to the edge of the lift, hitting out with her left hand again and again, as she banged down the ashtray with her right.

After a while she noticed that there were no more insults, but she could not stop hitting out for some time. Then, when Doctor Wilson's complete stillness forced itself on her notice, Willow held the ashtray still between her tightly clenched hands.

Her enemy lay half propped up in the corner of the lift furthest from the cot. There seemed to be an extraordinarily large amount of blood about. It was spilling out of a cut under the doctor's grey hair and dribbling down her face. There were smears on the stainless steel wall of the lift and on the floor. In half-dazed surprise, Willow realised that part of the edge of the ashtray must have been very sharp to have made such deep cuts. She looked away from the bloody face of her victim and saw that there were spreading blobs of blood in the yellow silk of her kimono, and a lot of her left hand, where she had broken her own skin as she got in the way of her own blows.

Forcing herself toward the control panel of the lift, Willow pressed the alarm button and then, thinking that she saw a movement from Doctor Wilson, flung herself on top of the woman's body, knocking her spectacles off her face. There seemed to be no other safe way of stopping her standing up again and perhaps getting to Lucinda after all.

Lying against the softness of the woman's body, smelling her cosmetics and a cloying, expensive scent, Willow wanted to be sick. Her only satisfaction was that Lucinda's screams had dwindled to the usual painful, attention-seeking wail. There was no more panic in the sound. Willow tried to block out every thought as she waited for help.

At last the lift began to move again. As Willow lay across Doctor Wilson's body, an appalling thought drifted into her muddled, adrenaline-intoxicated brain. Perhaps she had lost her mind. Some women did after childbirth. It was called postpartum psychosis. It sent some mothers raving mad and turned them violent. Perhaps the woman she had battered unconscious had been a genuine doctor, after all, legitimately trying to take Lucinda for some crucial tests.

Willow began to wonder what would happen to her, to Tom, and to Lucinda herself, if she had attacked a perfectly innocent woman, perhaps even killed her.

The lift stopped and there was a rush of cooler air as the doors slid open. Willow heard appalled exclamations and then felt strong, capable hands beginning to pull her away from Doctor Wilson. She looked down and saw the blood on her clothes and hands again. It was already beginning to turn brown. At last she let the ashtray drop from the fingers of her right hand. The aluminium circle fell on to the body of the doctor and then rolled on to the floor, where it spun round and round and then gradually settled with a fluttering clatter. Willow put out her right hand as though to make the ashtray completely still.

Suddenly finding it hard to see properly, she lifted her hand nearer her eyes. It was shaking and there was blood under the fingernails. The blood was already dark, as though it had begun to dry and granulate. She must have scratched the woman as well as hitting her. Beyond the bloody hand, Willow could dimly see the white, horrified faces of a group of nurses and an overalled porter. They began to move towards her.

Her mouth sagged open and she shook her head. All doubts about what she had done disappeared. No one was going to get to Lucinda if she could help it. No one was safe. No one could be trusted. Willow's eyebrows twitched together over her nose and she looked at the body at her feet and then over her shoulder. A man's hands pulled her towards the lift doors.

'Leave me alone,' she shouted.

'Come along now.'

'No. I'm not going anywhere without my baby,' she said, still looking back over her shoulder at the cot.

'She'll be fine,' said the man in a strong cockney accent. 'Come with me, love.'

'No. Let me go. Leave me alone. Don't touch me. Don't touch me.' As he pulled at her arm, Willow started to scream.

'Someone get one of the obs and gynae staff quick,' said an authoritative voice. 'Hurry up. She's got to be...'

'I won't go,' Willow screamed at the man who was trying to drag her out of the lift. 'I won't leave her. Stop touching me. Leave me alone.'

Her bare feet were sliding on the shiny floor of the lift and she could feel blood, still wet, under her toes. A familiar voice reached through her own screams.

'Now, calm down, Mrs Worth.'

'I won't go. Leave me alone.'

A slap across her face finally shocked Willow into silence. She looked at her attacker and saw the calm, kind face of Sister Lulworth.

'That's right, Mrs Worth. Now, come along like a good girl. You must try to stop screaming. It's not good for Lucinda. That's right. Well done. No one will hurt you. Good girl. Come along.'

'It's not safe. It's not. I can't leave Lucinda. Don't touch me. Stop him. Stop him.'

Willow wrenched herself out of the porter's grip and hurried backwards away from Sister Lulworth. She looked quickly from right to left and back again to make sure no one was about to jump her. When she felt the hard edge of the perspex cot in the small of her back, she stood still, looking from one to the other, breathing hard and fast. She wanted to pick Lucinda up and soothe her cries, but she could not. It was not safe to look away from them all. She began to feel dizzy and put both hands behind her to hold on to the cradle. They were probably all in league with Doctor Wilson. They were bending down over her, worrying about her, taking care of her. They

were obviously in league with her. They would do anything
to protect her and themselves.

Willow's knees began to sag and she clung even more
tightly to the edge of the cot, telling herself she must not fall
down or faint. She forced the dizziness back, biting her tongue
hard, and stood her ground with her back pressed into the foot
of Lucinda's cot, the other end of which was jammed into the
steel wall of the lift.

Sister Lulworth had joined the nurses bending over Doctor
Wilson's inert body. One of them was checking her pulse.
Willow did not care what happened to her, but she was not
going to let them move either Lucinda or herself.

'You can't take me. I'm not moving from here.'

'Don't worry, Willow.' Sister Lulworth's voice was firm but
kindly enough. She stood up. 'Nurse Brown will take Lucinda.
She'll be quite safe. Nurse!'

'Yes, Sister.'

'Take Lucinda to the ward and stay with her there. Now,
come along. We must get you out of here so that we can sort
everything out. Lucinda will be perfectly all right. Come with
me.'

As the remaining panic began to ease and some rationality
returned to Willow's brain, she said more calmly: 'Not until
my husband is here to see that she's safe. Then I'll go anywhere with you.'

As a familiar pain gripped Willow's abdomen, she became
aware that some of the blood on the floor of the lift and on
her kimono might be her own. The first blow to her stomach
must have started the wall of her womb bleeding again.

'But not until he's here. It's not safe,' she said more firmly
and was glad to hear that she sounded a lot less mad. 'Look
what's happened here. It could happen again.'

'Now, don't be silly,' Sister Lulworth said. 'We'll give you
something to calm you down and…'

'You damn well won't. I'm not mad. I don't need Largactil
or anything else. If you give it to me, it'll be assault, and I'll

sue. That woman…' She pointed at the still body that was lying on the floor outside the lift. One of the nurses was taking her pulse. 'That woman tried to kidnap Lucinda and attacked me. I don't know why, but I'm not prepared to let any of the rest of you get anywhere near Lucinda until I do know. Get my husband.'

'We've already rung him. You!'

The porter stepped forward.

'Yes, Sister.'

'Fetch a trolley for this woman. Willow, who is she?'

'I don't know.' Willow was relieved to hear that her voice was almost steady again.

'You don't know!'

Willow was still hurting and feeling very sick, but the wild, irrational terror had gone. She held out her right hand. The blood was there still, but the trembling had stopped. The buzzing in her brain had eased, too, and her tongue felt less woolly. She could even think.

'There's no name badge on her coat,' said Willow, not even aware of who had produced the furious exclamation. 'That's why I was suspicious. That and her wanting to take Lucinda for an X-ray at this time of night. And in the basement. And she sounded odd, too. At first she was pretending to be Scottish, but then that changed when she got angry. I don't know who she is. She attacked me. I had to defend myself.'

'What's going on, here?' Doctor Kimmeridge pushed his way through the crowd, looking even more tired than usual and extremely worried. 'Sister Lulworth, what is all this?'

'Doctor Kimmeridge,' said Willow before the midwife could say anything at all. 'I'm sorry you had to be disturbed, but look.'

She saw his eyes widen as they took in the body on the floor and the blood all over the lift. She nodded.

'We don't know…'

He put up a hand to silence her and turned to the nurse who was holding the so-called Doctor Wilson's wrist.

'Why hasn't she been moved?'

'I've sent for a trolley,' said Sister Lulworth. 'Ah, here it is.'

Doctor Kimmeridge oversaw the raising of the unconscious woman on to the trolley, covered her with a red blanket and checked her pulse for himself. He then raised one of her eyelids and then examined the worst of the cuts, before feeling her scalp with extreme care. Willow was relieved to see that most of the cuts in her face had already stopped bleeding. Kimmeridge ordered the porter to take the trolley down to the casualty department and dictated a short message for the doctor on duty. In a very short time he had got rid of all the spectators except for Sister Lulworth, Nurse Brown and a hospital security guard in the familiar grey-and-yellow uniform Willow had first seen on the night of Lucinda's birth.

'Now, Mrs Worth, will you come out?' said Kimmeridge.

The security guard edged into the lift and gingerly put his hand on her arm.

'I won't leave until Tom comes,' she said, still standing with her back pressed against Lucinda's cot. 'Or the police. Have you called them yet?'

'All in good time.'

'What the hell is going on here?' said Tom, bursting out of one of the other lifts and seeing the security man standing guard over Willow.

'Tom. Thank God,' she said, still not moving away from Lucinda's cot. The security guard was much too close for comfort.

'What's happened? Who did this?' Tom demanded.

'She did it,' said the security guard crossly, tightening his grip on Willow and pointing at her with his other hand. She pulled away but he did not let go.

'Will?' Tom walked into the lift, stepping carefully over the bloodstains. 'Let her go, man.'

The guard took his hand away, but he did not move any

further off. Tom ignored him and took Willow in his arms, stroking her hair. 'Tell me.'

She did, leaning against him, but still keeping one hand on the cot behind her. Lucinda's cries had lessened as soon as the shouting stopped and were now no more than occasional breaks in her breathing. As Willow spoke, giving Tom all the details she could remember, she was endlessly interrupted by the security guard or by Kimmeridge and Sister Lulworth.

Eventually Tom, still holding her head, said to the others: 'will you all please be quiet? Thank you. Now, has anyone contacted the police?'

'Not yet,' said Kimmeridge. 'I was trying to find out what had happened before we bothered them.'

'Call them at once. The team dealing with the Ringstead murder. Where is the woman who attacked my wife?'

'She's been taken down to Accident and Emergency,' said Kimmeridge in a professionally soothing voice. 'She'll be fine there. They're equipped to do everything that's necessary. The injuries were not nearly as serious as they looked at first sight. I suspect she hit her head on the wall she fell and knocked herself out, but they'll check everything downstairs.'

'I'm sure she'll be fine, but who's going to make sure she doesn't abscond?' asked Tom.

'She's unconscious, man,' said the security guard. 'Your wife beat her senseless.'

'Nevertheless, get down there and make sure she stays put,' said Tom. 'She may come to and she'll leg it if she can.'

Seeing that the man was about to argue, Tom reached into his breast pocket for his warrant card. The guard looked surprised and quickly did as he had been told.

Kimmeridge told Sister Lulworth that she had better call the police and she went reluctantly, taking Nurse Brown with her.

'Will?' said Tom, who still had an arm around her.

At last she moved away from the cot. There were some splashes of blood on the outside of the perspex walls, but none had reached the baby, who had opened her eyes and was stick-

ing her tongue in and out against her bottom lip. Willow made
sure she kept at least three feet away from Lucinda's face. She
did not want her to see any blood, and she wished that she
could do something to disguise the smell of it too.

'She's all right,' said Tom, sighing in relief.

'I hope so,' said Willow.

'And you?'

'I don't know. The woman didn't hurt me much, if that's
what you mean. Although I'm bleeding again. She hit me in
the stomach.'

'What?' said Kimmeridge. 'Why didn't you say so before?
Come along at once.'

Tom stayed behind to ensure that the lift was deactivated
and sealed to await police examination, while Kimmeridge
took Willow into an empty single room. When she was lying
down with Lucinda's cot within reach at her side, Kimmeridge
fetched a nurse, examined Willow and then gave her another
injection.

'D'you know who the woman was?' Tom asked as soon as
the nurse had gone and Willow was sitting up again, looking
very pale under the blood splashes on her face but in control
of herself again. She wanted to wash her hands and face, but
Tom would not let her do anything else until the police had
examined her.

'No. She said she was Doctor Wilson and that she was a
paediatrician here, but she had no name badge. She wasn't a
doctor. I know she wasn't. And she hit me.'

'There are no paediatric specialists called Wilson in this
hospital,' said Kimmeridge with authority.

'What about a locum?' suggested Tom. 'You must be short-
handed without Ringstead.'

'Yes, but none of the locums are called Wilson, and none
are that woman's age.'

Willow shivered. Tom sat on the edge of the bed and held
her carefully.

They were still there, waiting in silence for the police, when they heard a female voice calling from outside: 'Superintendent Worth?'

'I'm here,' said Tom, adding a moment later: 'Inspector Boscombe. Good. You know my wife, don't you? And this is Doctor Kimmeridge, who has taken over from Ringstead here.'

'We've met.' The police officer nodded to them all and waited to be told what had happened.

Tom quickly explained. Inspector Boscombe left the room for a short while to issue orders over her mobile telephone. When she came back to question Willow, Tom asked whether the woman in the A and E department had been identified.

The inspector shook her head.

'There's nothing on her that gives us any idea who she is. We'll find out in due course, but we may just have to wait until she's conscious again—or someone reports her missing. But that might take some time. Now, I need to ask Mrs Worth some questions.'

'Do you mind if I stay?' asked Tom, watching Doctor Kimmeridge rather than the inspector.

'Not at all, sir,' she said.

Kimmeridge took the hint and removed himself and his nurse from the room. Willow told her whole story again, listing the various things that had made her suspicious about 'Doctor Wilson' and describing as much as she could remember of the fight.

'Right,' said the inspector, sounding marginally more friendly than she had when she had been interviewing Willow for her memories of Alex Ringstead's last appearance. 'And have you really no idea who she is?'

'None,' said Willow. 'But it's possible that she could have been a patient here, recently discharged from the psychiatric wing.'

'You sound as though you've been talking to Sister Chesil.' There was a hint of humour in her brisk voice.

'Yes, I have. Why? Don't you think she might be right about the person who murdered Mr Ringstead?'

'No, I don't. That sort of killing tends to be random and immediate—usually by stabbing. Ringstead's death was planned. Any other ideas?'

'I suppose she could have had something to do with WOMB,' Willow said slowly, and then wished she had not as she saw incredulity and contempt passing across the police officer's face.

'What makes you say that?' Inspector Boscombe sounded barely polite.

'One of their leaders came to see me today. She'd been told that I was back here because of a complication of my daughter's birth. She wanted me to fight for compensation from the hospital and she got quite angry when I showed her that I found her motives suspect.'

'She'd hardly have got someone else to launch an attack on you just for that,' said the inspector.

'I don't know,' said Willow more crisply. She was getting angry. 'Someone did it. And there may have been more to Ros's anger than irritation that I wouldn't join her campaign.'

She went on to explain her suspicions of Ros and Durdle as succinctly as possible. It did not do her much good. Inspector Boscombe continued to look deeply sceptical. Tom was kinder, but he did say: 'That sounds pretty far-fetched, Will.'

'Maybe, but WOMB have been getting information from somewhere and Durdle hated Ringstead.'

Lucinda started to cry and Willow got up off the bed at once. 'It's time for her feed, but I can't even hold her like this. I must wash off the blood. She can't wait much longer. Please.'

'Could we get one of the doctors here to take samples?' Tom asked Inspector Boscombe. 'The police surgeon could be hours yet.'

After a moment the inspector nodded and went to find Kimmeridge. He took scrapings from under Willow's nails and removed some of the blood from her hands and face with sterile swabs, which were carefully enclosed in sample pots and bags. Tom had Lucinda in his arms by then and was walking up and down the small, grey room, jiggling her and trying to quiet her. But her crying was beginning to sound frightened again.

Willow waited with as much patience as possible for Kimmeridge to finish and then, escorted by Inspector Boscombe, shuffled towards the basin to wash. She could not bear the thought of having any traces of blood on her when she fed Lucinda.

Looking in the mirror above the basin, Willow was disgusted by her reflection. Her skin was greyish white. With the streaks of brown blood and the dark shadows under her eyes, which themselves looked huge and mad, she could have been the model for some medieval gargoyle. Bending down until her back ached, she sluiced cold water over her face, shuddering, and then scrubbed at her hands with soap. Standing up again, she dried her skin and then combed her cold fingers through her hair. The final result was not encouraging but at least she was clean and blood-free.

Lucinda was shrieking by the time Willow had finished washing. Tom handed the baby over with a mixture of apology and relief and watched Willow unbutton her nightdress. She saw that Inspector Boscombe had tactfully left the room. As soon as Tom saw that Lucinda was sucking and that Willow looked calmer, stroking the baby's small downy head and crooning to her, he joined his colleague just outside the door.

Willow could not hear what they were talking about and decided that she was not very interested. Some milk ran out of Lucinda's mouth and over Willow's breast. She withdrew it from the baby and held her upright, gently patting her back. At that moment it seemed far more important that Lucinda should take milk from her once more than that any of Inspector Boscombe's questions were answered.

FIFTEEN

INSPECTOR BOSCOMBE did not leave until she had arranged for a constable to sit outside Willow's room for the rest of the night. Tom wanted to stay too, but Willow eventually managed to persuade him that she would be safe enough and that he ought to go home for some rest.

For the first hour after Tom had gone, she found the constable's presence outside her door reassuring. It was only later, when she woke from a shallow sleep that had been spiked with nightmares, that she wondered whether Inspector Boscombe had put him there less for her protection than to stop her leaving. She even began to wonder, as she turned uncomfortably on to her sore front and then back again, whether her attacker had returned to consciousness and persuaded the police that she had been the innocent victim and Willow the deranged aggressor.

Soon after five o'clock in the morning Lucinda settled into a deeper sleep, but Willow could not follow her example. She poured herself some water from the jug beside her bed and sat in the dim light that came through the glass panel in her door, forcing herself to work through everything that had happened and to face the possible consequences. Only then, she thought, might she be able to stop her racing thoughts and sleep properly.

Once more afraid that she had lost her reason and imagined Doctor Wilson's first assault, Willow pulled up her nightdress and was comforted to see a large spreading bruise on her swollen abdomen. The woman had definitely hit her, and the blow had been very hard indeed.

Given that, it seemed virtually certain that she must have been involved in the killing of Alex Ringstead. It would have been too much of a coincidence to have had two completely unconnected violent assaults in the same part of the same hospital in so short a time. Equally certain was the fact that it must have been the questions Willow had been asking that had triggered the attack. After all, her questions were the only connection she had had to the dead man beyond that of every other woman in the obstetrics unit.

'Doctor Wilson' had seemed vaguely familiar, and yet Willow was certain that they had never met. That being so, whatever threat she had represented must have reached the other woman at second hand. Willow tried to see which of all the people she had talked to about Alex Ringstead could have been the conduit, but she failed.

Frustrated, she turned her mind instead to the woman herself, trying to track down the source of her elusive familiarity. Wondering whether it could have been a photograph of 'Doctor Wilson', Willow reached into the locker that had been wheeled into her room the night before to pick up the leaflets she had there.

There were plenty of photographs in the publicity material for the Friends of Dowting's Hospital, but they were of buildings, the garden, and some of the senior doctors, including Alex Ringstead. There was no one who looked at all like 'Doctor Wilson'. In the WOMB leaflet the only pictures were of babies, unidentifiable nurses (who all looked too young) and some newly delivered mothers.

Going back over everything that had happened from the moment she woke to feel the woman's hand on her shoulder, Willow castigated her memory for letting her down so badly.

'Her smell,' she said suddenly and quite loudly. Luckily it did not wake Lucinda, and Willow was free to follow her thoughts wherever they took her.

The fake doctor had been wearing a heavy, exotic scent that Willow had recently smelled somewhere else. It was not something she herself had ever worn; she rarely used any kind of scent any longer. She did not know its name, but she had definitely smelled it recently. Where?

After a moment her brain produced the answer to that as well and she slumped down on the bed in frustration. It was the same scent that Petra Cunningon had been wearing at the bridge lunch—and whoever 'Doctor Wilson' really was, she certainly was not Petra Cunningon in disguise.

They may have shared a taste for expensive scent, but they looked completely different from each other. Petra was a good four inches taller than the woman in the lift and neither her face nor her voice was remotely similar.

Feeling useless, Willow lay down again and tried to sleep. That did not work either. She was tempted to wake Lucinda so that she could feed her, which would at least have given her the illusion of doing something worthwhile, but she should not disturb her for such a selfish reason.

Eventually Willow remembered the post that Mrs Rusham had brought her the previous evening. Leafing through the telephone messages, she found that there was one from Jane Cleverholme, which Mrs Rusham must have written down verbatim from the answering machine:

Willow, you'll never believe it, but I've got it. The job, I mean. Isn't it amazing? Editor. I still can't believe it myself. We must have lunch as soon as you're up and about again. There's lots I want to tell you and ask you, too. How are you getting on with the Roguelys? I've got lots of gossip. Ring me as soon as you can.

PS Can't resist telling you one bit: did you know that the Chief Executive of the Hospital Trust for Dowting's once worked for George Roguely?

Willow looked at the postscript for a long time, wondering whether it had any significance at all and eventually decided that it could not have. But it did remind her that she had meant to telephone Mary-Jane about her lost scarf. Checking the time, she saw that it was still far too early to telephone anyone.

It was a blessed relief when Lucinda woke of her own accord wanting to be fed and then needing to be washed and changed. As they lay back in bed together, Willow searched her daughter's apparently contented face, wondering how much she had heard or sensed of what had happened in the lift. Before she could worry too much, one of the nurses brought her a breakfast tray and put Lucinda back in the cot for her.

Willow dawdled through the unappetising meal, trying to spin it out for as long as possible. Soft snuffling sounds from the cot told her that Lucinda was asleep again, and she had nothing else to do except telephone Mary-Jane in due course and wait for someone to bring her news.

The first visitor knocked at her door a few minutes after half-past nine.

'Come in,' Willow called, glad that she was going to be told something at last. She pushed herself into a more dignified position.

To her complete surprise, it was Mark Durdle's well-kept face that peered round the door. Her palms began to sweat and her heart speeded up. She was extremely glad to remember that Inspector Boscombe had posted a constable outside the door.

'May I come in?' said Durdle, sounding meek and very far from dangerous.

Willow saw the constable standing behind him, looking enquiringly at her. Believing that the officer's ability to identify Durdle would be enough to keep her safe, whatever he might have tried to make someone else do to her or even want to do himself, she nodded.

'Yes, do come in, Mr Durdle,' she said, speaking his name with deliberate clarity. 'What can I do for you?'

He came in and shut the door behind him, but he did not approach the bed. Instead he stood with his back to the door, rubbing his hands over each other again and again as though he were trying to wash them.

'Well?'

'I came,' he said at last, shifting from one foot to the other, 'to express my profound regret for what happened to you last night, and to…to apologise for it without of course in any way suggesting that the hospital could carry any kind of liability for it.'

Watching the colour in his face fluctuating from a rich red to an interesting pale greyish-pink as he hopped and rubbed his hands, Willow could not help thinking that her first assessment of his character must have been the right one. Emma might have thought him a likely murderer, but she had never seen him.

Even from where Willow was sitting she could see that his hands were trembling. He looked quite incapable of doing any physical harm to anyone. Her own fears began to seem almost silly.

'I see,' she said coldly because she had been so afraid. 'You're worried that I might sue the hospital over its rotten security, are you? Well, I can understand that. How would it be if I undertook not to sue in return for some information from you?'

'I don't understand.'

'I want to know exactly what has been going on in this hospital, and I think you could tell me. I know that you're in cahoots with WOMB—Ros let out that much. But I want to know just how far your involvement has gone.'

Durdle looked at Willow as though she had just pulled off all his clothes and paraded him in some public place.

'You didn't really think no one would find out, did you?' she said, feeling amusement for the first time since she had been assaulted. 'If so you were incredibly naive. And what on earth were you doing taking Ros out to lunch in the smartest restaurant in the area? You must have been mad if you wanted to keep your conspiracy secret.'

'There was no conspiracy,' he said quickly. 'I can assure you that my interest in her group is wholly above board and solely to do with my wish to ensure the wellbeing of women who come here to this hospital to give birth.'

'Yeah, yeah,' said Willow, copying Rob Fydgett's favourite expression of disbelief.

Durdle flushed deeply, his skin taking on the rich, bluish pink of cochineal-coloured icing.

'And I would like… You are making this very difficult for me, Mrs Worth.'

'Oh, I am so sorry about that,' she said with heavy sarcasm. 'Did you set up WOMB yourself?'

'Certainly not.'

'Then at what point did you become involved?'

When he looked as though he were going to deny any involvement, Willow pretended to lose her temper.

'Don't even think about it,' she said furiously. 'I saw you outside the hospital on the night of the riot, the night when Mr Ringstead was murdered. I know you've been feeding WOMB information so that they could cause trouble for him. What I'm not sure is why you wanted them to produce such a brouhaha on that particular night and how much you knew about the plans to kill him.'

'Nothing. What do you mean?'

'You're in a very difficult position even if you are innocent of that,' said Willow implacably. 'If I go to the police with what I know—or even to the chairman of your trust—you'll have to answer a lot of difficult questions and quite possibly find yourself without a job.'

Durdle looked so appalled that Willow thought that she must be getting somewhere at last.

'When exactly did you become involved with them?' she asked again.

'Once it became clear that Mr Ringstead was going to do everything he could to prevent all the actions we had to take to ensure the profitability and hence viability of this directorate,' Durdle said, speaking very fast as though that might make his admission less damaging.

'I see,' said Willow, not sure whether she could believe him. 'And what were you trying to do? Get him sacked?'

'Good heavens, no. Anyway it's almost impossible to dismiss a consultant,' said Durdle, betraying exasperation rather than fear or embarrassment for once. 'But there are plenty of them suspended on full pay from other hospitals. There's no reason why we shouldn't do the same.'

Willow said nothing, but her feelings must have been clear in her face, for Durdle rushed into another gabbling explanation.

'It wouldn't have been bad for him and it would have allowed us to get on with shovelling this hospital into the modern world. There was no malice in it. I didn't want to do him any harm; I just wanted him out of the way. It was for the good of the hospital and all our patients. Something had to be done. He was blocking all the modernising we had to do, defying and humiliating everyone who tried to control him, and spending far too much time and money on babies who should have been dead anyway.'

Willow could not say anything.

'You don't have to look at me like that,' he burst out. 'All I wanted was to get him suspended. He'd have been paid his full NHS salary and he could have gone on taking private patients. He wouldn't have lost by it. And we'd have been able to get on with our work. It would have suited everyone.'

'You really are a despicable little worm, you know,' said Willow, finding her voice at last. 'You didn't even have the guts to challenge him directly.'

'You may think he was a saint,' said Durdle nastily. He suddenly looked less wormlike and she had a moment's doubt about his weakness. 'Lots of people did, but then none of them knew him. He was a shit, an arrogant, selfish, self-regarding shit.'

'What can you mean?'

'I don't have time to go into it all. And you probably wouldn't believe it anyway. But I'll give you just one of the myriad examples: there was a woman who worked here, a nurse, one of the best.' For a moment he looked and sounded as though he might burst into tears but then he controlled himself. 'And he wrecked her life for a selfish whim. That's the sort of man he was.'

He turned and without another word left her room, banging the door against the wall, leaving her to think hard about Marigold Corfe and to wonder whether she knew just how many champions she had left behind her in Dowting's.

'Are you all right, Mrs Worth?' asked the constable, who had got to his feet as Durdle stormed past him.

'Yes. But I was jolly glad you were out there while he was ranting and raving at me. Look, do you know whether the woman who assaulted me last night has been identified yet?'

'I wouldn't know anything about that,' he said, looking stupid. Willow was not entirely convinced by his expression.

The sound of hurrying footsteps echoed along the passage, distracting them both. The constable looked to his left and all traces of stupidity vanished from his face as he straightened up. He looked both alert and intelligent.

Tom appeared in the doorway a second later, panting heavily. 'God, am I glad to see you,' he said, leaning against the door frame. 'Oh, Will.'

'What's happened? Come in and sit down, Tom.'

'That woman's disappeared.'

'What?'

'I know. I looked in to find out whether they'd identified her yet. To everyone's embarrassment, she's gone. Boscombe's got people trying to track her down now.'

'Wasn't there a guard on her?' asked Willow in outrage. 'I had one.'

'Yes, there was, but he left her for a few minutes soon after five this morning. I know, of course he shouldn't have done it, but he looked through the glass door, saw her sleeping "like

a baby'' and nipped away for, he says, three minutes at the
most. When he got back, she'd gone. He raised the alarm at
once, but they haven't found her yet. How she did it, I can't
imagine, and she can't have gone far. I legged it up here as
fast as I could.'

'You shouldn't have worried, Tom.' Willow smiled at him
and held out a hand. 'I was quite safe with my constable.'

He took her hand and clung to it. She could not decide
whether the unmistakable anger in him was directed at the
police for not hanging on to the woman or at Willow herself
for having provoked her. After a moment he let her hand go
and said more lightly: 'Anyway there is one good thing about
her disappearance.'

Willow raised her eyebrows in a silent question and was
surprised to see Tom's lean cheeks flushing.

'Oh, no,' she said. 'You're not going to tell me that you
thought I might have been the one who launched the attack,
are you?'

'No,' he said at once. 'But there's no doubt Boscombe had
it in mind. Look, Will, I know you, and I know that you
wouldn't do something like that in a million years, but if it
had come to it there'd have been nothing to prove it one way
or the other. It would have been the woman's word against
yours, and before she ran away like this there was very little
to suggest that her word might not have been believed.'

'You must have had a bad night worrying about it,' said
Willow coolly, not sure that she believed him or that she could
forgive him for the doubt, however slight, that seemed to have
been in his mind. Then she decided to let him off for a while
and asked whether anyone knew when the woman had re-
gained consciousness.

'For a minute or two when they were treating her cuts and
bruises last night. She only surfaced briefly, and she was so
confused that the doctors didn't think she should be questioned. They had her wheeled into a room, checked at inter-

vals, and otherwise left alone. The nurse who saw her last thought she was sleeping normally.'

'She'd probably been faking for hours and nipped down to the basement as soon as she saw her chance,' Willow said.

'Why the basement?'

'Because that's where she was trying to take us last night and she must have had an escape route planned so that she could make an exit as slick and unobtrusive as the one she achieved after she'd drowned Ringstead.'

Tom shook his head.

'She must have been his killer,' said Willow impatiently. 'It's ludicrous to think there could be two…'

'I know,' he said, gripping her hands again. 'I wasn't contradicting you. I just can't bear the thought of the danger you were in.'

'Hello,' said a young voice, making them both turn towards the door.

Rob was standing there with a huge bunch of red and white roses in his hand and an expression of serious disapproval on his face.

'Hello,' said Willow. 'Look, Tom, here's Rob.'

'So I see,' he said, getting up off Willow's bed and rubbing his hands over his eyes. 'You look very cross, old boy.'

'I brought Willow these,' he said gruffly, laying the roses on the bed.

'They're lovely, Rob. It's very generous of you. Come and sit down and tell us what the matter is.'

He grasped the rail at the foot of her bed and shook his head as though he did not know how to say whatever it was he wanted to tell them. Willow waited patiently. Tom had turned away to pull up the blinds so that he could look out of the window.

'They said you nearly got yourself killed,' he said at last. 'And Lucinda too.'

'Who said?'

'Everyone. I was buying you flowers downstairs and the

two women in the shop were talking about it. And people waiting for the lift did as well. One of them isn't working and everyone seems to know why. You wouldn't let me help you and now look what's happened. It's not fair. You could have died.'

For a moment Willow did not know what to do or say. She sat with her left hand over her mouth, looking at Rob's furiously unhappy face. Then she saw Tom turn and come to put his hands over Rob's as they clung to the rail.

'Rob,' he said gently. 'We're all shocked by what's happened and very worried. But it's not Willow's fault and she has even more reason to be shocked and upset by it all than anyone else. The last thing she needs now is either of us ranting at her. I think we ought to let her rest. Will you come with me now and have a late breakfast?'

'You should have let me help. Both of you.'

'Come on, Rob.' Tom was beginning to sound firm. Willow relaxed in the knowledge that she could leave this one to him. 'We must leave her in peace. She's got a copper of her own just outside the door now, so she'll be safe. She and Lucinda.'

Tom looked at Willow and she nodded, blowing him a kiss to show how thankful she was. He mouthed at her: 'I'll be back.'

'Good. I'm sorry, Rob. When I'm up and about again I'll explain it all. Thank you for the flowers.'

It was a relief when Tom eventually managed to get Rob out of the room and Willow lay back with her eyes closed, smelling the gentle scent of his roses, trying not to feel guilty about the danger into which she had put Lucinda.

Some time later she remembered that she was supposed to be ringing Mary-Jane and sat up to dial the number.

'Willow,' said Mary-Jane when she had got through. 'How nice! I *am* glad you've rung because I wanted to say how sorry I am to have been so silly and emotional when I came to see you. You and your housekeeper were so kind to me. It was really miles beyond the call of duty. I'd like to make it up to you somehow, take you out to lunch perhaps. Would you come?'

'There's nothing for you to make up,' said Willow, realising that Mary-Jane could have no idea what had happened to her. She tried to make her voice sound normally light and cheerful. 'But I'd love to have lunch with you in due course. I'm back in Dowting's at the moment, and I'm not absolutely certain when I'll be out. That's really why I'm ringing.'

'How awful! I'm so sorry. Are you ill? Or is it little Lucinda?'

'It was me. I'm much better now. There was a bit of a drama, but it turned out to be a lot less awful than I'd thought it was going to be. But that's why I wasn't at home when Miss Wilmingson came round for your scarf.'

'Miss Wilmingson? D'you mean my husband's secretary? What on earth was she doing bothering you?'

'Well, according to Mrs Rusham, she called to collect the Hermès scarf your husband gave you. Not something you'd want to lose, I can quite see that. The only trouble is that it's not at the mews. Mrs Rusham made a thorough search for it, but in fact, I don't think you were wearing a scarf when you arrived.'

'I never wear scarves, Hermès or otherwise.'

'That sounded very determined.'

There was a short laugh from Mary-Jane.

'Did it? Sorry. It's just that they're like scent. I gave up wearing both when I discovered they were what my husband hands out to loyal employees.'

'What?' Willow said even before Mary-Jane had finished talking. 'Sorry to make such a noise. I stubbed my toe. What employees?'

'Any of them he wants that little bit extra from. Women, I mean. He doesn't give men anything. Didn't you notice Petra Cunningon wearing an expensive scarf and heavy, heavy scent when she came to the bridge lunch? She always does. Unlike me, she hasn't noticed that they're badges of servitude.'

An explanation of what had been happening began to build in Willow's mind.

'As does Miss Wilmingson?' she suggested.

'Oh, yes. And in spite of what she thinks she doesn't know me very well either, so when she wanted an excuse to spy on you she can't have realised how unlikely a lost-scarf story would be.'

'And why should she have needed to spy on me?' Willow thought that the answer was pretty obvious by then, but she wanted to hear it spoken.

'Because she thinks I'm a witless child who will cause all sorts of trouble to George if she doesn't check out what I'm doing. I loathe it, but she's so useful to him that I try to put up with it. I can't tell you how sorry I am that you came in for some of it.'

'Why should she have thought I might be a source of trouble? After all, she can't know anything about me.'

'I'm afraid she does actually, and that really is my fault. God, I'm sorry, Willow,' said Mary-Jane. 'You see, when I got home after making that idiotic scene in your house I found an urgent message to ring George. He only wanted to tell me that he was going to have to cut our dinner that night, but he realised that I was in a state and asked why. I was so full of it all that I told him about you and how you knew such a lot about Alex and what had happened to him. She must have been listening in. She often does.'

'Yes, I see,' said Willow, wondering why Mary-Jane could not see the significance of what she had been saying. 'What does she look like?'

'Grey permed hair, plain. About five-foot six and pretty stocky. And huge hands. I've always wondered how she could fit them on the keyboard to type,' said Mary-Jane, sounding bitchy for the first time.

'I'm sorry, Mary-Jane. I'm going to have to go—the doctor's just arrived,' said Willow without waiting for anything more. 'Goodbye.'

'Constable!' she called. A moment later an unfamiliar figure looked round her door.

'Yes, Mrs Worth. Can I help?'

'You're different,' she said stupidly.

'That's right. I've just taken over. You seemed rather busy at the time or I'd have made myself known.'

'I see. Right. Look, would it be possible for you to get hold of Inspector Boscombe for me? It's very urgent.'

'I'll do my best.'

'Thanks.'

While she waited, Willow went over everything that had happened and everything she had learned so that she could present Inspector Boscombe with a carefully reasoned account of why it must have been Noel Wilmingson who had assaulted her in the lift.

All sorts of things that had made no sense fell into place, not least the fake doctor's habit of addressing her as 'Mrs King'. The only person who had done that had indeed been Sir George Roguely's snooping secretary and she had done it both the times Willow had spoken to her, the first in her search for information about the Friends of Dowting's Hospital and the second when Willow had answered the telephone in Mary-Jane's bedroom. That must have been quite a shock for Noel Wilmingson.

Twenty minutes later Inspector Boscombe was sitting opposite Willow, listening to her story in silence and looking as though she did not believe a word of it.

'I see,' she said when Willow came to the end. 'If I understand you correctly, you are telling me that Sir George Roguely's secretary tried to kill you last night because she had murdered Mr Ringstead and thought you had tracked her down and were about to produce evidence of what she had done. Have I got that right?'

'Yes,' said Willow. 'I know it sounds ludicrous, but I've just been speaking to Lady Roguely and her description of

Miss Wilmingson fits the woman who called herself Doctor Wilson.'

'I see. And what evidence do you have for believing that she drowned Mr Ringstead?'

'It's all circumstantial so far, but I'm sure you'll be able to get real evidence. You know that Ringstead was Lady Roguely's lover?'

'Yes, I did know that.'

'Good. Now, you have to remember that Miss Wilmingson does everything for Sir George to make his life as easy as possible. I think she has sublimated all her own needs in the work she does for him and can't bear it when the life she's arranging for him is not perfect. It takes everything she has to make his path as smooth as it is, and yet there are still bumps and potholes to trip him up. She's come to feel that she must make ever greater efforts to level them out because achieving perfection in his life is the only way she is going to be able to feel that hers has been worthwhile, and that's the only way she can get her own needs met. I think she has gone way beyond the point where she can weigh up the magnitude of what she feels compelled to do for him against the triviality of the difficulties he might face.'

'I don't know of any reason to refute any of that, but there's no evidence to suggest that you're right.'

'No. But there's a lot of highly suggestive hearsay. Listen: for a start there's what I heard from Lady Roguely on the telephone this morning about Miss Wilmingson's opinion of her and attempts to spy on her. There's also what I saw in, and heard from, Petra Cunningon when I met her at the Roguelys' house.'

'Are you suggesting that Ms Cunningon is also potentially murderous in the cause of Sir George Roguely's happiness?'

'No, of course I'm not,' said Willow, determined not to lose her temper and to wipe the contemptuous expression off the inspector's face. 'I told you about her because she's such a good example of the way that I think Roguely used Miss

Wilmingson. Petra is just tougher and didn't get sucked in quite as far.'

'What exactly are you saying he did to them?'

'He absorbed their lives,' said Willow, wondering whether the inspector was really as obtuse as she seemed to be pretending to be. 'I'm sure he had no idea of the ways in which Miss Wilmingson persuaded herself that what she was doing for him was both right and necessary, but I do believe that he made it happen. It is clear that he expects his staff—his female staff anyway—to be completely loyal to him and his company and to put everything they have into their work. Petra has retired and yet clearly has so few friends of her own that she has to rely on his wife, whom she both dislikes and despises, for her social life. She made it clear to me—a total stranger—that she thinks that Sir George is wonderful and has suffered in being married to Lady Roguely.' Willow sighed. 'Do you really not see what I'm getting at?'

'Not altogether.'

'I rather think that he'd discovered some time ago that one of the easiest ways to get female staff adequately devoted to him was to hint—if not actually say—that his wife made him unhappy because she wasn't good enough for him or aware enough of his needs. The suggestion, always unspoken, must have been that the employee in question would have been quite different, but that he could not do anything about it. A man as honourable as he would remain loyal to his wife, however unsatisfactory or difficult she might be, and however great the temptation of turning to someone more sympathetic, more loving, more in tune with him.'

'But perhaps she did make him miserable,' said Inspector Boscombe in a voice of cool amusement. 'That does happen, after all.'

'Of course it does,' agreed Willow. 'And his is a technique that hundreds of people use for lots of different kinds of seduction. "My wife doesn't understand me." We all know that. He didn't want them to sleep with him, but he did want them to pour their all into his business. He can't have had any idea that Noel Wilmingson's boundaries were so weak that she would progress from thinking that she had to tell his wife how to behave to him—and she did do that—to believing that it was up to her to stop the affair with Ringstead. Presumably the only way in which she could make absolutely certain of that was to remove him from the earth.'

The inspector said nothing.

'And that's what she did with all her customary efficiency. Oh, come on, Inspector Boscombe, it fits everything that's happened. You must see that. And you haven't managed to come up with any likelier suspects, have you?'

The inspector looked as though she had just trodden on some disgusting insect from a heap of putrid rubbish. Willow smiled in unfair satisfaction.

'All you've got to do now is pick Miss Wilmingson up. That shouldn't be too difficult because she can't run away and cut herself off from Sir George for ever. She'd be nothing then; I don't suppose it has even crossed her mind. I suspect if you got to his office you'll find her there. Then once you've got her, you can have her identified by any of the hospital staff who found us in the lift this morning. You'll be able to charge her with the assault on me and take it from there. When she was planning the murder she made sure that she chose a time when he was known to be out of the country. If she thought there were something that might connect him to it, I bet she'd cough.'

'Say you're wrong,' said Inspector Boscombe with the first glimmer of cooperation Willow had divined in her, 'about her determination to break up the relationship between Ringstead and Lady Roguely, how do you think she managed the killing?'

'Easily enough,' said Willow. 'Anyone can get hold of a white coat and a stethoscope and wander about the hospital looking as though she belongs. Wilmingson certainly convinced me last night until I noticed that she had no name badge. I suspect she rang the bleep exchange from one of the public telephones by the lifts and had Ringstead called to the birthing pool. We know that he was bleeped just before it happened. When he got there she must have asked him to investigate something she had already put in the pool. Once he was on his knees, reaching into the water, she will have put her right hand on his neck and forced his head down. I imagine that she must have straddled his back, too; otherwise he probably would have been able to throw her off because she's much shorter than he was and weaker too. Perhaps she even sat on him. That might not have made any marks on his skin through his clothes. He had a suit on, didn't he, as well as the white coat?'

'Yes. And,' said Boscombe reluctantly smiling at Willow, 'some rather odd bruises on either side of his ribs.'

I wonder if Tom knew about them, Willow asked herself grimly. Aloud she said: 'Once you start interviewing her you'll probably be able to shock her into an admission. And in any case you'll be able to get evidence easily enough if she doesn't. Presumably you can match the bruises to her measurements after all.'

'I think you can safely leave all that to us,' said Boscombe, beginning to look quite friendly. 'It is what we do, you know.'

'Yes, I know it is,' said Willow, laughing. 'I wonder what she did with the coat? It must have been very wet. Not that it matters much. If it were me, I think I'd have just rolled it into a supermarket bag I'd brought with me and walked out, pretending to be a concerned relative taking a patient's dirty nightdress home to wash.'

Inspector Boscombe's mobile telephone started to ring. She got to her feet, saying: 'I'll be back.'

SIXTEEN

WILLOW HAD BEEN home for two days by the time Noel Wilmingson at last made a full confession to the police. At first she had refused to admit anything, even the assault on Willow, although there was plenty of evidence for that, not least the identification independently made by several different members of Dowting's staff. The breakthrough came when Inspector Boscombe confronted her with the evidence that the marks left on Alex Ringstead's neck corresponded exactly with the size and shape of the fingers of her right hand. Boscombe warned her, too, that the forensic scientists would be carrying out DNA matching to prove that the samples taken from the splashes of blood on Willow's hands and clothes belonged to her.

Willow was deeply relieved when she heard the news, but her prime concern was for Lucinda. She showed no signs of trauma or distress, but Willow could not forget what had happened only a few feet away from her cot. She could not possibly have understood what was happening, but the noise must have been frightening in itself and Willow could not help thinking that some intimation of violence must have reached Lucinda.

Once they were back at home in the mews, Willow got hold of every book she could find about infantile memory, birth traumas, and the psychological development of very young children. Tom tried to stop her reading them, assuring her that what would matter to Lucinda was the way she was treated in the years to come. Even if some of what had happened in the lift had registered in her developing brain, which was by no means certain, he believed that she was most unlikely to be affected by it, provided both her parents behaved to her with intelligent, gentle kindness as she grew.

Knowing that he had not convinced Willow, Tom eventually asked Doctor Kimmeridge to come and see her to support his conviction. She tried to believe them both, but for several days she could not be comforted, although she tried to hide her doubts from everyone.

Rob Fydgett seemed quite unaware of her fears when he came every day to make sure that she and Lucinda were all right. He appeared to have forgiven Willow for shutting him out of the investigation and soon began to talk admiringly about the brilliant way she had trapped Noel Wilmingson into betraying herself.

Willow was not sure that Tom had absolved her so easily, but he said nothing about it. He continued to listen to her fears with as much patience as he could muster, and told her over and over again that Lucinda was physically thriving and that that would hardly be the case if she had been traumatised. He reminded Willow that the baby was putting on weight, that she was no trouble when feeding and that for the few hours she slept, she appeared to sleep well.

'And,' he added one night as a clincher, 'she shows absolutely no sign of fear of you at all. I've seen her when she hears your voice or when you pick her up. She finds you reassuring, Will. Try to relax, or you'll make yourself ill and that won't help her at all.'

'It all makes sense, Tom,' she said, lying in bed, holding his hand, 'but I can't...'

'You can't stop worrying about whether you've damaged her and whether you will be able to love her more than your mother loved you. I know all that. But you do love her. That's very clear and her response to it is just as clear.'

Willow looked at him in dumb gratitude. She, whose job was words, could not think of any to use.

'Now,' Tom went on more briskly, 'that's enough of all this for tonight. You must sleep. D'you want a pill? Kimmeridge said it was more important for you to sleep at the moment than to avoid them.'

'Perhaps,' she said. 'but if I do, you must wake me if she cries.'

'I will,' he said, handing her the bottle of ten sleeping-pills that Doctor Kimmeridge had prescribed.

Whether it was the pill or Tom's reassurance, Willow never knew, but she slept better that night. He was able to go off to Scotland Yard the following morning in the knowledge that she was at last beginning to contain her fears. She went back to bed after he had gone and ate another of Mrs Rusham's delectable breakfasts there before taking Lucinda into the bath with her.

They got on beautifully and Lucinda seemed perfectly happy. When she was dry and back in her cot in the nursery, Willow slowly dressed herself in her sunny bedroom. She could hear Mrs Rusham moving about downstairs and the sound of Lucinda's soft, regular breathing came comfortingly through the baby alarm. She heard the front doorbell ring and Mrs Rusham's footsteps on the polished parquet floor of the hall.

Two minutes later, by which time Willow had brushed her newly cut hair and even stroked some mascara on to her pale-red eyelashes, Mrs Rusham appeared in the doorway with a great sheaf of lilies in her hands.

'Heavens! Those look extravagant,' said Willow, swinging round on the stool in front of her dressing-table. 'Who are they from?'

Mrs Rusham carefully closed the bedroom door behind her and moved closer to Willow to say quietly: 'Sir George Roguely. He's downstairs and he wonders whether he might have a word with you. He says that he will quite understand if you don't feel well enough or if you'd rather not see him.'

Willow made a face but then she shrugged. After all, Lucinda was asleep and did not need her for the moment.

'Poor man. It must be awful for him; and to have been stuck

in New York when it was all happening. I'd better see him. Is he in the drawing-room?'

A mocking expression flashed over Mrs Rusham's normally impassive face. Willow felt an instant's outrage until she understood. Then she even managed to laugh.

'I know, I know,' she said. 'You're hardly likely to have put him in the coal hole even if that's where you usually put visitors.'

'I do beg your pardon, Mrs Worth.'

'No, don't do that. It was a wholly reasonable reaction, and I was being silly.' She felt that she must make some kind of gesture and added deliberately: 'I'm sorry, Evelyn.'

At Willow's unprecedented use of her Christian name, Mrs Rusham smiled. As she left the room, Willow turned back to the mirror to finish dealing with her face. She put on a pair of tights, too, as though they would help her to cope with the coming encounter.

When she opened the drawing-room door, she saw a big, dark-haired man sitting slumped at the end of the pale-grey sofa, staring into the fireplace. It was empty but for a large jar of pink and white peonies.

He was dressed in a dark-blue, faintly pin-striped suit. His shirt was striped, too, and hand-made from thick poplin, and his cufflinks were smooth-edged ovals of plain but heavy gold.

'Hello,' said Willow.

Roguely's head jerked as he looked round and then he pulled himself to his feet and stood as though at attention.

'Mrs Worth, I had to come to offer you my deepest apologies for what has happened,' he began, sounding as though he were reading from an Autocue. 'I need hardly say that I had no idea that Miss Wilmingson was in any way disturbed, let alone to the extent that has been suggested. If I had, naturally I should never have employed her. On the other hand, her behaviour...'

He frowned and licked his lips. It was as though he had lost his place on his script and could not begin again. Willow moved forwards and put her left hand on his arm. She noticed that the small cuts she had inflicted in her own skin as she brought the sharp-edged ashtray down on Noel Wilmingson's head had almost healed.

'Won't you come and sit down, Sir George?'

'Thank you.' He sat down on the sofa, while Willow took a chair at rightangles to it. 'I don't…I can't…I had to come to find out whether you were all right, to apologise and to ask you…to ask…'

'What did you want to ask?' Willow tried to make her voice sound gentle.

'I know that you are a friend of Serena Fydgett's as well as my wife's. I respect Serena so much that her good opinion of you leads me to think that you might be able to help me,' he said a little more fluently.

'In what way?' asked Willow, surprised that he had brought Serena's name into the conversation.

'My wife appears to think that Alexander Ringstead's death is my fault.' Roguely frowned down at the floor. 'It is important for her as well as for our future life together that we manage to get rid of that fantasy quickly. I mean, I…'

Willow, who had once been incapable of admitting any kind of doubt or fault, thought she could understand, and she leaned a little nearer him. As though he could feel her increasing sympathy, he looked up. A tiny part of the inside of his lip was caught between his teeth. Eventually he looked away again, saying unhappily: 'May I ask whether you believe that as well?'

'No,' said Willow, drawing out the vowel. She tried to work out how much she could express of what she really did feel and eventually decided that the question he had asked was far too important to be answered with anything but the truth. She also reminded herself of Richard Crescent's description of Roguely's ruthlessness and her own knowledge of his business successes. He must be tough enough to take anything she had to say.

'I don't know enough of the way you nurtured Noel Wilmingson's adoration of you to judge,' she began.

'I did nothing that any successful businessman does not do,' he said coldly enough to make Willow feel less gentle.

'Really? Did you never say or do things designed to keep her just on the boil?'

'That's absurd, if you'll forgive me saying so.' Roguely had ceased to sound at all uncertain.

'Is it? It sounded to me as though you gave her just enough in the way of presents, affection, and probably nicely judged confidences about your feelings, to keep her besotted, while taking care to ensure that she knew she could never expect any feeling from you in return.'

Roguely looked taken aback. After a moment he said with a defensiveness that surprised Willow: 'I could hardly be expected to know that a few scarves and bottles of perfume were going to make her form the kind of sick passion that would lead her to feel she had to murder people who might have annoyed me.'

'No, I can see that,' said Willow fairly. 'But did you really never talk to her about your wife's relationship with Alex Ringstead?'

A faint colour seeped into Roguely's perfectly shaven cheeks.

'I suppose I may have remarked once or twice on how tiresome I found it, but no rational person could have interpreted that as an order to murder the man.'

'"Oh, who will rid me of this turbulent priest?"' quoted Willow.

'You really ought not to make such damaging allegations,' said Roguely, no longer bothering to display any of his undoubted charm. 'I never said anything of the sort. It is irresponsible in the extreme to suggest that I might have done.'

'But perhaps you let her see just a teeny-weeny bit of bravely hidden distress,' suggested Willow, who was rarely intimidated by anyone.

Roguely got to his feet.

'I'm sorry that you have chosen to take this tone,' he said. 'I came in good faith to enquire about your health and to express my regret for what happened to you.'

'I'm not trying to insult you, believe me. You asked me what I thought.'

After a while, Roguely produced a smile, but it looked more like a grimace or perhaps even a baboon-like challenge, displaying the strength of his teeth.

'If you know so much, Mrs Worth, what do you suggest I should do now?'

'I don't suppose you will be called upon to do anything. For the next ten years or so she will be taken care of in prison—unless the jury go completely mad at her trial and let her off. But I can't imagine that. Juries do not like violent women.'

Roguely shook his head.

'I meant about my wife.'

'I'm afraid I have no answer to that.'

'She won't even let me through the front door.'

'Give her time. She's been through a terrible experience.'

'Haven't we all? But it's no excuse. The rest of us can carry on normally. Why can't she?'

Willow stood up, wanting to be rid of him. He clearly had no idea what his wife must be feeling, and he seemed to see the whole tragedy only in terms of its tiresome effect on his own life. Willow realised that his manipulation of Noel Wilmingson had been less Machiavellian than she had originally supposed. He genuinely did believe that the world and everyone in it should be ordered for his convenience. Understanding at last why Mary-Jane had turned to Alex Ringstead, Willow hoped that she had found more imaginative sympathy from him during the short time they had had together.

'Perhaps we have,' she said, trying not to show her dislike. 'Thank you for coming, Sir George. And thank you for the magnificent flowers.'

'Goodbye, Mrs Worth.'

TOM CAME HOME soon after half-past five that afternoon. Willow recognised the effort he was making not only to put up with her moods and fears but also to control the demands of his job, and she tried to show her gratitude.

He fetched them both drinks, loosened his tie, sat in his familiar chair, stretched out his long legs and smiled at her. He looked almost as relaxed as he had done in the old days, but not quite.

'How was your day?' he asked.

'All right. What about yours?'

'Interesting. I gather that the great Sir George dropped in today.'

'Yes. He said he came to apologise for what his secretary did to me.'

'And what did he really come for?' asked Tom, understanding the tone of her voice without trouble and glad to hear that familiar hint of acerbity in it.

'He wanted me to go to Mary-Jane and tell her to stop being horrid to him.'

'Oh, dear. And so you sent him off with a flea in his ear, did you?'

Willow smiled. 'I suspect it would have had to be bigger and noisier than a flea. He might have noticed a hornet, but nothing much smaller, I fear.'

'Ah. Sensitive sort of bloke is he? Like the rest of us men?'

'Not you, Tom,' said Willow, raising her glass to him. 'I know perfectly well that you would notice the most microscopic little aphid in your ear. And I'm grateful for it, believe me.'

He laughed then and they talked about other things, but there was still a constraint between them that she did not completely understand. Later in the evening, when they had eaten the dinner Mrs Rusham had left for them and Willow was peeling a peach, a thought occurred to her.

'I say, Tom, did anything ever happen about Ringstead's suspicions of the ambulance crews?'

'You're like a terrier, aren't you, Will?'

'No,' she said crossly. 'A gloriously elegant red setter, if it must be anything canine.'

'Yes, perhaps that is better.' Tom laughed. 'Don't worry about the ambulancemen. Surely I told you that I tipped off Inspector Boscombe some time ago? She will have dealt with it. She's very efficient.'

'Did you? I must have forgotten. My memory's been up the creek ever since Lucinda was born. Did you tell her how you knew?'

'No. She asked, of course, but I came over mysterious and told her that I'd stumbled on the information in the course of something completely different and couldn't jeopardise my sources.'

'Good for you!'

'Thank you.' Looking at Willow and seeing how much better she was, he decided to take a risk. They could not go on avoiding each other's scars for ever. 'I could hardly tell her what you'd been up to and what you'd almost got Rob to do.'

'Tom, I apologised for that weeks ago,' Willow snapped. 'What do you want, abasement?'

'An attic would do.'

For a second, she could not think what he was talking about and then she started to laugh. The peach slipped from her fingers, fell on to the plate, bounced over the edge and slithered on to her lap, probably staining the green linen of her dress for ever. She laughed and laughed.

'I know I'm pretty funny,' said Tom at last, 'but it wasn't that good a joke.'

'No, I know,' said Willow, wiping first her eyes and then her dress with the napkin. 'But somehow it shows we're still on the right track. You and me. We will be all right.'

'I know. You, me and Lucinda.'

Yes, said Willow to herself as she felt a surprising if short-lived burst of pain, it's not only me he cares about any more. How ironic! I used to worry so much about what his love might do to me and now I mind sharing it with my own daughter. And yet her well-being matters to me so much that I've thought about almost nothing else for a week.

She told herself that it was not surprising that Tom was as concerned for Lucinda as she was herself. For the next few years at least his primary allegiance and greatest care would have to belong to the child. That was how it should be because it would be Lucinda who had the greatest need of him. It was natural.

'So's arsenic,' said Willow aloud, startling Tom, who peered at her in the dim light cast by the single candle between them.

After a moment a smile of indescribable affection crossed his face.

'It's different,' he said and reached out to take her hand.

'How do you know what I'm thinking?'

'Because I've thought it too and been just as afraid.'

'Have you?' she said, beginning to trust him properly again.

'Yes. But what I've worked out is that she's our child; she needs our strength and physical protection. You don't need mine—as we saw that appalling night at the hospital—or I yours; at least not in the same way. What you have of me—and I believe I of you—is all my adult-to-adult love and all my loyalty. What Lucinda has of me isn't taken away from you. It's extra—different.'

'So it's all going to be all right, after all,' said Willow after a while.

'Did you really think it wasn't?'

'Yes, I did. But until now, I didn't realise why—or quite how much I was afraid.'

There was a pause until Tom said: 'Thank God for words, Will. They're the parachute. Provided we use it, we'll make it safely, and so will she.'

FOWL PLAY

A MOLLY WEST MYSTERY

Birds of a Feather

After fifteen years in rural Ohio, Chicago native Molly West is still considered an outsider, but as director of the local meals-on-wheels program, she's becoming more at home. The murder of a local woman and the abduction of a prize rooster are on everybody's minds.

Intrigued, Molly starts digging into the mystery. The trail leads to illegal doings and into the sport of cockfighting. However, the fowl deeds of the ring are minor compared to the blood sport of murder....

Patricia Tichenor Westfall

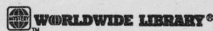

MYSTERY™ **WORLDWIDE LIBRARY**®

WPTW273

Prove The Nameless
An Owen Keane Mystery

Obstructed View

Working for an Atlantic City newspaper, Owen Keane is intrigued by the unsolved murder of a local prominent family—even more so when the sole survivor asks him: why was *she* spared?

With his talent for uncovering murky pasts, Owen, ex-seminarian turned seeker of lost souls, starts digging. But to confront a killer, Owen must also face himself—and the myriad fears locked in the hearts of those trying to prove the nameless....

Terence Faherty

MYSTERY W🌐RLDWIDE LIBRARY®
TM

WTF269

Mad Season
A Vermont Mystery

Downhill Slide

Spring. A time for renewal, growth, hope…and mud, at least in Vermont farm country. But something sinister had turned this season into one laced with fear and panic. An elderly couple is murdered in their home. A string of barn burnings adds to the uneasiness about town.

Running the family farm alone, Ruth Willmarth is stuck smack in the seasonal mess and getting deeper by the minute. Another murder hits close to home, and then her ten-year-old son disappears. Ruth valiantly tries to solve the puzzle, which is uglier than anyone dares to imagine.

Nancy Means Wright

MYSTERY W**O**RLDWIDE LIBRARY ®
TM

WNMW270

UNTIL IT HURTS
AN IKE AND ABBY MYSTERY

WHO'S GOT THE SHOOTER?

When a shotgun blast drops basketball superstar the Big Chill at Madison Square Garden, it's another murder for Ike and Abby, co-workers at TV's "Morning Watch." As the bickering exspouses dive into the world of New York's biggest hoop gods and into their strange rivalries on and off the court, a trigger-happy killer nearly cancels Ike and Abby permanently.

One thing is for certain: the divorced duo must keep moving because this killer is playing a game of sudden death.

Polly Whitney

WORLDWIDE LIBRARY®

WPW272

DEADLY PARTNERS
A KATE KINSELLA MYSTERY

SEASON OF DISCONTENT

A working holiday to the Isle of Wight is just what nurse-medical investigator Kate Kinsella needs to revive her lagging funds and sagging spirits. It's a missing-person case: hotel owner Nigel Carter has disappeared.

Posing as an heiress interested in buying a hotel on the island, Kate steps off the ferry and into a bizarre murder, then into a jail cell as the chief suspect. With the help of her friend Hubert Humberstone, Kate draws closer to the shocking truth that lies at the heart of a very elaborate deception.

CHRISTINE GREEN

MYSTERY **WORLDWIDE LIBRARY** ®
TM

WCG274